The 375-year Journey
of One Family
1638 – 2013

by Robert W. Bitz

Copyright ©2015 Robert W. Bitz
Published by Ward Bitz Publishing

All rights reserved. Printed in the United States of America. This book may not be
duplicated in any way without the expressed written consent of the publisher, except
in the form of brief excerpts or quotations for the purposes of review. The information
contained herein may not be duplicated in other books, databases or any other
medium without the written consent of the publisher or author. Making copies
of this book or any portion for any purpose other than your own, is a violation of
United States copyright laws.

LCCN: 2015916142
ISBN: 978-0-9859504-5-3
First edition, published 2015.

Ward Bitz Publishing
Baldwinsville, NY

The author may be contacted at:
2472 Virkler Trace
Baldwinsville, NY 13027

Preface

Many families have little information pertaining to their lineage simply because it hasn't been passed on from one generation to another. Other times we ignore the information shared with us by our elders. The life we enjoy today wouldn't exist if it hadn't been for the paths of progress paved for us by earlier generations over many centuries. Knowing some of their experiences brings us closer to them and helps us appreciate more what they have done for us.

As I write about my ancestors, each one becomes more than just a name on our family tree. I begin to feel their presence in my life and I actually became a meaningful part of my extended family.

There is a great deal of factual information available to me concerning the Ward branch of my family. My mother's maiden name was Ward. That name became my middle name. I gave my oldest son the middle name of Ward and he passed that name on to his two sons. We all grew up on the Ward family farm, which was purchased by my great-great grandfather William Ward in 1835. My wife and I lived in the house he built and raised our children in that home. There were numerous old artifacts, letters and pictures that were saved and passed on to me.

Back in 1851, Andrew H. Ward issued a book on our Ward family. Artemas Ward published *The William Ward Genealogy*, which included information from Andrew H. Ward's book and brought it current to 1925. In addition, I used material from *Puritan Village* by Summer Chilton Powell, which is a comprehensive record of the founding of Sudbury and also is very informative regarding the founding of Marlborough.

In this book all of the Ward names, dates and locations are accurate. All of the conversations and most of their daily activities are fictional. I attempted, however, to have their experiences accurate in regard to the time and place where they lived. I felt that if I stayed strictly with facts the reader wouldn't think of each of my ancestors as a person but simply as a name. Obviously, I had no way of knowing exactly what role Abner Ward played at Concord, but the records clearly show that he was a participant there. Neither did I know the role Peter Ward played in Cuba, but records show he received the promotion to Sergeant and died there about a month later. (I have his original promotion certificate.)

The recent 200 years of my family's history is very accurate because of the written records and the information passed down to me by my mother over many years. By traveling only a half mile, I can view the grave stones of four generations of my Ward family. Next to the cemetery is the church constructed in 1854, which the Ward family helped build and held one of the original pews. Sitting in the church, I can enjoy the beautiful stained glass Ward window and the stately baptismal font.

To help the reader gain as accurate a picture of my characters' lives as possible, in the appendix I share additional information as to what is fact and what portions are fiction. This Ward family history pertains not just to my branch of the family. Thousands of other Ward family histories could be written, some branching off on another limb of the family tree at each generation. Hundreds of Ward family histories, however, could follow the same branches for at least six of my thirteen generations.

Because I enjoy history, writing this book has brought me enjoyment beyond being just a family history. The changes that have occurred during each generation in housing, transportation, food and leisure time are truly facinating. In agriculture one can clearly see the planting and harvesting methods magically evolving over the years. Without question it helps me to appreciate the life I am enjoying today more than it would without this knowledge.

Seldom does anyone have the opportunity to share a family's history that covers 375 years with the amount of substantiated records that were available for me to use in writing this book. Royal blood lines, where the lives of each generation are documented, would be the major exception. Another fact regarding my family that is unusual is that beginning with William Ward, in 1637, each generation, up through the author and his son, made its living on the farm. Rather than being the same farm through all the generations, during the first 175 years these farms were in two different countries and four different states.

An author seldom knows who will enjoy reading his writing and perhaps benefiting from it. I do hope it will help my children, grandchildren and their children, read this and obtain a better understanding of their heritage. Perhaps some other Ward relatives, totally unknown to me at this time, will also benefit. Regardless of whether another person enjoys this book or not, it has been a great pleasure and learning experience for the author.

About the Author

Bob Bitz's 'roots' run deep in Plainville and in the 72-acre farm purchased by his great-great grandfather in 1835. He has lived in the 1835 home, constructed by his ancestors, for the past 59 years and previously lived in the home built by his grandfather in 1883.

Generations of Bob's ancestors, from several branches of his family, have been laid to rest in the Plainville Rural Cemetery, which sits peacefully behind the Plainville Christian Church. The three Plainville schools – first a log cabin, then a brick three-room school and last a wooden two-room school – attended by generations of his family, have all disappeared.

The family's home farm gradually increased in size from the original 72 acres to well over 1,000 acres. The team of oxen that originally pulled the walking plow evolved into tractors of several hundred horsepower which pulled behemoth plows and other equipment. The few hundred bushels of wheat and homemade butter, originally produced to purchase the farm, contrast to millions of turkeys sold throughout the country during the early 21st century.

Bob went to the Plainville school for eight years, then to Baldwinsville Academy and on to Cornell University before returning to the farm. He chose to specialize in turkey production and marketing, which had been a portion of the farm's business since 1923. Bob led the farm's operations for over 30 years before gradually turning leadership over to his son Mark in the early 90s.

While operating the farm Bob was involved in numerous local organizations, visited all 50 states (including museums in many of them) and numerous countries scattered around the world. He strongly believes that anyone fortunate enough to have 'roots' is blessed, and that they help provide a deeper sense of being.

Bob has written several books including A History of Agriculture in Onondaga County, Four Hundred Years of Agricultural Change in the Empire State, A History of Manufacturing in Baldwinsville and the Towns of Lysander and Van Buren, Transportation in Central New York and the Baldwinsville Area 1600 to 1940 and Tales of a Turkey Farmer.

At one time he had a museum on his farm entitled The Pioneer Experience and is a past director and president of the Witter Agricultural Museum. Recently he received a medal from the Onondaga Historical Association for his contributions to the history of Onondaga County.

Table of Contents

CHAPTER 1
Leaving the Old World for a Better Life

"Elizabeth, would you be willing to become my wife and start our life together in 'New' England? There is no opportunity to prosper here. My wife, Rebecca, has passed away and left me with five little ones. I can't offer you anything but my love and hope for the future, but I would be honored to have you as my wife."

William Ward had been married to Rebecca at the age of 22 and during their 12 years of marriage produced five children. Rebecca died a few days after giving birth to their daughter Deborah in 1637. Deborah had a wet nurse and, along with her siblings, was being cared for by her grandmother Sarah.

England was in turmoil. King Charles the First had succeeded to the throne and the Parliament of England had not met since 1628. The economy was suffering with slowdowns in shipbuilding and the woolen industry. This, coupled with high taxes and religious intolerance, took almost all the joy out of life for many. The gallows seemed to be in almost constant use. Even the prohibited catching of a wild rabbit for a hungry family's dinner was sufficient cause for a hanging.

News of the Pilgrims' venture and their heroic fight against hunger and disease had been big news among the the farmers and laborers throughout the East Anglia countryside. Dreams of religious freedom and the opportunity to own land away from the oppression of the King, church and large land owners, fueled the imagination of thousands of England's common men.

With the 1629 charter creating the Massachusetts Bay Colony, a Puritan fleet of 17 ships transported a thousand settlers from England to what would later become the state of Massachusetts in the single year of 1630. A book, Wood's *New England Prospect,* had been published in 1634 and enjoyed a large circulation throughout England. It was a main item of discussion at many gatherings. The book outlined the advantages and disadvantages of life in New England: the climate, crops, animals, birds and flowers. It told of the clothing and equipment needed and of the several "plantations" already established. It also described the Indians, accounts which greatly fascinated readers.

It is likely that William and Rebecca discussed the possibility of settling in the New World before Rebecca had succumbed. Now, in an even more helpless state, William was in need of a wife and a new start in life.

Elizabeth slowly responded, "Master Ward, your proposal flatters me. You are almost as old as my father, but you are respected and have greater resources than many of your fellow farmers. For several years I have wanted to leave home and start a new life in New England, but held little hope because of my family's position in life. Yes, I happily accept your proposal and will do my best to be a good mother to your children and be a dutiful wife."

Elizabeth's grandfather had been a substantial landowner, leasing portions of his land to a number of small farmers, but had fallen out of favor when King Charles I came into power. The King had granted a knighthood to one of his supporters who illegally took her grandfather's property, sold it and passed the money on to the King in payment. The King looked the other way and accepted the money while her grandfather and his family were left penniless. Now her grandfather, father and family worked part of the land they had previously owned and were forced to give half of everything they produced to the new landowner. One year there was a drought that left them with barely enough food to survive. Help from their neighbors, one of whom was William Ward, helped their family survive. With no resources, it was impossible to find funds to go to New England unless you committed yourself to many years of servitude to an unknown master.

Much had to be accomplished before they could sail to New England. After a simple wedding, William booked passage for his family aboard one of eight ships planning to sail as a group the following spring. It was essential for them to take enough food to maintain the family for at least a year. They might not get to New England in time to plant a crop that could be harvested and had no knowledge if there would be food available for purchase in New England or what it might cost. Often ships sat in port for several weeks before setting sail because of the lack of favorable winds. Sometimes, crossing the Atlantic took longer than the estimated weeks when conditions were unfavorable.

An auction to sell the items they could not take with them was scheduled for early March 1638. William had been fortunate to sell his land to a neighbor who was helping his oldest son get started farming. It brought less than he had hoped, but with so many people deciding to move to New England and the weak English economy, land was cheaper than it had been for many years. They were lucky to be the only family in their village to leave that year. Fortunately, the sale brought enough to pay for their passage. They hoped that what they had left would be enough to help them get a fresh start in New England.

There was a great deal of excitement in the Ward family once the decision was made to leave England. John, who was 12, and Johanna who would soon be 10, had heard many stories about New England from neighbors who received letters from family members who had sailed three years earlier. Of course, the experiences of the Pilgrims, who had settled at Plymouth 18 years earlier, were well documented and had been discussed in their family as long as they could remember. Understandably, Obadiah, who was five and his younger brother and sister were quite oblivious to the changes that were about to occur in their lives.

The families of both William and Elizabeth had lived in or near Glemsford Parish for generations. Many of their neighbors in and around their little village of Steeple Bumpstead were close or distant relatives. Elizabeth's father and mother both shed tears at the news of her leaving because they realized they probably would never see her again. She went with their blessing, however, because they knew any future she might have in England was likely to be as the wife of a poor sharecropper struggling to survive. Her two brothers told her that they envied her, and within the next few years would sign up for servitude in exchange for their passage to New England.

Goodbyes, which included parties and dinners with family and friends, went on for several weeks. It was most difficult to say goodbye and many tears were shed, especially by grandmother Sarah who had mothered the Ward children since Rebecca's passing. More than once, in whispered conversations, before heading to the ship anchored in London, William and Elizabeth shared their concerns and prayed they were making the right choice for their family. Elizabeth kissed William on the cheek and softly stated, "The name of our ship is 'Hope'. That is a good omen, William. I am full of hope and feel sure our family will prosper and find happiness."

London was 60 miles to the southwest of the little village where the Wards lived. Arrangements were made to hire a stagecoach to transport the family, with all their worldly possessions, to London, a two-day trip with one night at an inn along the highway. It would not be safe for the family to travel at night because of possible attack by highway men. Also, the four horses pulling the heavily laden stagecoach would need to be fed and rested overnight to complete a journey of that length. Goods were lashed to the back and top of the stage and the family set off amidst many shouts and tears.

William had been to London, on one previous occasion, to see some of its sights before he had married, so he had a good idea of what to expect. But Elizabeth and the children could hardly believe their eyes. The largest village they had ever seen had less than 5,000 inhabitants; London, at the time, had a population of over 250,000. The buildings were mostly wood and of one or two stories. It was a rambling city largely stretched out for several miles along the Thames River. The Wards couldn't believe the great number of people and the many horses and oxen pulling wagons and carts. It seemed to them that the city of London sprawled on forever.

THE LONDON OF THE TIME OF WILLIAM WARD'S EMIGRATION
From the "View of London," by C. J. Visscher, 1616.

There were many boats from all parts of the world anchored along the Thames, which served the city as its major "highway". Ox carts and horse-drawn wagons moved merchandise from the docks to the stores and businesses scattered in and around the city. Boats plied the river hauling all types of merchandise, serving as the shipping of railroads, airplanes and tractor trailers of today. Oars and sails propelled boats of all sizes moving merchandise a few hundred yards or across thousands of miles of seas.

Even before locating their ship, John, who had gone ahead came running to his father and family and breathlessly exclaimed, "The ships have stopped loading their provisions! The Privy Council has ordered the Lord Treasurer to detain every ship going to New England and to put any passengers already on board, and their goods, on shore! We won't be able to sail."

William told his family to stay with the stagecoach and he would try to locate the ship *Hope* and its captain. When he did, the captain told him that what he had heard was true. The ship and its crew sat idle for a week trying to determine what action, if any, they might take. The King felt too many people were immigrating to New England and this was England's resources. The decree, however, was seriously affecting ship owners and merchants. They were violently protesting the decision hoping the decree might soon be rescinded. The captain told William to store his goods at the dock. He was quite sure it would be only a matter of days before the ban was lifted.

William returned to his family and directed the stagecoach driver to the dock where the *Hope* was moored. The children marveled at the size of the ship, almost 100 feet long, with a 24 foot beam and three masts soaring into the sky. The other seven ships sailing out together were moored nearby. Each vessel flew the Red Cross of St. George, which was respected by most English privateers. They learned the ship's captain had booked 96 passengers on this trip. Although the Ward family was not taking any cattle or livestock with them, one of the other families had two cows, two calves, chickens, hogs and sheep. Two other families also had some chickens and sheep. William hoped that the cost of purchasing livestock in New England would be less than the cost of transporting them and their feed across the ocean.

When the Wards had their goods piled on the dock and the stagecoach departed, they had time to see the stacks of goods on the dock belonging to the other passengers traveling on the *Hope*. They couldn't believe it could all be fitted onto the ship and successfully reach New England. Elizabeth received some satisfaction when she learned that the captain and crew previously had made three successful voyages to the New World. The crew of 28 men, counting the captain, were veteran sailors.

Each ship had several cannon and large caliber guns aboard along with a gun and a sword for every man. Every hand might be needed if pirates or privateers attacked the ship. Although the eight ships were to set sail at the same time, it was nearly impossible to maintain their respective positions during the night or in storms. Usually each ship was on its own within a few days.

The type of ship which carried William Ward and his family across the ocean

The first night was spent on the dock sleeping next to their provisions to assure that none would disappear. Other passengers were also sleeping next to their goods so they felt additional safety in numbers. The docks along the Thames were a lawless area and a family by itself would be in great danger during the night.

The family awoke the next morning to a buzz of excitement. Word had just been received that the ban preventing ships from taking settlers to New England had been lifted. There was much jubilation among the passengers waiting to board their ships. The captain advised the Wards that they would be able to spend the next night on the ship.

The captain was a solid and sturdy man with a leathery lined face who appeared to be in his 40s but was probably even younger. You could tell he was a man of few words and used to being in charge. He demonstrated this in his shipboard welcome to the Wards, "You can all call me Captain Jack. This is going to be a difficult voyage for each of you and the rest of the settlers. I will do my best to get you to New England safely and as quickly as possible. We will be fortunate if we arrive within 60 days. I expect absolute cooperation from each of you. I don't want to hear any complaints. It will be easier for each of us to make the best of every difficulty we encounter and there will be many! My second mate will show you to your cabin."

The family's cabin had a double bunk on each side with barely enough room for two people to pass each other. John asked, "Where do Obadiah and I sleep? We can't all fit in here."

William sternly replied, "John, we are fortunate to have this much room. I had to pay extra for a cabin to give our family a little privacy. This is not just where we will sleep but also where we will spend much of our time. We will be in here when the seas are rough and even eat in here when conditions are bad. By the time we reach New England you will be thankful for this little cabin."

As the Wards explored the ship they found that the passengers' goods, the ship's provisions and the fodder for the cattle were in the hold. The crews' quarters were in the forecastle and Captain Jack's cabin was below the poop deck not far from their cabin. Most of the passengers were located on the common deck as was the common cabin where they were to have most of their meals. Food was allocated from the ship's stores to each family to be cooked in the ship's galley. Cooking equipment was furnished on the ship but most of the families had brought some of their own cooking ware and would supplement the ships provisions with some of their own. The Wards had brought a limited supply of potatoes, carrots and beets along with some dried apples and prunes. Some families cooked together with the women helping each other or taking turns in the responsibilities. On stormy

~ MAYFLOWER DIAGRAM ~

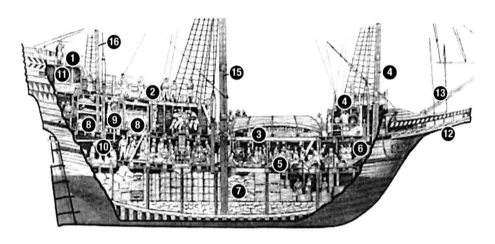

KEY TO DRAWING

1. Poop deck
2. Half deck
3. Upper deck
4. Forecastle
5. Main deck where most of the Pilgrims were housed
6. Crew's quarters
7. Large hold
8. Special cabins
9. Helmsman with whipstaff controlling the tiller
10. Tiller room
11. Captain's cabin
12. Beak
13. Bowsprit
14. Foremast
15. Mainmast
16. Mizzen mast

This cut-away view shows passengers and crew as they would have been packed into the Mayflower for the 1620 crossing. The Mayflower was similar to the ship that William Ward and his family sailed on, from England to Boston, 17 years after the Pilgrims.

days there was no cooking because of the ship being tossed about by the sea.

Fitting all of the ships with necessary provisions and loading the passengers with their goods usually involved several weeks. Fortunately most of the ship's provisions had been stored on the boat before the Ward's arrival so only the passengers, their gear and last-minute provisions were left to put aboard.

The families eagerly explored the ship and were amazed how every nook and cranny was filled with the passengers' goods and the ships provisions. Johanna was puzzled as to why there were so many barrels. Her mother explained that the barrels held water, beer and an assortment of food for the trip including biscuits and salted meat. She turned to the children explaining, "We all will be drinking beer, including baby Deborah. You must never drink water because it will make you sick. Sometimes people even die from drinking the water. The water will be used only for washing and cooking. It is different than the water we were able to drink in our little village."

One family had brought many more provisions than their allotted space would hold. Captain Jack told them, in no uncertain terms, that half of what they brought was staying on the dock if they were traveling on his ship. They violently protested and he told two of his rugged seamen to forcibly put them on shore. The family relented and tried to find space for the extra goods on another ship. There was no space available for at least a month so half of their goods remained on the dock. Another family had excessive livestock. Captain Jack told them they could bring it on board but part of it would be slaughtered, cooked and served to all on board during the trip.

"John, I hereby appoint you, as our eldest child, to dump the chamber pot contents over the side of the ship every morning and every night. And don't drop it! Furthermore, make sure the wind is at your back when you toss its contents over the side of the ship! Scrub it out each time you dump it."

Three days after the Wards were packed onto the ship, Captain Jack announced the the ship was loaded and ready to sail as soon as there was a favorable wind to take them down the Thames and out into the channel. He also told them not to wander more than a few feet from the ship as it was not possible to tell when the wind was right until it arrived. "On my last trip," the Captain added, "two boys wandered off and we embarked without them."

Time dragged for everyone. All were eager to be on their way and there was nothing to do but wait. Everyone stayed on the ship or next to it on the dock. The meals consumed as they waited were cutting into the provisions taken on board for the trip. Would there be enough to last the entire trip? Someone mentioned that two years previously a ship that had been thrown off course by a violent storm had arrived in Boston with passengers that were nothing but skin and bones.

The passengers became well acquainted while they were waiting. There were 16 families on board, four young couples and about a dozen single men representing a variety of trades. One of them was a blacksmith and another a preacher, both of whom would be needed in a new community. The families were all farmers, as was most of the population of England in 1638. The adults all seemed to be under forty with the exception of two older widows who came with their children.

After five days of seemingly endless waiting, Captain Jack announced that the ships were heading out. It was fascinating for all the passengers to see the sailors prepare the ship and put up sails. April 15, 1638 was the beginning of a new and unknown life for the Ward family! One by one the eight ships in their little fleet headed down the river, accompanied by many other ships, heading to unknown destinations around the world. After days of waiting for favorable winds, a large number of ships were anxious to sail.

They observed numerous boats tied up along the Thames and little settlements on both sides of the river as they sailed the Straits of Dover into the Channel heading south, then west toward the Isle of Wright, slightly south of the English mainland. The passengers got their first taste of difficult sailing in the English Channel where the winds refused to cooperate and the seas were rough. "Mommy, I feel sick," moaned Johanna as the undulating waters of the Channel pitched the ship back and forth, up and down, sending Johanna's breakfast on a return trip.

Fortunately, the rough seas lasted only a day and the ship gradually made its way past Portsmouth to Yarmouth, their last and only stop scheduled before their destination of Boston Harbor. They anchored at Yarmouth to take on provisions. The passengers were able to spend a few hours on land; a most welcome opportunity for Johanna and the others who had experienced their first taste of seasickness. The water casks that had been emptied were filled, additional wood for cooking in the galley was taken aboard along with a good supply of fresh fish.

After a night in port, the *Hope* set sail from Yarmouth exactly a week after leaving the dock in London. The Ward family stood on the deck watching land slowly disappear from view. They settled into a routine of talking with fellow passengers, eating in the common cabin and looking out over the endless ocean to see how many of the little fleet of eight ships they could sight. On their first day out of Yarmouth, Obadiah, who was learning his numbers, was able to count all seven of the other ships. The following day he was only able to count three and in two more days there were none to be seen.

Elizabeth, who had been taught to read and write by her grandmother, spent some of her spare time teaching Johanna, who was nine and Obadiah, who was five, some alphabet letters by showing them small words from their bible. Each evening, when the weather was good, William read to the family from their Bible. He had been fortunate to come from a family that found time to make certain their children could read and write as well as to do numbers. John, who had just turned 12, was already able to read and write, but likely his education would end when they reached New England because of the demands of settling in a new land. Elizabeth, of course, spent time in the galley each day working with some of the other ladies in preparing their food.

For several days the settlers and crew enjoyed the fresh vegetables and fish that they had taken on board at Yarmouth but all too soon that was gone and they settled into a diet of salt beef, salt pork, salt cod, cheese and smoked herring. These meats were supplemented by cheese, cabbage, turnips, dried peas and biscuits, which was actually hard tack taken on board in barrels. As the vegetables on board became gradually depleted, Elizabeth supplemented the ship's food with the vegetables they had brought with them.

Unfortunately, six days out of Yarmouth the weather changed and the ship began to be tossed about by the seas. What had been a relatively easy 13 days on the water since leaving London, changed for the worse. Settling into their bunks for the night in relatively calm seas the Wards were awakened by the sounds of high winds and waves hitting the ship. "Daddy, is the ship going to sink?" cried Obadiah. His father reassured him that storms on the ocean were very common and that the ship had probably weathered far more serious storms than this. Actually, William, who had never been on the seas before, was as concerned as Obadiah but had to keep up a brave front for the sake of his family.

Baby Deborah, who had been sleeping with her mother and father, remained sound asleep as had two-year-old Richard, both oblivious to the fury of nature tossing the ship about. John was extremely frightened, but since he was nearly a man he felt he had to appear unafraid. Johanna was whimpering, "I feel sick." Soon she was retching all over the bedding in her bunk.

William exclaimed, "Everyone stay in your bunks. It isn't safe to try to get up. If you have to relieve yourself do it where you are. We will clean things up after the storm. Pay no attention to the water coming under the door. That is from waves crashing over the ship. We aren't sinking!" The storm was relentless. The ship was tossed around like a cork in the water all night and the storm continued unabated the next morning.

After what seemed like an eternity and feeling it must now be morning, William advised his family to stay where they were and he headed out of the cabin grasping whatever he could reach to keep from being thrown about. Outside the cabin he could tell it was daytime even though it was almost like night because of the sky's darkness from the storm. He could see a man a few feet away. It was Captain Jack returning from checking with the helmsman who operated the tiller. The captain told William that he had checked all stations on the ship and it was surviving the storm satisfactorily, but to get back to his cabin because the storm was not getting any better.

When William fought his way back to the cabin he was shocked to find Elizabeth lying on the floor with water that had come into the cabin sloshing about her. John was holding her head and he shouted to his father, "Mother got up to get something for Deborah and was thrown against the bunk and probably hit her head. I don't think she is dead but she hasn't said anything or moved since." William carefully reached over and put his hand on his wife's forehead and then took her wrist. He could feel her pulse and told the family she would likely come to within a short time.

Soon, Elizabeth started to move an arm and open her eyes. "What happened?" she asked. William told her she had taken a bad fall and to lie still for a few minutes until she felt better. Meanwhile, John was still nestling her head in his arms showing as much concern for her as if she had been his birth mother. Gradually Elizabeth raised up and William helped her get back into their bunk. Meanwhile, baby Deborah started crying and, in apparent sympathy, Richard also started crying. While this continued, Johanna was still retching in her upper bunk. She had long since emptied her stomach.

In William's 35 years of life he had experienced many difficulties, but nothing resembling the situation he was now experiencing. The cabin smelled worse than a pig sty. The odor was a combination of accumulating human waste, vomit and sea water. How long would the storm last? What could he do in the meantime? He decided he could do nothing at the moment but try to calm his family and pray for a quick end to the storm and the ship's safety.

The day seemed to last an eternity. Toward evening they noticed the wind was not as loud and the ship was not pitching around as much. William told his family to still stay in their bunks. He would venture forth to get some food so they could have something in their stomachs after going without eating for almost 24 hours.

In the common cabin, two of the ship's crew were passing out beer and biscuits to passengers who felt like eating and to those who were taking food back to their cabins. Each person was sharing their stories of the horrendous night and day they had experienced. One of the crew reported that a young man, who was a passenger on the ship, had foolishly gone onto the upper deck and was swept into the ocean by one of the huge waves. There was nothing anyone could do to save him.

When William returned to the cabin, he offered each of the children beer from the tankard and a couple of biscuits. He told them to be sure and suck on the biscuits to soften them before they attempted to chew because they might break a tooth. There was a small beaker in the cabin that Elizabeth used to soften several biscuits in beer for Deborah and Richard. Johanna moaned, "I don't think I'll eat again, I feel so bad." Elizabeth told her she must drink some beer to replace some of the fluids she had lost from all her retching. She also told her that it would help make her stomach feel better.

Everyone wanted to get out of the confinement in their filthy, stinking cabin but the ship was still pitching too much. The captain ordered everyone to stay below deck until daylight the next morning. The Wards settled in for another difficult night. To everyone's surprise, they slept quite well.

By the next morning the winds had subsided and the ship again seemed to be in harmony with the sea. The hungry passengers headed to the main cabin for some much needed breakfast and to the upper deck to breathe some rejuvenating fresh air. The sails were in place and the ship was again heading to the west. Captain Jack told the passengers that the ship had weathered the storm without any major damage but they had been thrown off course. It would take two or three days make up what distance had been lost.

The passengers were using every spare spot on the deck to air out their bedding and dry it in the sun. Johanna had come back to life and was working with John and Obadiah to help their mother and father clean up the terrible mess in the cabin. William was on the upper deck cleaning some of the family's bedding when Obadiah came running up shouting, "Father, something is seriously wrong with mother and she said to have you come to the cabin immediately!" William hurried to their cabin and found Elizabeth lying in her bunk in apparent agony.

Elizabeth was in tears and softly whispered to William, "I think I'm having a miscarriage. I'm so sorry. It would have been our first child and now I think I am losing it, probably because of the bad fall I had in the storm." William, seeing her obvious pain and feeling his inadequacy, knew she needed immediate knowledgable care. He had heard that one of the older women on the ship had helped dozens of babies come into the world. He soon found her and upon hearing of Elizabeth's plight, she followed William to the Ward cabin.

It took her only a moment to determine that Elizabeth needed help. She ordered Richard out of the cabin, told William to take baby Deborah with him and bring her daughter back to the cabin so she could help take care of Elizabeth's needs. The daughter was a mother of three young children and had helped her mother deliver several babies for other women.

Richard was outside the cabin crying and tears were starting to show on Obadiah's cheeks. Johanna looked to be in a state of misery and asked her father, "Mother was in a lot of pain. Will she live?" William did his best to assure the children that their mother would be fine but inwardly was seriously worried.

Minutes seemed like hours as William waited for news from the inside of his cabin. He was holding baby Deborah, two year old Richard was clinging to one of his legs while Johanna and Obadiah were quarreling.

Each of them had learned to love Elizabeth dearly even though she had been their mother for only six months.

Their waiting came to a happy end when the midwife's daughter came to them with a smile on her face and told them all was well. She told William that she would hold Deborah a few minutes and keep track of Richard, Obadiah and Johanna while he went in to see her mother and Elizabeth.

William, now with a heavy load being removed from his mind, cautiously entered their cabin. Elizabeth was resting quietly in their bunk with the midwife standing next to her and holding her hand. The midwife turned to William and softly said, "Your wife has had a miscarriage, probably because of her fall yesterday. The baby was not fully developed and could not have survived. Elizabeth will be fine in a few days. I will check back on her tomorrow. She should feel much better after a good night's sleep. I'll take Deborah with me and look after her tonight."

William got on his knees, bent over to give Elizabeth a gentle kiss and whispered, "I love you." She roused, opened her eyes and softly murmured, "I love you so much. I'll make this up to you. We will have a number of fine children together."

Gradually life returned to normal on the ship. Bedding and clothes were cleaned and aired, and the cabins scrubbed clean. There was a feeling of camaraderie among the passengers. Occasionally tempers did flare because of the daily close proximity of the passengers and crew, but Captain Jack ran a tight ship and never allowed things to get out of hand.

The continuous diet of salt pork, salt beef, salt cod, smoked herring, peas, beans, biscuits and beer was becoming monotonous. How the passengers longed to have some fresh meat and vegetables! Before the storm the crew had slaughtered two sheep and some chickens that had been part of the ship's provisions, but that feast was a long ago memory. There would be no more fresh meat until they reached Boston Harbor. Sometimes passengers looked longingly at the livestock a few families were taking with them to New England, but realized that they could be slaughtered only if the ship was unable to reach port before its provisions ran out.

Six weeks out of London a shout rang out that a sail was sighted in the distance. Captain Jack again reviewed each passenger's responsibilities if the ships should make contact and if it happened to be a pirate or a privateer. A constant watch was kept during daylight hours and fortunately the sails didn't seem to be coming any closer. Was it one of their sister ships, a friendly cargo ship or a pirate ship? Everyone settled down for the night with a sense of uneasiness.

With daylight the sails had disappeared and everyone breathed a sigh of relief. Perhaps they would reach New England safely. They had weathered a bad storm and to this point had avoided enemy ships. All the crew and passengers were still safe except for the one young man who had been swept overboard.

One morning the seaman on watch sighted an iceberg and later that day several more. The passengers had marveled at the unfamiliar sight of the huge mounds of floating ice. Captain Jack told them that they always have a double watch when they are near icebergs because it would be fatal if the ship were to hit one. He also explained to them that the icebergs were much larger than they looked because most of their bulk was beneath the water.

Seven weeks and four days out of London, the early watch spotted some birds flying in the distance. Everyone shouted with joy since sea birds indicated they were near land. Captain Jack advised them "The land is Newfoundland. It will still be some time before we reach Boston Harbor." He also said that on one of his previous voyages they had been able to catch some cod. They should drop some lines over the side and try their luck.

John turned to his dad and queried, "Can we?" Fresh fish would be a wonderful relief from that everlasting salted cod. William was more than willing. Captain Jack supplied them with hooks, line and bait. A baited line was soon in the water. Anxiously waiting for a strike, they took turns watching the line. Several times they pulled the line up but the bait was still attached. Not even a nibble!

Captain Jack came by to inquire as to their luck. He suspected that the ship hadn't reached the waters where cod thrived. He encouraged them to try again the next day. Obadiah, who had been observing their lack of success, pleaded, "Let me try my luck. I caught a good mess of fish last winter in our river back home." William responded that fishing in the ocean was very different than fishing in their little river back home and a big fish might pull him over the edge of the ship and into the sea. However, he condescended and told Obadiah that he could hold the line but, he would tie the end to the ship's rail in the unlikely event that he hooked a big fish.

Obadiah took the line and bait while his father tied the other end to the ship's rail. Obadiah then took the bait in his hand and spit a juicy amount of his saliva on it. His father was shocked and wondered why he did that. Obadiah responded, "Last winter when I caught those fish in the river back home it worked, so I am going to try it again."

No sooner were the words out of his mouth and the bait hit the water, that the line took off like a racehorse out of the starting gate. Obadiah yelled, "I've got a fish." Immediately his father was at his side and holding the line, which was stretched tight as he forcibly tried to pull the fish toward him. They soon landed a 30 pound cod, a real beauty!

As they unhooked the fish, William said to Obadiah, "Try your luck again." Obadiah spit on some new bait and threw the line over the side, again with immediate success. This happened three more times with beautiful cod hauled in, each almost as big as Obadiah. Everyone on board feasted on fresh fish that evening and marveled at the magic Obadiah had.

Captain Jack knew the secret of Obadiah's success. It was pure coincidence that Obadiah had thrown out the line just as the ship was entering a section of the sea teeming with codfish. Anyone would have had similar luck. The captain, however, let Obadiah bask in glory thinking that his spit had attracted the fish.

The next few days bird sightings became more common as the ship sailed southwest along the eastern coast of North America. On a clear day it was occasionally possible to catch a glimpse of land in the distance. On their 63rd day out of London, Captain Jack announced that they should be seeing Boston Harbor soon.

On their 65th day at sea, there was tremendous joy among the ship's passengers to see buildings along the water. Soon they could see the three large hills of Boston rising in the distance. As they neared the harbor they met several ships and shouted greetings to each other across the water.

The Ward family and the other passengers had successfully reached New England. Each had his own vision of what life would be like for him in this new land. Even though they had read and heard numerous reports of what life was like in New England, the experiences that were awaiting them were beyond their wildest imaginations.

CHAPTER 2

Transition from the Boat to Their New Home

The Ward family and the other passengers on the good ship *Hope* joyfully crossed the gangplank and stepped on to the shores of a new world, one that would be their home for generations. The Wards knelt to the ground in a close circle giving thanks for their safe voyage. Johanna, after her 65 days on the ship and numerous bouts of motion sickness, bent over and gave the soil beneath her a long kiss of joy. Even little Deborah seemed happy, as she softly cooed.

The city of Boston, a sight that at first filled them with joy, was also a disappointment. It could be honestly described as a pioneer town. Only eight years old, with dirt streets and ramshackle buildings, it didn't compare with the neatness of the little villages in England and certainly there was no comparison with London.

There were few wooden buildings. Most of the homes and many of the commercial buildings were composed of clay and sod with thatched roofs. In the entire city there was only one brick building and perhaps 30 frame homes. There were very few trees on the 800 acre peninsula where Boston rested, so logs and lumber had to come by water. The one church in the city was on State Street. Adjacent to the thatched roof church was a whipping post. Obadiah asked his father what that was. William responded, "Obadiah, that is used to punish people who do not obey the laws of the church or disobey the laws established by the city. It helps make a safe community.

An artist's view of what Boston Harbor may have looked like in 1638.

Just as they were leaving the area, they saw three men forcibly bringing a man toward the whipping post. They watched as he was stripped of his shirt and tied to the post. Then, one of the men took a whip, reached back with his arm and swiftly lashed the offender across the back. Soon the shouting turned to screams and some strokes later, to whimpers. The man in charge of the whipping exclaimed, "Next time you will think twice before you try to steal another person's property. We will leave you there until sundown and then give you something more to think about!"

The Wards watched in utter amazement. They had seen people back home with their head and hands in stocks for a few hours but never a whipping like this. William explained that because there were so many people coming to Boston, along with sailors from all over the world, punishment needed to be severe. He went on to tell them that in the new "plantations" being settled the population would be more stable and there would be less crime.

As they walked around the little city of Boston they discovered that most of the trades that existed in the villages back in England were already represented in Boston. There were butchers, wine merchants, a linen draper, an apothecary, carpenters, plasterers, tailors, shoemakers, shipwrights, blacksmiths and others. The activity of shipping in and out of the little port of Boston, and the constant influx of immigrants, furnished business opportunities and employment for the unskilled. William's love of the country and his life's experience as a farmer gave him no interest for a life in Boston. Even though there was good land on the peninsula that would grow corn and gardens, William could readily see that there was little room for livestock to graze and that as the city grew the farm land would rapidly disappear.

William and Elizabeth had talked with other settlers back in London while waiting for the ship to sail. They had heard that the Watertown "plantation" had been settled a few years earlier and might be a place where they could live. William discovered it was only a few miles west of Boston and there had been good reports about the new community.

Arrangements were made for the Wards to stay with a Boston family for a few days. William then set off on foot to Watertown to determine its suitability for their new home. His trip turned out to be a disappointment. He discovered that few people were allowed to own land, and it even required approval by the community for any new person to buy land. Allocations of land had been closed since 1634. There would be little opportunity for William to be more than a common laborer in that community.

He reported the sad news to Elizabeth and the children. Elizabeth had learned from the couple they were staying with that there were other new "plantations" being formed. One they thought might be promising was in the Musketaquid valley about seven miles north of Watertown. Musketaquid was the Indian name for grassy ground. It was reported to have the best expanse of grassy ground, which was important for cattle fodder, within 10 miles of Watertown. There was also a good spring to furnish drinking water for the settlers and the valley was located on a longtime trail used by Indians that extended many miles west from Boston.

With further exploration they discovered that a man by the name of Peter Noyes, along with some other men, had petitioned the General Court of Massachusetts for a grant of a new town below Concord on the Musketaquid River. Noyes and 11 others of the petitioning group, owned land in the "Watertown" plantation. For the court to give approval for a new grant over half of the settlers had to be those that had been denied land in Watertown or owned no other land.

It did not take William long to locate Peter Noyes. After a long discussion, he urged William to become one of the settlers. Peter told him that he would be awarded land as soon as the court gave its official approval. The tract was five miles square so there would be plenty of land for each of the settlers. In the meantime, the petitioners had been preparing a map, which would allocate four acres near the center of the community for each settler's house lot. Later, there would be allotments for meadow and additional crop land for each of the settlers. Adding the Wards to the list, since they owned no land, would give additional strength to the petition. He also said that it was very likely the petition would be approved. Some of the settlers were already in the process of clearing land and building homes so as to move in before cold weather.

William reported the good news to Elizabeth and the children. He also told them that Mr. Noyes seemed honest and had a reputation as a strong leader. The new settlement, to be called Sudbury, was very isolated and about 15 miles inland from Boston, but had strong possibilities for the family to be free and to prosper.

After much discussion, William and Elizabeth decided that Sudbury seemed to offer them the opportunities they were looking for and to take the plunge. William enthusiastically told Peter Noyes to add his family to the list of settlers. Peter showed William the proposed map and gave him several choices for his house lot. He also told William he did not have to decide the exact location until he had visited the Sudbury "plantation".

The couple that the Wards had been staying with, Tom and Ann Belcher, had taken a liking to the Ward family and upon hearing of the their decision to settle in Sudbury, offered to have them stay as long as necessary while they built a home and until they were ready to move. The Belchers had no children of their own and were overjoyed to have children in their home.

William announced to his family, "John and I will travel on foot to Sudbury. We will take our axes, other tools and food for a month. Since the sun is now close to giving us our longest days we will take along some beans and corn to plant. If we can prepare a plot of ground, we may have a small harvest this fall." Obadiah begged to go but his father reminded him that he was only six and would have to wait until his mother and the rest of the family came.

John and his father were fortunate to be able to follow a long-used Indian trail the entire distance to Sudbury. The trail was made easier to follow as ox carts to Concord and other Massachusetts plantations regularly used a portion of it. The further they went on the trail, the narrower it became and as they neared Sudbury there were no more signs of ox cart travel. They had set out at the first signs of daylight to avoid the heat of the afternoon and were surprised and pleased to reach Sudbury about the time the sun was directly over them.

Despite being hot and tired from their load and the heat of the sun, they felt like they had come home. They were welcomed by several men who had been busy clearing ground, cutting small trees and trimming the branches from them to make shelters. They said that there were five settlers with six sons working on the site and that probably a few more would be coming soon. Any settler who didn't get started clearing, building, planting and cutting wood for the winter soon wouldn't be able to stay through the winter.

Two of the men owned land in the Watertown plantation but were going to settle at Sudbury. They told of the snow and cold during the past two winters and warned William that it would take a lot of wood to keep the family warm. When fall came the two men were going back to their cabins in Watertown for the winter and would be bringing their families in the spring.

The men had cleared about a half acre of land and had planted some corn, beans and squash as Cato, the Indian who had sold the five mile square tract of land to the Massachusetts Court, had suggested. They told William that Cato and his family were about the only natives who lived on the tract and that they were very friendly. They also told William that if he and his son spent half of their time working on the plantation's common sections, his family could have a share of the crops when they were harvested.

William and John immediately went to work and constructed a small lean-to, which was open on the south. The frame consisted of small trees, limbs and branches. The top was covered with some of the tall grass growing along the river. In only a few hours they had a shelter that would protect them from the summer rains. Tall grass laid on the ground inside the lean-to provided a comfortable bed for two very tired people that night.

As light started to show in the eastern sky the next morning, they heard some men talking and arose to join the others in whatever work was planned for the day. One of the men had managed to bring a team of oxen to Sudbury that he had used on the Watertown plantation. The oxen were being used to pull small trees from the ground after the larger trees had been cut and hauled out of the way. Others still were felling trees and cutting them into short logs to split in the fall for firewood while others were trimming branches from the logs or working with the oxen.

John and the other young boys were assigned the light duty work of trimming and piling the branches and helping the teamster pull the small trees with the oxen. John had used an axe many times in the past but not for so many hours at a time. Before the day was over he had a few blisters on his well callused hands. Even William, who had spent a lifetime of hard work on the farm, found his callused hands becoming tender from wielding an axe all day.

The men had a proposed map of the Sudbury plantation and went over it with William that evening after the day's work was complete. The lots near the center of the proposed village had all been spoken for. After considering the lots that Mr. Noyes had said were available, William chose one on the northern edge of the settlement. That evening before retiring for the night, William paced off the boundaries as closely as he could and marked a few trees on each of its four sides. He intended to look it over more closely the next day, then determine the best location for their cabin.

John had never worked so hard as he did during the their first four weeks at Sudbury. Although only 12-years-old he did almost as much work as some of the men. After the first few days, he was quite discouraged. But once he made it through the first week he found it didn't seem so bad. He began taking pride in what was being accomplished and the camaraderie among the men and boys.

John's favorite days were when he and another boy were assigned the responsibility of procuring food to feed the group. Every other day two boys received the assignment of catching fish in the river, shooting wild game and gathering wild fruits and berries. They were also responsible for cooking the large evening meal.

The food that they enjoyed was very similar to what the Native Americans had lived on for centuries. The streams were filled with salmon, pickerel, shad and alewives. There were deer, wild turkeys, bear, beaver and squirrels in abundance. Wild strawberries, raspberries and blackberries were theirs for the picking. They worked hard but they ate well.

The men were astounded at the number of pigeons that occasionally appeared. They could almost reach up and pluck them from the air as they came to roost in the trees and feed in the grasses. They found that with a long stick they could knock them from the lower branches of the trees. The pigeons were small but tasty when cooked over their open fire.

William had told Elizabeth and the Belchers that he and John would return in a month. The other men and boys working at Sudbury had gone back to see their families occasionally, so when William announced that he and John would be leaving for a few days they wished them well. They also asked that William try to find out if there was any news about approval of Sudbury by the General Court.

There was wild rejoicing when Elizabeth and the children saw John and William approaching the Belcher's home. Elizabeth was amazed by how much John seemed to have grown and how healthy he looked. She also was pleased at how good William looked. She had worried they wouldn't have enough to eat and that they might get sick while in the wilderness of Sudbury.

John had much to share with Johanna, Obadiah and little Richard. They listened with awe as he told them about the many experiences he had. They wanted to know if he had seen any Indians. He told them that some had passed by on the old Indian trail and even joined them for a meal and spent the night. He told them how Cato had showed them the Native American way of growing crops and how well the corn, beans and squash were growing.

William shared with Elizabeth and the Belchers how well their crops were doing, the clearing of the common land and the progress of settlers constructing homes. He told them that he and John had cleared the four acre site for their cabin and would be clearing an adjacent plot for a family garden once they had completed their cabin's construction in about two months. The Belchers were pleased that William's family would be staying with them a little longer. They considered Elizabeth to be like the daughter they never had and that the children were, in their minds, their grandchildren.

Mr. Belcher reported that he had seen Peter Noyes just the day before and that he was there to consult with the Massachusetts General Court regarding their petition. William immediately set out to find Peter. Peter eagerly appraised William of the Sudbury situation. He told him that it was almost certain to be approved within a month or two as they had met all the settlement criteria.

Peter wanted to know what William thought of the Sudbury location and what was going on there. William responded that the location was excellent with plentiful drinking water. The natives were friendly and the men were working well together and accomplishing a great deal.

Before returning to Sudbury, William purchased a new axe that one of the men had requested and secured some flour, salt and sugar. Obadiah again asked that he be allowed to go along and help. William agreed affirmatively since the corn was growing well and it would soon be necessary to have someone watching the garden during all the daylight hours to keep the birds from destroying it. Because of the convenience of the Indian trail William promised Elizabeth that they would return in another month since it only took them about seven hours to make the trip.

The trip to Sudbury took a little longer this time because of Obadiah's short legs. The first few miles he easily maintained the pace, at times even running ahead of his father and brother, but then he began to slow. William told him, "Obadiah, you are getting to be a big boy. In Sudbury you will be with just men and I want you to act like a man. You may be tired but you will find you will be tired every night and you might as well get used to it." Obadiah wondered if he had made a mistake about his desire to travel to Sudbury, but it was too late to change his mind. So took his father's advice and picked up his pace.

When they arrived at Sudbury the sun had started dipping toward the west. The excitement of reaching the spot where they were going to live and being introduced to the others gave Obadiah new energy. His inquisitive mind generated many questions, like "Where will our house be? When will we have it done? Will any Indians attack us?" "Hold on," said his father. "No Indians are going to attack us, but I don't want you wandering off by yourself because there are bear and wolves in the forest. They are usually looking for a meal. Stay around the men who are working and in the area that we have cleared and you will be safe."

William reported to the men what he had learned from Peter Noyes, He also reported that Peter had said it was unlikely that any more men would be coming to clear land and build houses until after winter.

At that time there were nine men with 12 sons, including the Wards, clearing land and building houses on the plantation. One of the recent arrivals had brought a team of oxen. Now with two ox teams they were making good progress on the plantation. They had cleared an additional two acres of land to plant crops which they planned to sow with wheat and rye in the early fall. These would provide them with the flour they had been used to in England. They all preferred wheat flour to the corn meal flour they had been forced to use as a substitute. They had heard that the soil in some places didn't produce a very good crop of wheat so they would plant some rye to use as a substitute if the wheat didn't grow.

Because the length of the days had been decreasing for over a month, the group had decided to spend most of their time during the next two months working on their homes in order to have them livable before cold weather. Five of the men had decided to try to finish their homes and have their families join them before bad weather. The other four were going back to Watertown plantation for the winter and move to Sudbury in the spring.

Obadiah was put to work the first day keeping the birds away from the garden. An older boy, who had been very successful keeping the birds away before Obadiah's arrival, explained what he was to do. Whenever birds approached with the intent of landing in the garden he was to run toward them and make all the noise he could. For the first hour Obadiah thought it was great fun. The birds were persistent, however, and when they tried to come back every few minutes the fun part of it soon disappeared. His little mind went to work and he took off his white linen shirt, tied it to a pole and waved it at the birds whenever they tried to swoop in.

At lunch time Obadiah's father checked to see how he was getting along and noticed that Obadiah's skin was starting to get red. Before scolding him he realized that his son had shown ingenuity by coming up with an easier way to keep the birds away and tempered his words. He kindly remarked, "Obadiah, the sun burning your bare skin isn't good for you. As evening approaches you will also be a feast for the mosquitos. Put your shirt back on. I have a worn out piece of linen cloth that will work as well and you can use that tomorrow. This afternoon you can help John and I work on the cabin. One of the other boys will take over your job of bird watching this afternoon." Obadiah was elated to be able to spend the afternoon helping John and his father.

William and John had set eight poles in the ground, with three on each side, to form a rectangle of 16 feet by 20 feet to serve as a frame for their cabin. This afternoon one of the men who owned a team of oxen was helping them. They had cut some of the tall grass along the river and put it in piles. Then they had taken their shovel and spade to cut the sod into chunks about 12 inches wide and 18 inches long. The teamster had a sled made from split logs, hitched behind his oxen. They loaded the chunks of sod on the sled and hauled load after load to the cabin site. As they unloaded the sod chunks they placed them around the perimeter of the cabin, in between the poles as they interlaced the chunks of sod, one on the other. A three foot opening was left near the middle of one side to leave space for the door.

Cutting and drawing the sod took several days. When they reached the height of four feet they left three openings for windows, which later were covered with greased paper to allow some light to enter the cabin. Long poles were lashed to the end poles about a foot apart for the roof. The tall grass that had been cut was also brought to the cabin on the sled and used to thatch the roof. It was laid on the roof poles and placed in strips, starting from the eves. The next layer overlapped the prior one which kept the rain and snow from coming in. A pole was lashed on top of each layer to keep the wind from blowing the long grass off the roof.

One afternoon Obadiah's father didn't need his help. Bored, he decided to explore around the little plantation of Sudbury. He hadn't seen any wolves or bear so wasn't afraid of them. He wandered down to the river, threw a few stones into the water like most boys do and headed along one of the small streams that flowed into the river. He saw a tree that had fallen across the stream and decided to walk across it to the other side. Further up the stream he saw a beaver dam and was intrigued to see a beaver busily gnawing on a tree. In fascination he watched the beaver busily making inroads into the trunk of the tree with its teeth. After much gnawing the tree started to lean and came crashing to the ground.

Obadiah marveled that the small animal, not even as large as Obadiah could fell a tree over six inches in diameter simply by chewing on its trunk. Then he noticed that the sun was setting and realized he had better get back to his father or he would be in serious trouble.

He found a tree across a stream and thinking it was where he crossed earlier, walked across it thinking he was headed home. After about an hour it was very dark and he couldn't see any signs of the Sudbury settlement. He was lost and alone in the forest. He yelled and yelled for help but got no response. Soon his yells turned to tears and concern that a bear or wolf would find him. He found a large tree that had fallen but was lying over a hollow in the ground and crawled under it. He was tired, hungry and afraid! He sobbed himself to sleep.

Meanwhile, his father was becoming more and more concerned about Obadiah's whereabouts. He inquired of the others if any of them had seen Obadiah. One of them reported seeing him heading toward the river. William headed in that direction to no avail. He returned, admonishing himself for bringing such a young boy into the wilderness. Finally he retired for the night, fitfully turning and tossing, eventually finding sleep. Had Obadiah drowned in the river? Had wolves gotten him? He heard wolves howling in the distance every night. What had happened to his son?

The next morning after a quick breakfast all of the men and boys gathered to search for Obadiah. As they made their plan, their Indian neighbor Cato, approached them, with a bundle in his arms. Cato spoke, "Does this young brave belong to one of you? I found him sleeping in a hollow under a fallen tree. I wrapped him in a blanket since he was shivering and cold. He went to sleep immediately."

William joyfully thanked Cato. He took Obadiah, who was now wide awake, in his arms and gave him a kiss. He then looked Obadiah sternly in the eyes. "Obadiah, I am pleased you are safe, but you disobeyed me and left our settlement. I will help you remember never to wander again." William then took a knife and cut a small sapling. He told Obadiah to stand next to a tree and put his arms around the trunk and hang on tightly. He then took the switch and swung it against Obadiah's bottom. Once, twice and several times more. Obadiah tried to be quiet but soon the tears were running down his face and he sobbed, "I promise to never wander off by myself again!" His father replied, "If you ever do leave this area by yourself again, your punishment will be much worse. Now head to the garden and make sure you keep the birds away!"

John and his father had been working on the home for the Ward family for over a month. The sumac was beginning to change color, the dough in the corn kernels was hardening, the fruit on the squash plants was beginning to show signs of ripeness and Obadiah didn't have to keep birds away from the garden any longer. With the plants ripening, the birds lost all of their interest in the garden. Every few days Obadiah would ask his father when his mother, brother and sisters would be coming to live in the new house. The answer was always the same: "Not until our house is completed." Today when he asked, the answer was different. "Obadiah, if you and John continue to work as hard as you have this last month they will be here in a fortnight."

Both Obadiah and John were joyous. They missed their brother and sisters and their mother's good cooking. Stones were laid on the dirt floor in one end of the cabin to serve as a hearth, a mortar of clay and water was layered on the wall above the hearth and a stick and mud chimney was constructed from a few feet above the hearth through the roof sufficiently to obtain a good draft. John wondered why the chimney extended several feet above the thatched roof and his father explained that they didn't want sparks to fall on the thatched roof and start a fire. He told them that there would be plenty of smoke in the cabin on windless, damp days even with the chimney extension.

Whenever William didn't need John's help, John was assigned the chore of scouring the neighboring wooded areas to collect dead limbs and cut them into shorter lengths for later use in the fireplace. He was also told to cut the smaller dead trees and chop them into appropriate lengths with his axe. Obadiah helped him stack the wood near the cabin for use during the winter. They would be burning wood from living trees during the winter but needed the dry wood to start the fire.

On the end of the cabin, away from the fireplace, beds were constructed from slabs of wood fastened between two of the cabin's logs on three corners and a post set deep into the dirt floor on the other corner. Beds for John, Obadiah and Richard were bunk beds about three feet above their parents' and the girls' bed. A table for eating was similarly fashioned but designed to be slid under a bed when not in use. Grass, was used for mattresses. It was a bit prickly but William assured the boys that when they came back with the rest of the family with ticks, made from flax and similar to huge bags, to hold the grass they would be quite comfortable.

Leaves were beginning to cover the forest floor and the air had a sharp nip to it on the happy day they set out for Boston to be reunited with their family. William had sent word with one of the other Sudbury settlers, who had returned a few days earlier, of the completion of their cabin and their impending arrival. Upon hearing that news, Elizabeth, Johanna, Richard and even little Deborah were excited in anticipation of the family's reunion and moving to their new home. Elizabeth, helped by Ann, had been busy spinning and weaving during the last several months. Tom Belcher had been fashioning a work table and several chairs for them to take to their new home.

Elizabeth greeted the boys and William with great joy. The Belchers had been like parents to her but she sorely missed having the happiness of all her family members under the same roof.

She had some important news to share with William. They could now move to their new home knowing it would truly be theirs. Only a month ago, on September 6, permission had been granted by the General Court for the Sudbury settlers to move to their plantation. It would have been catastrophic for William to have worked all summer and then they not be allowed to settle there.

William set out to obtain what items they lacked to settle at Sudbury. The money he had received for the goods and land they had sold in England had been slowly disappearing but he was fortunate to have enough left to purchase what was needed.

At the top of his list was a team of oxen and an ox cart. He had chosen not to bring any livestock from England hoping that since 18 years had passed since the arrival of the Pilgrims, the number of cattle and livestock would have multiplied enabling him to purchase them at a reasonable price. He was vindicated in his belief and was able to purchase a bred heifer, three sheep and two pigs.

He was limited as to what livestock he could purchase because they would have to be fed all winter. The oxen and heifer could winter easily in the forest but feed would have to be furnished for the sheep and hogs. The sheep could survive on grass, similar to what he had used for the thatched roof, and the hogs could get most of their food from scraps that the family couldn't eat.

Their goods were assembled, a small crate was fashioned in a corner of the oxcart for the pigs, and almost exactly one year since they had decided to move to New England, they set out for Sudbury. A spot was made in another corner of the oxcart for Elizabeth to sit holding Deborah and where Richard could sit when his little legs became tired. The heifer was tied to the back of the cart with the sheep following behind. John and Obadiah were responsible for seeing the sheep didn't stray.

It was a bittersweet moment in the lives of the Belchers, as well as the Wards, because they had all become very close. William promised the family would be back next summer to see them, and they hoped to build a new home within two years where there would be enough room for the Belchers to visit.

It had been a busy morning getting the family around and everything loaded. The small caravan set out following their tall shadows as the sun came up in the east. Amidst shouts of farewell and tears of sadness the Ward family headed toward their new home on the Sudbury plantation.

CHAPTER 3
Settling in Sudbury

It was a long day. The oxen were slow and it was necessary for them to stop along the way so they could drink and eat. Meanwhile, the family enjoyed a lunch prepared for them by Mrs. Belcher and had some time to relax. It was fortunate that it had been a dry fall. They had no problems crossing the mostly dry stream beds. When they were almost to Sudbury, the Sudbury River presented a slight challenge. There was a fording location nearby, however, and they were able to drive the oxen across in only a foot of water. William told the family that when he and John had first come to Sudbury in June there was three feet of water in the river.

William had described the work that he and the other men had accomplished at Sudbury. But Elizabeth had never been to a plantation when it was first being settled and she was shocked. She kept her composure, knowing how hard William, John and the other men had worked and expressed her admiration for all that they had accomplished. William pointed out where the main part of the settlement was located. He then took them toward its northern edge where their family and three other families would be living. It was about a mile west of the path to the Concord Plantation.

As they came to their cabin, John and Obadiah expressed their pride in helping their father build such a fine home and rushed the family inside to show them the fruits of their labor. Elizabeth's mouth dropped open when she saw how small and primitive the cabin was. How could their family of seven survive through the winter in that little sod house? Her thoughts traveled back to England and William's marriage proposal of a year ago. She had little idea, at that time, that they would be living under such conditions. At this point, however, there was no way out. She realized she must keep a positive attitude as well as carry her share of whatever load they might face over the next few years.

Instead of expressing her concerns, she exclaimed how proud she was of their new home. She gave William, John, and Obadiah hugs and thanked them for their fine work. Ten-year-old Johanna didn't hide her thoughts, however, as she blurted out, "Even the cows and pigs had a better place to live back home in England! We can't stay here. I want to go back to the Belchers' home!"

Her mother understood her thoughts but knew she had to challenge them. She immediately warned Johanna that if she ever again heard similar words come out of her mouth she would demand William take drastic action. "We are here as a team. By working together we will tame this land and have a far better life than would have ever been possible back in England. The next one of you who complains will spend three nights sleeping on the dirt floor of this cabin. Now, each of you get to work and let's make this cabin a nice livable home! Johanna, you can start by filling the ticks with grass. Then, put a blanket on each bed. Obadiah and John help your father unload the oxcart and take care of the livestock."

William smiled with with pleasure at Elizabeth's remarks. He was already impressed with what she had accomplished while staying with the Belchers. Now he knew that he and Elizabeth would become strong leaders of a team of family members that could conquer any adversity they might face.

After unloading the cart, the pigs and sheep were put in a nearby enclosure that William had built before going to retrieve his family. He had cut down small trees about four inches in diameter. He cut them into six foot posts and then dug a narrow trench about a foot deep and 100 feet in diameter. The posts were placed in the trench about six inches apart and then vines were interlaced at several places on the posts making a tight fence to protect the pigs and sheep from night time predators. Next, the trench was filled and the dirt packed around the posts. He had also made hobbles to put on the oxen and heifers' front legs, so they could graze during the night but not wander off.

There also was a simple three-sided shelter in the pen that would provide the pigs and sheep a bit of shelter from the winter elements. The oxen and heifer needed only the shelter from the forest to survive.

Elizabeth had been busy preparing food for the first meal in their new home. It was dark by the time William and the boys came in to eat. The glow from the fireplace and three grease lamps provided a dim light while they enjoyed their evening meal. Before eating, the family held hands in a circle thanking God for their new home. Everyone was tired and hungry after the long walk, so the younger children went right to bed. The older children listened to their parents discuss what they would need and what they do during the next several months of late fall and winter.

William told Elizabeth that in the morning he would take her to meet the other two families that were already settled in. He said that both of these families had oxen and other cattle, so they had made plans to have one of the boys in each family rotate cow herd duties. A cow herder's job was to take the cattle out for grazing each day, see that they didn't wander off and return them at night. Two other families planning to spend the winter in Sudbury were expected to arrive within a week or two. The five men had started fencing a common pasture where the cattle could safely spend their nights, but it would not be complete for about another fortnight.

The community garden, planted similarly to the way the Indians planted their gardens, had thrived. The corn, squash and beans were divided into five equal portions. William had helped one of the other men dig a large hole into the north side of a nearby hill. They placed all the squash in the hole, except for what they would eat in the next several weeks.. They then covered the squash with dry grass and the opening was covered with several short logs. This would prevent the squash from freezing and keep it away from animals. During the winter they would uncover the squash and take it from the hole for later use.

The corn and beans were well dried when they were harvested and stored in a small lean-to attached to the cabin. They checked daily to make sure no rodents or squirrels got into them. The beans had been shelled and were stored in a bag woven from flax. The corn was shelled from the cobs as needed and pounded into flour.

The stump of a maple tree had been hollowed to about the size of a 12 quart bowl to serve as a mortar. A hickory limb, weighing about eight pounds, served as a pestle. Grinding the corn was one of the jobs that John and Johanna hated most. It seemed to take forever to break the corn down into flour. When they brought it into the cabin, Elizabeth almost always sent them back out to pound it into finer particles.

Everyone was very tired after the long hike from Boston to Sudbury so all slept soundly in their new home. William and Elizabeth had a joyful reunion, snuggling together in the bed. Johanna and Richard felt like they had only been in bed a few minutes before they heard their father and mother busily starting the new day's activities.

William put John and Obadiah to work gathering more firewood. He then took Elizabeth and the rest of the children to the homes of the Johnsons and the Freemans, both closer to the center of the settlement. Elizabeth was pleased to meet her neighbors who were both about 10 years older than she. They found that both families had similar backgrounds – they each came from farm families in East Anglia, England. This was about a two-days walk from where Elizabeth and William had lived. Each woman assured Elizabeth that they hoped to see her often and that they would be pleased to assist her whenever she might need help.

William joined the other two men already at work on the pasture enclosure. Rather than taking the time to split logs for rails, they cut poles about 16 feet long to use instead. They used shorter tree lengths crossing them to form an X. They used vines to bind them together in the middle and also used vines to fasten the rails to the X members. It was a slow process because it required several hundred small trees to construct a fence to surround the common pasture area. Next summer they might increase the size of the enclosure depending upon the number of cattle the rest of the settlers brought with them.

When William and the boys came in for dinner, Elizabeth had a fine meal waiting for them. They were ravenous not only because they had been working hard, but also because Elizabeth was a much better cook than the men who had cooked all summer. She had several requests for them. She needed a place to set some of the food items they had brought. Would they build her some shelves? She was concerned that since Deborah was now almost a year and a half old she might wander into the fireplace. Would they build her a little chair with enclosed sides to keep her confined? She also wanted them to build her a box that could be slid under their bed that would hold a variety of items.

Since John was becoming handy with the axe, saw and hammer, William assigned him the tasks. This also enabled William to continue helping the other men build the cattle enclosure.

Johanna and Obadiah were assigned the chore of taking two of the smaller flax bags to gather walnuts and butternuts. These could be dried and easily stored for shelling and eating during the winter. Obadiah, having been at Sudbury about two months now, was knowledgeable as to the location of these trees.

They set out and soon found some walnut trees. They were busily gathering nuts when Johanna blurted out, "Obadiah look over there. It looks like two Indians. They might scalp us." Obadiah looked up, saw the Indians and waved to them.

He said, "Don't worry, they are our friends. One of them, Cato, saved me when I was lost. Occasionally they spent the night with us when hunting near our settlement." The Indians, who had their bows with them, came over and Obadiah introduced them to his sister. While talking with them they told Obadiah of a nearby hickory grove, where they could easily pick up more hickory nuts than they could possibly carry home.

By following Cato's directions it didn't take them more than 10 minutes to find the hickory grove. There were indeed many nuts, but Johanna and Obadiah noticed they had formidable competition in the form of almost a dozen squirrels! They went to work and soon had as many hickory nuts in their bags as they could carry. On the way home, they stopped several times to rest and began to wish they hadn't picked up so many.

One morning Obadiah went out to the pen to feed the pigs and discovered that one of them was missing. He carefully looked around the pen and couldn't find it. He ran back into the cabin to tell his father. William and John, quite concerned, immediately came outside. The pig was intended to be used for a special treat during the winter. It would have provided a much needed improvement in their diet.

William examined the pen and found that by pushing against the inside bottom of the gate in the fence that it could be forced open enough to let the pig escape. This was where the pig probably got out. He immediately fixed the gate and cursed himself for being lax and letting it happen. He then sent John and Obadiah out looking for the pig. It wasn't long before they returned with a well chewed pig's head. They reported there was very little of the pig remaining except some meatless bones. William told them that the wolves had probably had a feast and that each of them should check the security of the pen each time they fed the animals.

With a comfortable though crowded cabin, a good pile of fireplace wood nearby, squash, corn and beans from the garden and bags of nuts to crack, the William Ward family felt they could comfortably survive their first winter in the new world. But, as November winds whistled around the cabin and as the temperature dropped below freezing, they found the little cabin wasn't as snug as they thought.

The first big change they made was to almost entirely fill the oiled parchment windows with chunks of sod. This took away all natural light, leaving all the interior light to come from the fireplace and the grease lamps. The next improvement, in their fight to keep nature's ravaging elements away from the interior of the cabin, was to fit a heavy woolen blanket that Mrs. Belcher had woven for them, over the door opening. It helped a great deal but an opening had to remain at the bottom of the door to allow sufficient air to enter the cabin. It was necessary to replace the air used by the fireplace and also maintain a chimney draft to keep the smoke level down.

Except in the nastiest weather, the family members spent as many of the daylight hours outside to get away from the confinement and smoke that was always a part of cabin fever. There was plenty of outside work to keep the men warm. They cut, split and gathered wood, but much of Elizabeth's work required her to be inside and to keep track of young Deborah.

To help solve this problem William built a simple lean-to with three sides and a roof to serve as an outdoor kitchen. On many days Elizabeth cooked their meals here and the family sat on logs around the campfire eating. Back in England, some wealthy families had what was called a summer kitchen to keep the heat from the fire out of their home. William joked and said that they were a step above their wealthy neighbors back in England because they had not only a summer kitchen, but also a winter kitchen.

Not all of their time was spent in isolation. Often they got together with the Johnson and the Freeman families to share a meal. Each of these families also had an improvised summer kitchen to escape the confinement of their cabins. These were enjoyable visits as the children played together and the women and men shared their experiences and thoughts with each other. One day a week each of the three women took turns caring for all the younger children. This gave the other women two days s week to do major food preparation and other chores that could be completed more expediently without interruption.

November turned into December with more and heavier winter blasts. These were surmountable, but as the days stopped getting shorter and the winter deepened, the wintry blasts were accompanied with more and more snow. The snow made it difficult to go very far from the cabin to cut and gather wood. Snow drifts piled higher and higher on the leeward sides of the cabin.

One winter morning William and John parted the blanket over the door to go outside and bring in a fresh supply of firewood. When they opened the door a huge pile of snow came into the cabin and they were faced with a snowdrift as high as the door. Elizabeth ran over to the door at their cries of surprise and felt the cold air rushing in over the top of the snowdrift. William groped with his hands to find their homemade wooden shovel leaning against the door. Fortunately, he soon found it and started making his way to the top of the drift where he could begin to cut through its top and make room to remove the snow in front of the door and inside the cabin.

After a great deal of effort William and John were able to make a path through the snow drift and reach the firewood. Upon reaching the outside they found that they were faced with another problem. The drift was so high on one side of the cabin, that it extended up onto the thatched roof. Their next job was to lower that drift and pull the excess snow from the roof. If they didn't remove the snow, it might stay on the roof and become hard. Then, as it melted, water from the snow would come through the roof into the cabin.

They found a basswood log in their fireplace woodpile. They chose basswood because it was much lighter than most other woods and was easily split. Next they used a wedge and axe to split it into several slabs. One of these slabs was fastened to the end of a long pole and used to pull the snow off the roof. Before they constructed the cabin, William had heard that sometimes there were heavy snow storms in New England. Mr. Belcher told him to make his roof at least twice as strong as he thought was necessary and to give it a very steep pitch to shed the snow that might come. William was now very thankful for Mr. Belcher's excellent advice.

The changeable weather they had been experiencing in New England was now a blessing. The sunshine and a gradual warming trend turned the huge snowdrifts into little ones and left many patches of bare ground. They could now go back to their normal routine. William had also been told that the New England winter was much longer than their English winters and not to expect the winter to come to an end until the trees started budding.

All five of the families that had settled in Sudbury were concerned that their food supplies might disappear before the end of the winter. They had enjoyed the nourishment of many deer, turkeys and squirrels but the squash, beans and corn that they had grown in their garden were about gone. As weather permitted, they caught fish from the Sudbury River to supplement their diet. But how wonderful some bread made from wheat flour would taste! Bread made from corn meal filled their stomachs but it could never begin to match the taste of bread from wheat flour.

The five men discussed their situation and decided that William and Jack Johnson would travel to Boston to bring back additional food supplies for all five families. They didn't know if they should take an ox team with ox cart or not. The road to Concord was nearby and Jack investigated to see if there had been any travel on the old Indian trail where the Concord road branched off. He reported that there were fresh impressions of cart tracks in the ground so they decided to take the cart with them. Without the cart they would not be able to bring back enough supplies to last them through the winter.

They hoped not to be gone more than three days – a day each way for travel and a day to gather supplies – but it was impossible to know what obstacles they might face. They set out very early in the morning equipped with their guns, axes and shovels to help them overcome whatever challenges might arise. The Sudbury River was well frozen so there was no difficulty making that crossing. Fortunately, the ground was still frozen in most places and there were no huge snowbanks to shovel through on their trip to Boston.

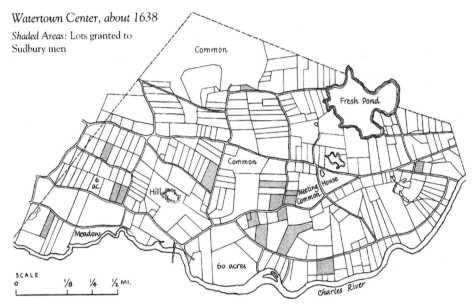

Watertown Center, about 1638

Shaded Areas: Lots granted to
Sudbury men

A number of the early settlers in the "Watertown Plantation" near Boston were
the proponents of establishing the new "Sudbury Plantation" because of severe
restrictions as to whom could own land at Watertown. Illustration from Puritan
Village copyright 1963 by Sumner Chilton Powell. Reprinted by permission of
Wesleyan University Press.

Print of forest being cleared, which would have been similar to what the Ward's
experienced in Sudbury, Marlboro and other new settlements they helped establish
over several generations.

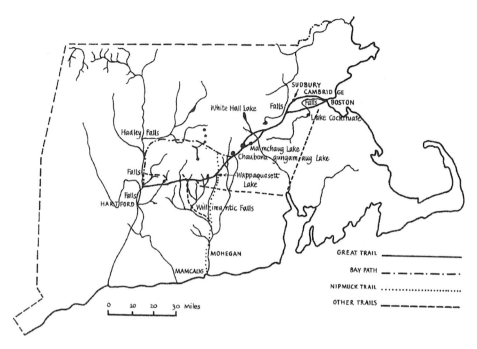

Print of a long time Native American trail from the area that is now Boston to the West. Illustration from Puritan Village copyright 1963 by Sumner Chilton Powell. Reprinted by permission of Wesleyan University Press.

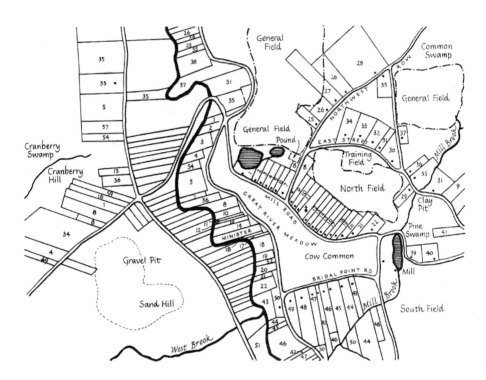

In addition to his house lot, William Ward owned 25 acres of meadow and 20 acres of upland in Sudbury. Illustration from Puritan Village copyright 1963 by Sumner Chilton Powell. Reprinted by permission of Wesleyan University Press.

The Meetinghouse served both as a place where decisions concerning the Sudbury Community were made and as the place where religious services were held. Illustration from Puritan Village copyright 1963 by Sumner Chilton Powell. Reprinted by permission of Wesleyan University Press.

When the Sudbury Plantation population increased beyond the capacity of the first Meetinghouse, a larger Meetinghouse was constructed. Illustration from Puritan Village copyright 1963 by Sumner Chilton Powell. Reprinted by permission of Wesleyan University Press.

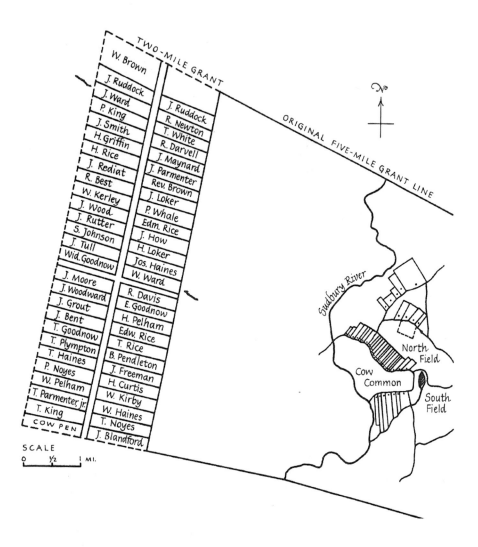

As the population of Sudbury increased the Massachusetts government granted
Sudbury an additional two-mile grant. This illustration shows that John Ward, oldest
son of William, had been granted property in addition to William. Illustration from
Puritan Village copyright 1963 by Sumner Chilton Powell. Reprinted by permission
of Wesleyan University Press.

John Ruddock was a friend of William Ward and the illustration of his house and barn are likely quite similar to those of William Ward. Illustration from Puritan Village copyright 1963 by Sumner Chilton Powell. Reprinted by permission of Wesleyan University Press.

A drawing of the location of the house-lot of William Ward
in Sudbury. From the William Ward Genealogy published by
Artemas Ward in 1925.

To the memory of
WILLIAM WARD
1603 – August 10. 1687

Emigrated from England 1638
One of the Founders of
Sudbury and Marlborough, Mass.

And to his wife
ELIZABETH WARD
1613 – December 9, 1700

The great grandparents of
ARTEMAS WARD
The First Commander in chief
of the American Revolution

HERE LYES THE BODY
OF ELIZABETH WARD
THE SERVANT OF THE
LORD DECEASD IN 87
YEAR OF HER AGE DE
CEMBER THE 9 IN TH
YEAR OF OVR LORD
1700

William and Elizabeth Ward Monument in Sudbury, Massachusetts. From the William Ward Genealogy published by Artemas Ward in 1925.

They were surprised and pleased to find the traveling with oxcart even better than what they had experienced the previous fall. They started out from Sudbury when there was just the slightest touch of pink in the eastern sky and were able to reach Boston soon after the middle of the day. They stabled their oxen at the Belcher's home and went searching for wheat, peas, beans and squash. They also hoped to find a pig they could butcher and load on the cart to take back with them.

They were sorely disappointed to find that wheat was scarce and expensive, costing more than they could afford. They had to be satisfied with purchasing corn to take care of their flour needs. They were able to purchase beans and peas, though, which were in abundant supply. The squash and pumpkins were scarce and expensive, so they didn't purchase any. They splurged on a special treat for all their families by purchasing a half bushel of apples, enough so each person would be able to have one. It seemed like it had been years since they enjoyed any fresh fruit, even though it had only been a few months. Each of them planned to save the seeds to plant in their individual orchards when spring arrived.

Finding a pig for butchering was also difficult. Most slaughter hogs had been killed earlier in the winter. Most of the remaining ones had been saved for breeding. William did find a young pig that had been bred three weeks earlier. He decided to buy it if the other four families would share in its cost. He would share the meat from the one he had brought with him in the fall in return. It would be a win-win solution as, hopefully, the pig he was purchasing would have a litter with several little ones in the spring. Jack agreed, so William purchased the pig.

Having made all their purchases, they loaded the oxcart that evening and decided to head back to Sudbury early the next morning. There had been almost no red in the western sky at sunset and the wind had started to blow from the east. Both of these were signs of ominous weather.

That evening they told the Belchers all the happenings at the plantation. The Belchers shared with them the latest news from England as well as news from other English colonies in the new world.

They told William and Jack that they had heard that there were about 50 families planning to be a part of the Sudbury settlement and that some of the men would be heading there very soon.

Early the next morning they said goodbye to the Belchers and headed to Sudbury. The traveling was slower going back because the oxcart was laden with food and supplies. A corner of the cart was turned into a pen for the pig. How it squealed when each of the men each took two of its legs and lifted it into the cart!

They were well on their way when the sun faintly appeared on the eastern horizon. The eastern sky was curdled with blotches of pink, reminding them of the old sailor saying: 'Red sky at night, sailor's delight; red sky in the morning, sailors take warning!'

When they were less than half the way back to Sudbury, the temperature began to drop and there was an occasional flake of snow in the air. As they moved along the trail the flakes became more common and the temperature continued to drop. They hated to take time for the oxen to eat the hay they had brought with them from the Belchers, but knew that the oxen would refuse to continue without being fed. It also provided a chance for William and Jack to eat and rest before continuing on.

Although they had stopped less than an hour, more than an inch of snow accumulated. Unfortunately, oxen don't have the ability of horses to find their way home. Once they guided the oxen in the wrong direction because they were unable to see the path and got off the trail. After finding the trail again, they decided that one of them would have to walk ahead and sing or regularly shout out so they could follow him on the trail.

They were probably only three miles from Sudbury when the oxen refused to go further. With no sun and a sky full of snowflakes it was pitch dark and the trail was almost impossible to follow. The oxen were tied to a tree, given the last of their feed and the men had to decide how to spend the night. There was no way that they could find their way to Sudbury and no shelter was available.

They decided to pile the front part of the oxcart high with their purchases and bed down next to the pig. William said to Jack, "I never thought the time would come when I would sleep with a pig! Probably, though, Elizabeth will be happier with me sleeping with a pig rather than one of those vixens who parade the Boston waterfront."

Feeling some warmth emanating from the pig, which weighed as much as either of them, they drifted off to sleep. Their stomachs were empty but they sensed that they would survive the night to tell of their experiences.

While they were sleeping the snow stopped. They awoke the next morning to a world of great beauty. The trees and shrubs wore a mantle of glowing white. The ground seemed to be covered with a layer of sparkling diamonds. Never in their lives had they seen such a beautiful sight. Jack turned to William and remarked, "I never had any idea that sleeping with a pig could make the world seem this beautiful the next morning. I couldn't figure out whether it was you or the pig snoring the loudest!" The two men roused the oxen, put the yoke back on them, hitched them to the cart and continued on toward Sudbury.

The Sudbury families were surprised to see them return so early in the day. William and Fred related their experiences of the last two days and got a big laugh from all the listeners. They suffered more than a little kidding from the rest of the men about sleeping with a pig.

Jack and William explained to the other three men the arrangement about the pigs. All were agreeable because the pig that William had fed all fall was even larger than the one William had just purchased. Since the new pig would probably fight with the other one they decided it would be wise to butcher the pig that day and put the new one in the older one's pen.

They knew that, back in England, Jack Johnson had often butchered hogs for his neighbors, so he was designated head butcher. The pig was brought from its pen and taken to the edge of the woods while Fred started a large campfire. He hung the largest kettle the group possessed over the fire. It was then filled with water. The men took time for lunch while the water in the kettle was heating. After eating their lunch the water in the kettle started to boil.

William and Jack turned the pig on its back while holding its feet. How it did squeal! Jack took his knife and made a deep cut across the pig's neck. They released the pig, which got to its feet and ran around in the snow leaving a dark red path wherever it went. It soon fell over and stopped moving. The men put a pole under the kettle's bail and lifted the kettle of water from the fire to the ground. Next, four of the men each took a hold of one of the pig's legs and lowered its back end into the boiling water. Since the kettle was not large enough to hold the entire hog, the two men who had released their hold on the hind two legs took a pail and poured hot water over the rest of the pig.

Some of the children had run into their houses when they heard the pig squealing, but Obadiah, who was always curious, asked his father why they were putting the pig in the hot water. His father explained they did that to loosen the hair on the hog so it could be easily removed. Next, the men hung the pig from a tree branch high enough so that the pig's nose was about a foot above the snow. Jack continued the butchering process while the other men scraped off its hair.

Back in England, a butchered pig would have been hung in a barn over night to gradually cool. The men knew that since there was no appropriate barn yet at Sudbury, they would need to remove the pig before nightfall or it would make a good meal for the wolves. Every part of the pig except the hair and the squeal was saved to provide food for the families. The pig was then divided into five equal portions for all the families to enjoy. The families relished the fresh pork for about a week, enjoying this delicious change in their diet.

Winter was losing its grip on Sudbury when one night the Ward family was awakened by what appeared to be someone trying to enter their cabin. William yelled out, "Who's there?" There was no answer but they could hear what seemed like someone trying to break down the door. William grabbed his gun, which he kept loaded and nearby for any emergency. Before he could bring it to his shoulder, the door of the cabin came crushing down. With a little moonlight silhouetting what was coming through the door they could tell it was a black bear.

William knew the bear had probably just come out of hibernation and was looking for a good meal. With only one lunge, in such a small cabin, the bear could quickly sink its teeth into one of the children. William fired his gun but with a moving bear and no time to aim the bear was only wounded. The bear, now feeling sharp pain, directed itself toward the source of the loud noise and bright flash. William was temporarily helpless. Elizabeth and all the children except for John, were huddled in the back corner of the cabin.

John, now almost 13, had his own gun and had used it many times to bring wild game to the family. Instead of cowering in the corner of the cabin, he picked up his gun and taking careful aim fired at the bear. It momentarily stood in a daze and then tumbled to the floor. William shouted out, "Everyone stay where you are. He might not be dead." He then picked up his hunting knife, went over to the bear, and thrust it deep into the bear. The bear was clearly dead.

John was the hero of the day! His father praised him saying that John probably saved his life. By this time, Jack Johnson and Fred Freeman had arrived at the cabin with their guns at their side. William filled them in as to what had happened. They also told John how they admired his presence of mind and fearlessness. The men pulled the bear from the cabin and then Jack and Fred returned to their homes.

William told Elizabeth that he would dress out the bear in the morning and maybe they could enjoy some bear meat and have a bear rug for their floor. It took the children a long time to settle down for the rest of the night. Little Deborah had slept through the entire episode but Richard was still hanging on to his mother's leg. Johanna told John how proud she was of him. Obadiah, now almost seven and not wanting

John to get all the credit, exclaimed, "If I had a gun I would have shot the bear even faster than John."

In the morning Jack and Fred came over to see how things were and to help dress out the bear. They found William repairing the door on the cabin that the bear had knocked down. They helped hang the bear from a tree and Jack went to work dressing it out. When he cut the bear open he remarked that there was almost no fat. The fat had been the source of food for the bear while it was in hibernation. He noted that the bear meat would have been tastier if they had been able to kill it the previous fall. After dressing out the bear he went to work removing its hide; the gunshots hadn't done any serious damage. He also noted that the bullet from John's gun had gone through the bear's heart.

The meat from the bear was divided among the five families making a good bear stew for each of them. William spread the bear's hide out in the sunshine to dry and later would use some hemlock or oak bark to cure it.

With the coming of spring a number of new settlers arrived at Sudbury. It was only the men and older boys who arrived that spring because the families that intended to live there needed to build their own cabins. The Massachusetts's General Court had given the power to Peter Noyes, Edmund Brown and Brian Pendleton to distribute the land. Even though the plantation was five miles square and consisting of over 15,000 acres, the men only distributed the four-acre home sites and meadow land varying from a few acres to 75 acres to each settling family. Some of the men had no intention of living in Sudbury, but participated because they wanted the free land. Accepting land and not moving to Sudbury was highly discouraged. In most later distributions families that didn't settle in Sudbury received none.

During the spring of 1639 there were about 20 families that were planning to have their homes constructed and move to Sudbury. The first general meeting of Sudbury's settlers was soon held and it was decided that each man was required to construct his share of the fence around two common fields. At succeeding meetings it was decided that each man was required to help repair the highways. It was also agreed that no hogs or pigs could run loose without being yoked and without rings in their noses. The five settlers, including William, who had spent a great deal of time building a common fence the previous fall were excused from having to help build the fence around these fields.

Fortunately, part of the land in the settlement had been cleared, planted and then abandoned by the Indians some years earlier. This land was much simpler to prepare for planting than the land covered with forest. All the men were busy preparing this land as well as some forested land for planting. They not only needed enough food to feed everybody the following year but, hopefully, some extra to sell.

The two acres of wheat and rye that the men had planted during the previous fall were showing a healthy green color. Barley, peas, beans and corn were all planted. Families planted their own turnips, parsnips and carrots on their four-acre home plots. Most of them also started an orchard with apples, pears and cherries. Apples were especially important because of the desire for hard cider and vinegar.

One spring day when William was busy preparing their home garden, Johanna, all excited and out of breath, came running to her father. Crying out, "Mother needs you! Come immediately!" William dropped his spade and ran to the cabin. Elizabeth was sitting near the door.

"William," she said, "My water just broke. I hadn't expected the baby for at least another week." William immediately sent Johanna to get Molly Freeman, who had often performed the duties of a midwife. He also told her to stay with the Freeman's little girl if one of her older sisters was unavailable to care for her while her mother was away. After he helped Elizabeth to her bed, William filled the kettle hanging over the fireplace with water to have it ready for Molly Freeman when she arrived. He bent over to give Elizabeth a gentle kiss on her forehead and whispering "Don't worry my love. This time everything will be fine and you will have a healthy baby. Our first one together!"

Molly Freeman was a take-charge person. She immediately soothed Elizabeth with some kind words, checked to see that the necessary supplies were ready and told William to have Susan Jackson come over to give her a hand. She also told William to go about his work and she would call him if he was needed.

William went back to his work in the garden with a light step because he was sure everything would go well and that he would be a father again for the sixth time. A large family provided many hands to accomplish the necessary work. It was also good to have enough children so at least one of them would be able to care for Elizabeth and him in their old age.

John and Obadiah came running to the house when they heard the news regarding the impending birth of a brother or sister. William assured them that everything would be fine and told them to go back to work. The hours dragged by and toward evening Susan Jackson came outside and called William over. She congratulated him on the birth of a healthy baby girl and invited him to come into the cabin.

Upon entering he heard the lusty crying of his new daughter. He went over to Elizabeth, kissed her and told her how happy he was. Elizabeth, with a contented look on her face, smiled back at him and told him that she was also very pleased. Now there were three boys and three girls in their family.

William reflected upon the past year of their lives together. In the one year they had left their homeland, sailed safely across the huge ocean and found a good place in the new world to settle. Now they had added another member to their family, who was the first child born in Sudbury. God had been very good to them! He smiled and thought, "We have no idea what the future has in store for us, but with God's help we have and will overcome whatever obstacles are placed in our path."

CHAPTER 4

The Marlborough Years and Beyond

Settling down for the night and nestled in William's arms, Elizabeth softly reminisced, "Will, do you realize it was exactly 20 years ago that we spent our first night together here in Sudbury?" (She had called him Will since their 11th child, William, was born nine years earlier.) She continued, "God has been good to us. We have 13 wonderful children, a daughter-in-law, two sons-in law and three grandchildren. And soon, we will be moving into our new home in Marlborough. We will also have two of our sons with their wives on farms next to ours. I never would have imagined anything as wonderful as this when you proposed to me 21 years ago."

Will gave her a gentle kiss and whispered, "No man could possibly have a better wife than you. Life in the wilderness hasn't been easy but it has been worth it. I hated to have to leave Sudbury, but I couldn't persuade enough of the others that we must make provision for the next generation or we would lose them."

There were 32 young men, sons of the original settlers of Sudbury, who had been given no meadow lands by the Select Board of Sudbury. There were still several thousand acres that had not been allocated, but they refused to provide land to these young men. Will, a member of the board, had worked hard for several years to persuade them, but the majority ruled. The minority, which included Will, petitioned the Massachusetts General Court to grant land for a new 'plantation' seven miles west of Sudbury. In 1657, the request was readily granted because of the previous success of their Sudbury settlement.

The General Court required that they must have the town settled with at least 20 families within three years. It granted them a tract, named Marlborough, six miles square containing over 20,000 acres. After the grant had been made, it was discovered that a previous title had been granted to a group of 'praying' Indians. The problem was soon solved by setting off 6,000 acres as a reservation for them. The Court granted the settlers additional land adjoining the grant to make up the difference.

House lots of from 16 to 50 acres were laid out for each of the settlers. Will received 50 acres, Obadiah 21 and Richard 18. Hannah had married Abraham How of Watertown a year earlier and they received 25 acres. Deborah and her husband, John Johnson, received 30 acres. John Ward, who earlier had seen no opportunity for land ownership in the tight knit Sudbury community, married eight years earlier and settled in Cambridge. Will and Elizabeth were now looking forward to having most of their extended family living near them in Marlborough.

The Ward family started to spend much of their available time building new homes in Marlborough while still living in Sudbury. With new homes needed for Obadiah, Richard, Hannah, Deborah and of course one for Will and Elizabeth, the years 1657 to 1659 passed quickly for the family. Obadiah remembered helping prepare Sudbury for settlement. Now, as a man, he took a major role in the development of the new community. Richard had only faint memories of that earlier time, but now at 23, was working closely with his older brother as well as one of his younger brothers and brothers-in-law.

By 1659, Marlborough was well settled with 38 families living in homes, building them or with intentions of living there. The next year the General Court confirmed that Marlborough had been successfully established.

Will, although now in his 50s, was still a very active man and deeply involved in building their new home. It was quite different than the one he and John had constructed in Sudbury 20 years earlier. The new home was of timber construction, had a shingle roof, was sided with clapboards, had glass windows and boasted a cellar. It even had several rooms since there were still eight children living at home. Bethiah, the youngest child, was only a little over a year old but with three teenage daughters Elizabeth had several good helpers.

Along with building new homes, land had to be cleared, fences built and barns constructed to house the livestock and store their crops. William sold some of his property in Sudbury since he wouldn't need so much land with his allotments in Marlborough. As the meadowland was distributed in Marlborough, an attempt was made to have the meadow land allotments as conveniently close to the home lots as possible.

Massasoit, the Indian leader who had befriended the Sudbury settlers since their arrival, died in 1661. While he was the chief, relations between the Indians and the settlers had been very good. After his death there was a gradual deterioration in their relationship. The Indians felt that the settlers were gradually taking away their hunting grounds. They saw what had happened to their land around Boston earlier. There were too many white men in that area for them to dare to attack Boston now, but in the outlying settlements like Marlborough the Indians felt that they were as strong as the whites.

Some of the settlers in Marlborough coveted the 6,000 acre reservation that had been set aside for the Indians. There were negotiations to purchase the land and it was finally sold to the settlers, but some of the Indians were very unhappy and resented its sale.

As tensions increased, the settlers began to think of the Indians as agents of the devil rather than as poor heathen, their original opinion. Eventually the Indians began to attack and they attacked stealthily. This method of warfare was totally foreign to the white settlers. For centuries wars were fought on the battlefield in good weather and postponed during the winter. The Indians might, from the cover of the woods, shoot a lone settler working in his fields. Sometimes one or two Indians waited, in the early morning, outside a settler's home for someone to open the door and then shoot that person as he started to come out. Other times they would attack a small white settlement, kill the men, women and children and then burn the buildings and destroy the crops.

The Massachusetts General Court, as well as the settlers in small communities like Marlborough became very concerned. A fortified blockhouse was constructed and manned in each of the larger frontier towns. About 30 soldiers were stationed in Marlborough and billeted at the resident's homes. The blockhouse was constructed of solid walls that were impervious to musket balls. There were slits in the sides so the defenders could fire at the attackers in relative safety. Even with the blockhouse constructed and soldiers stationed in Marlborough, a number of the settlers moved to older more populous communities when hostilities commenced. All the Wards, however, stayed in Marlborough.

Even the residents who stayed in Marlborough were not completely satisfied with their safety under the current plan. On October 1, 1675 they held a Council of War and voted to fortify eight houses as garrisons. These houses were chosen because of their readily defendable locations. The settlers could have shelter in these garrison houses in case of an Indian attack. Each garrison home was surrounded by a solid fence that was eight feet high. These garrison homes were stocked with arms, ammunition, extra food and water. Each settler was assigned to one of these homes or the blockhouse in case of emergency. Several of the militia, originally assigned to the blockhouse were also assigned to the garrison homes.

The fears of the residents of Marlborough was heightened when in late February the Indians passed through the village on their way to Medfield. Later they received word that Medfield had been attacked with much of it destroyed. The suspense increased during the next several weeks when they heard that large numbers of Indians were massing to their west.

March 26, 1676 was a normal Sunday morning. Most of the Marlborough residents followed their Sabbath routine by going to their meeting house for services. During the last several months, however, it appeared as if the men might be going hunting instead of the meeting house because they carried their muskets at their side. It now had become a precautionary practice to carry their muskets whenever they left their homes.

Suddenly, during the services, the meeting house door was thrown open and one of the militia yelled to those inside the meeting house. "Run for your lives! The Indians are upon us!" Everyone rushed to the nearest fortified home or to the blockhouse for safety.

Will and Elizabeth's home was one of the fortified houses and was almost across the street from the meeting house. "Run, hurry across the street to my house!" shouted Will. There was a mad scramble to get across the street and inside the stockade fence. One man, who wasn't at the meeting house came running down the street to join the others in the stockade. Just as he reached the stockage a bullet from an Indian's gun shattered his elbow and crippled him for life. The stockade's door was thrown open for him to enter and he stumbled in, bleeding profusely. The stockade's door was quickly closed and bolted. The slits, in the perimeter of the stockade, soon had muskets protruding from its sides like the quills of a porcupine. With muskets blazing from the inside the Indians quickly withdrew to a safe distance.

Soon great billows of smoke were arising in the air followed by orange flames of fire. The meeting house and the homes that were not fortified were going up in flames. One of the men in the Ward's fortified home violently exclaimed, "Let's go out and kill those heathen devils!" Obadiah, who could size up a situation with uncanny vision, held him back.

Obadiah exclaimed, "That is exactly what those devils want us to do. Once we open the stockade door they will be immediately upon us. Our scalps, as well as those of the women and children would be hanging from their sides. Marlborough would be nothing but smoldering ashes with dead bodies lying about when they left."

Gradually the flames died down and there were only occasional puffs of smoke rising into the sky. Most of the men in the stockade wanted to go out to inspect the damage and see if other members of their families and friends had survived in the other fortified homes and in the blockhouse.

Again Obadiah restrained them. He explained, "Those devils are very crafty. They will probably stay out of sight for hours, even days, waiting for us to come out. Be patient! We don't want to lose any lives."

The settlers waited, waited and waited. The men were continually peering through the stockade slits in all directions to discern if there was any Indian activity. Early the following morning, one of the men caught the glimpse of an Indian stealthily moving from behind one large tree to another. He passed the word on to the others and they resolved to continue to wait. Fortunately the barrels of water and the food that had been stored for just such a situation took away the hunger pains and made the waiting less difficult.

Finally, after almost two full days several of the members of the regiment, billeted at the blockhouse, came by and told them that from the second story of the blockhouse they had observed all the Indians heading west, away from Marlborough. Everyone breathed a sigh of relief. Will Ward, who was a deacon, led a prayer of thanks to God for saving their lives.

As the settlers ran to other fortified homes to check on their loved ones, there were many tears of joy when they discovered that no one in the village had been killed and the only injury was the one man's shattered elbow. There were sad faces, however, when they saw the small piles of smoldering ashes that had once been their homes. Now the possessions that many residents had were gone.

After taking inventory of the community, they found that the Indians had burned the meeting house, 13 houses and 11 barns. They had also killed all of the cattle they could find and destroyed the fences and orchards before they returned to their camp in the neighboring woods. None of the fortified homes had been destroyed.

The settlers of Marlborough were not about to roll over and play dead. The next night some of the citizens of Marlborough, along with the soldiers stationed there, made a surprise attack upon the Indian camp and killed and wounded a number of the Indians.

The surprise attack on the Indians delayed further attacks for a time. More of the Marlborough settlers decided to leave the community. They piled their possessions on ox carts to head east where it was safer. Some stayed in Marlborough, including all of the Ward family. The number of fortified homes was decreased to only four to make a stronger defense in each home.

On April 18 the Indians suddenly attacked Marlborough for the second time. Again lookouts alerted the settlers in time for them to reach the blockhouse and the fortified homes. The Indians destroyed every remaining unfortified structure. They kept a low profile around the community for two days hoping to murder any unwary settler who wandered outside the blockhouse or fortified homes.

Disappointed in their lack of success in killing the residents of Marlborough, the Indians then ventured seven miles east and attacked Sudbury. At Sudbury, as in Marlborough, they burned and destroyed everything except the fortified houses. There was also some loss of life at Sudbury. John Howe, Will and Elizabeth's son-in-law and their daughter Elizabeth's husband, was killed in the fighting. Elazer Ward, Will and Elizabeth's 25 year old son, was shot and killed by the Indians as he was riding from Marlborough to Sudbury to warn the residents of the oncoming Indian attack.

A relief party led by Captain Wadsworth, which was on its way and almost to Sudbury, was hit by a surprise Indian attack and almost annihilated. Soon larger military units were sent westward in an attempt to destroy the Indian menace.

Upon looking at the remains of their village, the residents of Marlborough were devastated. Only the blockhouse and the four fortified dwellings remained. The Ward family quickly buried John Howe and Elazer Ward due to concern of further Indian attacks.

One half of the Marlborough settlers had left for safer communities to the east. Those remaining had a huge task awaiting them. Houses and barns needed to be replaced, fences repaired and new orchards set out. Crops would need to be planted soon since it was almost May. But, what should they do? Perhaps the Indians would come back again and destroy everything.

There were a few cattle wandering in the woods that the Indians had missed. The fences had all been destroyed but portions of them remained and these were pieced together to make a pen for the cattle. Some of the smaller fruit trees had been overlooked by the Indians and they formed the beginning of new orchards.

Good news arrived when a small military unit arrived from the West. They announced that many of the Indians had been killed or had surrendered and that there should not be any mass attack from them again. This military unit of 12 men had been sent to help the remaining residents of Marlborough rebuild. There was another unit coming that would go on to Sudbury to help them rebuild. With a major Indian threat removed there were fewer men needed to search out any remaining Indians.

Will, now in his early seventies, turned to Elizabeth and remarked, "Elizabeth, we still have most of our family around us. John and Elazer's deaths were tragic but we will not give up. They gave their lives for these communities and those gifts must not be in vain. Our children and grandchildren are strong. They will overcome this setback and continue to enjoy the freedom here that wasn't available for us in England."

The numerous Ward families in Marlborough, along with the other remaining families, went to work rebuilding the community. The militia unit was a big help and stayed for over a month helping rebuild the community. Marlborough was getting back on its feet. A strong sense of camaraderie developed as everyone worked together.

Limited fighting in the West continued for an additional four months. Gradually the militia, through the killing as well as surrendering of Indians, eliminated the Indian danger. Some remaining Indians scattered to unoccupied areas in western Massachusetts. Upon the Massasoit leader's death, known as King Philip, the fighting gradually ceased. Life in Marlborough slowly returned to normal.

Gradually, over the next several years, the harmony that had existed in Marlborough began to develop some sour notes. Residents that had left the community because of the Indian danger gradually returned and wanted to again have the property they had owned before the Indians attacked. They also wanted to retain their same status in the local government body. Most of the residents that had not fled resented giving up several years of effort reestablishing Marlborough to those who had not been there to help. The disagreements continued for years and the formerly close knit community became divided.

In 1686, the colonials were even more shocked when England appointed a governor for Massachusetts. Home rule gradually disappeared as more and more authority was vested in the hands of the governor. The bottom fell out when the governor announced that King's patents were required for all land in town grants. All of the Marlborough settlers were to lose the land that they had carved out of the forest unless they paid prescribed fees and obtained new titles from the English government. What could they do? England was large and powerful. They had both a large army and a large navy. Massachusetts had spent a great deal of resources fighting the Indian menace. There was little left to adequately confront England. Their only consolation came from the fact that their relatives back in England had also lost their independence because of the new English government's dictatorial policies.

As the years passed and the children married one by one, Will and Elizabeth were finally living alone, something they had never before experienced. Realistically, other than during the nights they were hardly ever alone. Children and grandchildren would pop in to see them regularly. Elizabeth still retained her cooking skills and kept a

box filled with cookies on a table near her hearth for her children and
grandchildren to enjoy.

As children ,Elizabeth and William had both attended school in
England. They had become reasonably proficient in arithmetic, reading
and spelling. For a few years, before heading to New England, John and
Johanna had also been able to go to school. None of the other children
or grandchildren ever had the opportunity to attend school as a school
didn't come to Sudbury until 1692. This was long after the Wards had
moved on to Marlborough.

Teaching was entirely a man's profession. Even in the home, if there
was any teaching at all, it was done by the man of the house. Early in
their marriage, William had noted that Elizabeth enjoyed learning and
possessed the gift of being able to pass on the love of learning to her
children. William encouraged and supported it. Even on the good ship
Hope, that transported the family across the ocean, Elizabeth filled much
of the time teaching Obadiah both his numbers and letters along with a
few simple words. William was always subjecting the children to simple
math problems that would improve their skills in business dealings later
in life.

Once they reached New England both William and Elizabeth became
so busy building a new life in Sudbury and raising a large family there
was little time for teaching. A complete generation grew up with little
training. The children who rebelled against learning were not even able
to sign their name. In later life, when could only sign their name with
an X they wished they had been more attentive.

Once the family was established in Marlborough, Elizabeth again found
time to teach some of her grandchildren. Since Will was one of the
selectmen, he encouraged the other selectmen to form a school so that
the children in the community could receive some education. The
school was proposed but didn't come about until the fear of Indian
attacks had faded away and the community was rebuilt. Through Will's
continual urging a schoolmaster was hired to teach a winter session in

the Marlborough meeting house in 1680. Both Will and Elizabeth were overjoyed!

Elizabeth continued helping some of her grandchildren with their numbers and letters even after the school was organized. Grandson William had always been close to his grandfather, stopping by to see him regularly. Like his father, Obadiah, William enjoyed learning and when he wasn't sitting at his grandfather's feet he was with his grandmother learning to read.

Will especially enjoyed having Obadiah's oldest son William stop in. He was now a young man of 16 and had gradually developed a close relationship with his grandfather since he was a toddler. Maybe the relationship developed because they shared the same name but it seemed like it was because they had the same enterprising and adventurous spirit. Since William had been born after both Sudbury and Marlborough had been settled, he continually peppered his grandfather with questions about bringing Sudbury out of the wilderness and his experiences with the Indians. He often told his grandfather how he hoped he would be able to carve a new community out of the wilderness someday.

Will enjoyed sharing parts of his exciting life with his grandson. Without even realizing it, William was learning much about relationships with other people: what worked and the things to avoid.

Gradually Will left the work and decisions in Marlborough, and in the Ward family, to others. He began to take more satisfaction in their achievements than he ever had in his own. Finally on August 10, 1687 his busy life of 84 years came to an end. Twelve children, their spouses, dozens of grandchildren, an untold number of great grandchildren and dozens of friends and neighbors paid their respects. He was laid to rest in the Spring Hill Cemetery in Sudbury, the community he helped found. Elizabeth served as the family's matriarch for another 13 years before again resting next to Will in the Spring Hill Cemetery.

Marlborough, with the Indian threat eliminated, continued to grow because of the large families produced not only by the Wards but almost every family. Three years after his grandfather's death, William fell in love with and married Judy Carpenter. Following the Ward family tradition of large families, they produced seven children.

As Marlborough's population grew, so too did the squabbling among its residents. Land claims, by members of the community who had left years earlier at the time of Indian warfare and returned years later, continued. William, who often remembered his grandfather's stories about the settling of Sudbury and Marlborough, longed to fulfill his own urge to carve a new community out of the wilderness. He had often mentioned this to Judy, now mother to seven children ranging in age from seven to twenty.

One evening, after an especially argumentative and disorderly session of the Marlborough selectmen, William was bemoaning to Judy how difficult their life was becoming with the continued controversies in the community. Judy put her hand on William's shoulder, gave him a gentle kiss and said, "It's time to move on. You have always had the dream of founding a new community. We want our children near us and if we don't make the move now soon there will be marriages. Let's make the move while all of our family is under one roof."

A smile broke out on William's face. He gave Judy a big hug, lifted her off her feet, twirled around and exclaimed, "Honey, you are wonderful! I have heard that there are new towns being formed in the Connecticut Colony. It is about a three-day trip." Judy didn't want William to go such a long distance alone and it was finally decided that 14-year-old Jacob should go with his father, leaving the two older boys to look after the farm and the rest of the family. Provisions were put together for a 10 day trip in case they ran into difficulties or if extra days were needed to explore the area.

Early in the morning in the late winter of 1711, father and son started on their journey with heavy backpacks, rifles and axes, which they might or might not have to use. They had heard that there was still some hostile Indian activity in Eastern Connecticut where they were heading but didn't anticipate any problems until near the end of their journey. They were able to follow roads, heading southwest, through settled communities during their first and second day, traveling almost to Ashford. To William's satisfaction and Jacob's chagrin, no Indians were encountered and there were no pathways that needed to be cut through the woods.

They spent their first night camping on the edge of a small community and their second night they had planned on doing the same thing. In stopping at a farm to ask directions late in their second day out, however, they met a very friendly couple who invited them to stay overnight. While eating supper with the couple, William explained their mission and their desire to help settle a new community. The couple, George and Mary Hile, told them that they were only a half day's walk from the town of Ashford, where people were still taking up land and building homes. They said they had settled where they were living 20 years earlier when there was not another family within a day's walk. Ashford was just wilderness at that time.

During the evening's conversation the Hiles indicated that they would like to sell their land because they had no children left in the area and they were getting too old to live there by themselves. William told them that he wanted to explore Ashford and the area around it.

Saying goodbye the next morning after a filling breakfast, William and Jacob set out to explore Ashford and the surrounding area. Ashford was a growing town but had existed long enough so that there was no opportunity for a new settler to obtain raw land. He would have to purchase property that had previously been owned and settled. William inquired if they knew of any new towns being formed in Western Connecticut but always received the answer that they knew of none.

Another two days were spent exploring the areas around Ashford without success.

William was disappointed and dejected as they started their return to Marlborough. As they neared the Hiles home, Jacob suddenly blurted out, "Father, why don't we buy the property from the Hiles? They want to sell it." William thought for a few minutes and decided that they should stop and report to the Hiles about their lack of success in Ashford. While they were there it wouldn't hurt to ask a few questions.

They were again welcomed by the Hiles. William related their lack of success in Ashford. George Hile enthusiastically said to William, "We didn't mention to you when you stopped three days ago that we own, with good title, over 300 acres of land on this site. The land all around it is still owned by Connecticut and they have no immediate plans to remove that land from its wilderness state. Our land isn't part of a new town but it would be like you and your family would have its own town if you settled here."

William had no idea that the Hile farm was so large and immediately asked George to show him the boundaries. They set out on foot and found that even though much of the land was very hilly there was a stream on the property that flowed continually throughout the year. There was a sizable meadow along the stream and more than enough land for orchards and to grow farm crops. Except for not being part of a new town it was exactly what William wanted. But, how much would George want for the land and could William afford to buy it?

George explained that if they were to sell the property, he and Mary would buy a home in Ashford to be near neighbors. There was a meetinghouse in Ashford where they could attend Sunday services. William was surprised that the price George was asking might be within the family's reach. They agreed that if William could sell his Marlborough property successfully the deal would be consummated.

Lighthearted William and Jacob headed back to Marlborough. Once back William explained to Judy what they had found at Ashford and its vicinity. He told her that the Hile's home was small for their large family but that in a few months time he and the boys could build an addition that would give the family plenty of room. Jacob excitedly told his brothers and sisters about the stream full of fish and the good hunting that lay close to their new home.

Word rapidly spread throughout Marlborough that the William Ward property was up for sale. It wasn't long before three different parties were vying to purchase it. A deal was made with one of the interested parties who wanted the land and home for one of his sons who was about to be married. The sale was consummated by payments in gold coins, which filled William's money pouch to the brim.

This time the trip to the Hile's home and back would only take five days; two each way and a fifth day to explore their purchase and make plans for the move. Because of the gold he was carrying, William decided to take his oldest two sons William Jr. and Gamaliel, with him because of concern that highwaymen might be waiting to relieve him of his gold. Word had spread throughout Marlborough of the sale and the purchaser had bragged of paying for William's property with gold.

William's father Obadiah also volunteered to travel with William along with two of William's cousins. All of them had served, or were still serving, as militia members so the six of them were a formidable group for any highwaymen to tackle. In addition, they were all eager to see William Ward's new home near Ashford. All went well during their first day of travel and they enjoyed a good meal before they settled down for the night.

Obadiah suggested that he and the two cousins camp out of sight of the others but close enough to hear if there were any problems. Each of the three of them would take a turn on sentry duty during the night. William and his sons were soon snoring peacefully after their long day's trek. A few hours into their sleep each of them was awakened by a gun in their ribs. One of the attackers cautioned them to be silent and hand over their gold.

Thoughts of losing everything he had worked for passed through William's mind as he slowly reached for the bag of gold that was serving as a pillow. Suddenly each of the highwaymen slumped to the ground.

William looked up and there were his father and two cousins standing over the three highwaymen who were lying on the ground, writhing and holding their heads. Obadiah, who was on sentry duty at the time, had heard the highwaymen and made out their forms in the pale light coming from a quarter moon. He and the two cousins had quietly sneaked up behind the highwaymen and given each of them a hard rap on their head with a gun butt.

The Ward's planning had served them well. Each of the highwaymen was stripped of his clothes, which were thrown into a nearby lake. Obadiah cut a small maple tree about an inch in diameter for a switch. The three highway men were tied side by side to a large tree and soon appropriate punishment was rendered.

Since everyone was wide awake by this time, the Ward party continued on their journey with an extra three guns in their possession. Knowing that the highwaymen could work loose from their bindings in a few hours, they were left shivering while tied to the tree. Obadiah remarked, "Justice has been served. Those men will long remember this night!" They had recognized the three men as drifters in and out of Marlborough and knew that the men would never dare to show their faces in Marlborough again.

With their early morning start they reached the Hile's home by midday. The Hiles were both pleased and surprised to see William return so soon with the money. The gold changed hands after a refreshing lunch. George and Mary were pleased to be able to share with William that they had been to Ashford and found the perfect home to enjoy during their senior years. Obadiah and one of the cousins volunteered to accompany George with some of his gold into Ashford the next day to purchase his new home. William and the others spent the day planning the big move from Marlborough.

The trip into Ashford was successful with the men returning that evening. George reported that arrangements had been made for two oxcarts to arrive the following week to move his and Mary's belongings to their new home in Ashford. The return trip was uneventful. They passed by the tree where the highwaymen had been tied. All that remained was a loose rope around the tree.

There had been more gold obtained from the sale of their Marlborough property than was needed so some of the remaining was used to stock up on needed supplies that would cost more or be unavailable in Ashford. Plans for the move were made for the following week, about the time George and Mary would be moving to Ashford. William already owned a team of oxen and an oxcart. A pen was made to fit on a sled and one of the cousins volunteered to follow along with an ox pulling the sled with their pigs inside the pen. Obadiah volunteered to take his oxcart and team to help move William and Judy's goods. William's older children would drive the cattle, sheep and goats along behind but they knew it would be a simple task with the help of their dog, Nosey.

A few years earlier, one of their Marlborough neighbors had given Jacob a puppy from the large litter of a bitch known for her herding instinct. Jacob had named the puppy Nosey because he seemed to always have his nose near the ground ferreting out some unusual odor. Nosey and Jacob had become close friends and were almost always together. When Jacob had gone with his father to Ashford and was told that Nosey had to stay at home, Jacob was disappointed. Nosey was too. He whimpered and moped around because he missed Jacob so much. Nosey had inherited the herding skills from his mother and had been invaluable when the family moved their animals from one pasture to another or when one had managed to escape through a fence.

Goodbyes were said to the various extended family members and neighbors as moving preparations were made for the next week. It was early April, an ideal time to make the move. At a large family goodbye dinner William verbally relived some of the stories of the move from England to New England that his grandfather Will had shared with him. Obadiah chimed in with some of his own remembrances. The parallels were very similar except this time, 73 years later, it was not a permanent goodbye but only one of a few months. With this move the family was only two-days travel away rather than 60 days and a huge ocean separating loved ones.

Because of the slow pace of the oxen and the livestock, the caravan departed when there was just a hint of daylight in the eastern sky. William scouted out an overnight location with meadowland for the oxen to graze and a stream where there was plenty of water for the livestock. It was also necessary to locate a place where the animals could drink sometime near the middle of the day.

The caravan moved fairly rapidly because oxen, cattle, sheep and goats are all herding animals and normally follow the leader. The first ox cart was pulled by a young team of oxen that set a good pace for the rest of the caravan. Obadiah volunteered to walk ahead of the caravan to set the traveling speed and to make sure the path was clear. There was no problem with the livestock following along behind being able to keep up the pace because if one lagged behind, Nosey was immediately there nipping at its heels.

Animals and people were fresh and the weather cooperated so it was not difficult to reach the first day's stopping point in late afternoon. The animals were herded to the stream and then peacefully grazed on the meadow. A campfire was started and in less than an hour the cast iron kettle hanging over the fire was full of bubbling stew. With about 15 hungry mouths to fill the bottom of the kettle soon appeared.

Temporary shelters, one for each gender, constructed of limbs fastened between trees and topped with brush and meadow grass were soon ready for the travelers. The men agreed to take turns on sentry duty and the camp settled into slumber. The cattle had been hobbled and the sheep and lambs stayed in the area with the cattle.

The night quickly passed and the wake-up call was made by the sentry just as a little pink showed in the eastern sky. The animals were driven to the stream with Jacob and Nosey in charge. Jacob soon came running back to camp and shouted to his father, "Dolly, our yearling heifer is missing!" William quickly called to two of the children and ordered them to tend to the livestock drinking at the stream. He then told Jacob to take Nosey and circle the perimeter of the campsite to see if Nosey could pick up the scent of the wandering Dolly and find her.

They hadn't gone far before Nosey picked up a scent and with nose close to the ground, headed directly away from where they had camped. They didn't go far before they heard bleating. There ahead of them, in a marsh sunk up to her midriff, was Dolly. There was nothing that Jacob could do by himself so he and Nosey headed back to camp.

Back at the camp, the ox teams were being hooked to the carts and everyone was about ready to start the last leg of the trip when Jacob came running up to his father and reported on Dolly's situation. They couldn't leave Dolly in the marsh to die a slow death but they needed to start on their way if they were going to reach their new home by dark. William talked it over with the other men and decided that the caravan should get started but they would leave the ox and sled behind. The ox could pull Dolly out of the marsh and then they could pick up the trail of the others.

William, Jr., who had been driving the ox attached to the sled, was designated to go with Jacob and Nosey to extract Dolly from the marsh. William, Jr., who was known as Bill, sized up Dolly's predicament. He had Jacob find several large tree branches, which he put on the marsh so he could safely reach Dolly and tie a stout rope around her middle. He tied the other end to the ox's yoke. It took a substantial initial effort but as Dolly slowly came up out of the mire her feet touched solid ground and she came the rest of the way on her own. Similarly to a dog, Dolly vigorously shook herself and Jacob, who was at her side was well splattered with wet dirt. Bill was highly amused and told Jacob how much better he looked with his face covered with mud.

On the way back to where they had camped, Bill told Jacob that he was amazed that Nosey was able to tell Dolly's scent from the rest of the livestock. Jacob responded, "Nosey knows all of the livestock by name. When the cattle are all in a group, I simply tell Nosey which animal she is to separate from the others. He knows what I say!"

The ox was hooked to the sled and they were off. Dolly followed behind, then Nosey and Jacob. The group moved along very nicely because Dolly knew what Nosey's teeth felt like when he nipped at her heels. About the middle of the day Bill and Jacob caught up with the rest of the caravan while they were still on their mid-day break.

The rest of the trip was uneventful. The caravan arrived at the Ward family's new home just before the light of day disappeared in the west. The animals were placed in a temporary pen that had been prepared when the men were there earlier, and the oxcarts were unloaded while food was prepared. Two candles were lit and the food was hungrily devoured, but not before the family stood in a circle with William offering thanks for the successful trip and their new home.

The following months were extremely busy. The first priority was to build a fence around an area large enough to comfortably hold the livestock. More of the forest around their home needed to be cleared and the ground that the Hiles had previously used as a garden needed to be prepared for planting later in the spring. An addition to the house could wait a couple of months and after that a barn would be constructed to give the livestock some shelter during the winter.

Four years after settling at their new home, William made one of his quarterly trips to Ashford to pick up supplies. While there, he heard some disheartening news, which he dejectedly shared with Judy and the children when he returned. The British Governor of Connecticut had increased the size of Ashford by about 20,000 acres of land, which included the land that surrounded their farm. They were to be surrounded on all sides with new settlers and, like it or not, they were now residents of Ashford. The Ward family, previously enjoying its own happy world would now be governed by the leaders in Ashford and decrees from the English Governor of Connecticut.

Inevitably, with both the local laws of Ashford and decrees coming from the English Governor of Connecticut, the freedom the Wards had previously enjoyed was slipping away. In addition, new families were settling on nearby land. William still possessed his childhood urge to carve a new community out of the wilderness similar to what his grandfather had accomplished. There was more and more family discussion about moving.

About ten miles to the North, adjacent to the Massachusetts line, a new town in a wilderness area was authorized for settlement. It was to be named Union. Most of the Ward family were still living at home. If the family was ever going to move, now was the time. William signed a petition, which was approved by the state, to be a settler in Union.

The family made the move successfully and helped carve out the new town of Union. After more than 10 years of a difficult but enjoyable and successful life at Union, in 1731 William became the first white settler to die. He had the satisfaction of fulfilling his boyhood dream of, like his grandfather before him, founding a new community.

CHAPTER 5
The French and Indian Wars Years

Preamble: The French and Indian Wars encompassed the years 1689 through 1763. They were a series of intermittent conflicts which pitted Great Britain, its colonies and Native American allies against France, its colonies and its Native Americans allies. Later Spain became a French ally. The New England colonists and the Native Americans were both pawns of the English and French who were attempting to take control of lands in North America. Several generations of the Ward family, along with most of the other colonial families, served in their community militia; to protect their families and property during this period of time.

~

Both William, who was born in 1670, and his son Jacob, born in 1697, had served in the militia. William served as a member of the militia while a resident of both Marlborough and Ashford. Jacob served while living in Ashford, Union and Somers.

Jacob and Hannah's third child, Peter, was a bundle of energy who seemed to never stop moving. His mother emphatically remarked to Jacob, "If we are to have any more children like Peter, it will be the death of me!" She did have five more children, however, but none were as lively as Peter.

In 1742, when Peter was 12, the family moved to Somers, Connecticut about 25 miles northwest of Ashford. Jacob had been suffering from consumption for several years and the family could no longer maintain the farm. Although land was cheap at the time the farm was sold, Jacob received enough money to retire in Somers. Six years later he died.

Peter worked as a day laborer on a farm near Somers. In 1750, at the age of 20 he married Lucretia Jones. The farm work didn't pay very much but provided them with much of the food they needed. He was able to bring home cracked eggs, all the buttermilk they could use and a variety of fresh vegetables, during the summer and fall. Little of the food was salable so it was no loss for the farmer. By renting space in a wing of a large house, the family was able to survive. Farm work was boring for Peter, but with no special trade he had to take whatever work he could get.

Militia were an essential part of living on the frontier. It was required that every male old enough to use a gun be a member of the militia. This had been the situation in Sudbury, Marlborough and every community along the frontier. Peter, like his father, Jacob, and his grandfather, William, became part of the militia at an early age.

Peter's urge for adventure fit in nicely with service in the militia. He trained regularly with the Somers militia, which was often sent out to battle Native Americans who were loyal to France. The natives, in their attacks on frontier communities, were elusive and usually outwitted the bands of militia, preferring surprise attacks on unsuspecting settlers.

The war with France had taken a significant portion of England's resources and men. England's leadership felt that its North American colonies should help pay for the war and also furnish men to fight the French. In 1758, the English Governor of Connecticut put out an order that the colony furnish 5,000 men for a Provincial army to fight against the French and their Iroquois allies. The rank and file of the Provincials were to receive wages comparable to what they would have earned in civilian life and a signing bonus of three pounds.

Peter volunteered to be one of the Connecticut Provincials to help fill the quota. The signing bonus would provide Lucretia with enough money to live while he was away and his pay in the military would raise their standard of living. Lucretia was happy with the extra money and Peter was happy to have a life that was more exciting than the mundane life of a farmhand. While he was away a year earlier, fighting the Indians on the frontier with the militia, his third child, Abner, was born. This time, while he was fighting in the Provincials, his fourth and last child was born.

After a short training session and being issued clothing, he set out on a westward march with 1,000 other soldiers of the Connecticut Provincials. None of them had any idea when they would be returning to their homes. It all depended upon their success in battle and the whims of the English generals.

Peter spent five days marching across the Berkshire Mountains toward the Hudson River north of Albany. There was much speculation among the men as to where they might be headed. There was a rumor circulating that they were going to fight the French in Canada.

One thing they all knew was it was cold, especially for their feet. Every day they crossed streams with no bridges. At night they were able to partially dry their boots but they would become wet again the next day. Each morning Peter rubbed animal oil into the leather of his boots to help keep out the moisture but with wintertime weather and lack of sufficient sunshine, moisture seeped in. One of his buddies, Nate Pinney, had boots that had completely worn out. Peter gave him an old shirt, which they cut in two, to wrap around his feet. Fortunately, it was only one day before they reached the Hudson River where supplies awaited them and Nate was issued another pair of boots. Nate told Peter that he seldom wore anything on his feet unless the ground was covered with snow, but marching through miles of snow, the shirt really helped him.

Tents were set up in a large meadow along the Hudson River, north of Albany. Food was issued to groups of eight men, which they were to prepare on their own. It consisted mostly of dried beans and dried peas, which the men soaked overnight before putting them in a pot, adding some salt pork and cooking them. After a couple of days the diet was becoming monotonous so they decided to see if they could spear some fish along the edge of the river.

They located a dead pine tree, used an axe to cut its resinous wood into small pieces, attached the pieces to the grate of their small cooking stove and then attached a short pole to the bottom of the grate. Using coals from their campfire to light the small pine chunks, they soon had a torch to see into the clear waters of the Hudson. The fish seemed to be attracted to the light and soon they had speared enough fish to supply their needs as well as well as that of a number of others camped next to them. The fish were so tempting that they had a late evening fish fry before retiring for the night.

Another force of Provincials was to join them before they marched further north, so they waited and waited. During this time Peter and Nate found that they had much in common and became close friends. Nate's family had also come over from England to Massachusetts in the 1630s and had migrated to Connecticut. He also came from a farm family and had been helping his father until joining the Provincials. Nate had younger brothers who could work the family farm so he decided to seek adventure in the army.

The New York Provincials joined them bringing much needed supplies. They were even followed by some men driving a small herd of cattle. Chunks of beef, mixed in with the beans were a welcome change from the salt pork. The New Yorkers also brought some cannon, which traveled on the river in bateaux. They were able to move up the river by poling or rowing. The most difficult part of the journey was when they had to portage. Both the bateaux and the cannon had to be portaged around rapids and waterfalls. The rumor passing among the soldiers was that they would be portaging from the Hudson to Lake George and then another portage to Lake Champlain and the St. Lawrence River to Canada.

The men received the order to begin the trek up along the Hudson and across land to Lake George. It was a slow and tedious march. Some miles up the river they reached the end of the navigable waters and had to portage their cannons and other equipment across land to Lake George. At the head of the lake they saw the remains of Fort Henry, which the French had destroyed earlier.

It took several days for the soldiers to march along the lake to reach Fort Ticonderoga. There, the army's commander ordered the men to set up their cannon on top of a hill, well above the fort. The French, inside the fort, could see the massing of the English on the hill. A few Gannon salvos, periodically bursting down on them, convinced the French that it was time to abandon the fort. By the time all the English and Provincial forces had achieved their positions on the hill the French had disappeared. Peter was disappointed since he was looking forward to the excitement of a battle with the French. He remarked to Nate, "Now we'll have to chase them back to Canada! We'll get them yet!"

Peter soon had another disappointment. Most of the troops were heading to fight the French in Canada, but his contingent, including Nate, was to remain behind to make repairs to the fort and man it until a unit of regular English troops arrived. It was still spring so it was unlikely that the regulars would arrive before fall.

About 500 members of the Connecticut and New York Provincials received the assignment to stay and rebuild the Fort Ticonderoga. Peter hoped that there would be an attack on the fort so he could see some action but there was no French attack.

Finally, in November, the English and Provincial forces returned from their invasion of Quebec. They had overcome the French positions there, and in September 1759, the French Governor of Quebec signed a notice of capitulation. Quebec City was now occupied by the English and a garrison of English soldiers remained. The men returning to Fort Ticonderoga reported that most of them didn't even participate in the 15 minute battle for Quebec.

With Quebec fallen, Peter and Nate expected to return to their normal life in Somers. The Provincials were discharged and given a supply of food to last them a few days. Peter, Nate and most of the men from Connecticut headed home looking forward to seeing their families after almost a year's absence.

Lucretia and the children were overjoyed to see Peter. The oldest was eight and the baby, born soon after Peter left, was sitting up. It was a joyous reunion with neighbors and relatives. As anticipated, not every man returned, some were lost in battle while others died from disease, but most of the Connecticut men were fortunate to have escaped the major fighting.

With Spain becoming a French ally the battle fields extended to new parts of the world. England needed more men to fight and again called upon its colonies. Connecticut received another large quota. Once more, to obtain a sufficient number of volunteers, there was a signing bonus and pay equal to what they would have earned in their normal jobs.

Peter and Nate, who had remained in close contact since returning from Ticonderoga, discussed signing up again. Nate was single so it was an easy decision for him. Peter's love for adventure also made his decision easy. They went to the Somers Town Clerk's office to sign up. They were told they would receive their signing bonus when the Connecticut Provincials were called to duty. Peter spent some uneasy months waiting for his assignment but eventually, when the quota was filled, they set out. He was surprised to find that they were marching East toward Boston rather than West as they had the last time.

The Connecticut Provincials set up camp on a hill outside of Boston. Peter and Nate were in awe of the city of 20,000. They had never before seen a village with even 1,000 inhabitants! On a clear day they had a good view of Boston Harbor and the dozens of ships moored in its waters. They had been told that they would be boarding ships and sailing to an unknown destination.

The order came to move out. They marched through the city of Boston marveling at the many buildings and people. At the harbor more than a dozen ships awaited them. Peter and Nate marched aboard the frigate *Lyme*, a sleek, swift moving boat of about 500 tons armed with 28 guns. It carried three square sails and was one of the more recent additions to the English fleet. It was not a ship of the line but was built for battle as well as speed and maneuverability.

In a few days they moved out of the harbor and were joined by about 30 other ships. Ship life, which was unfamiliar to most of the Connecticut Provincials, was very confining, especially for Peter who thrived on action. When rough seas were encountered, many of the men suffered. But Peter enjoyed the bucking of the ship on the waves. Inevitably, the ships became separated from each other. After three days the winds died down and the sea began to calm. Fortunately the *Lyme* hadn't been blown against another ship, but only six of the original 30 were now in sight. There were two ships of the line, two cargo ships carrying Provincials and one other frigate. They maintained formation but were unable to locate any of the other ships.

A few days later the lookout sighted several ships in the distance and a cry of joy went out. The joy soon turned to consternation when it was discovered that they were ships of the French fleet. There was no outrunning them without leaving the two cargo ships carrying other Connecticut Provincials behind, so all ships prepared for battle. The two ships of the line, each with 64 gun,s took their battle stations with the two frigates in support. Soon cannons were blasting away and smoke was flying as each side tried to destroy the other. In the heat of battle it was discovered that the two relatively unarmed cargo ships had been cut off from the others by another four French ships. Greatly outnumbered, the two frigates were ordered to flee because tarrying would lead to certain disaster. The two cargo ships were sunk or seized but the fates of the two English ships of the line was unknown.

About the middle of July, after experiencing warmer and warmer weather, they located part of the missing British fleet. All of the ships had made it to Cuba except the two unfortunate cargo ships carrying the 500 Provincials. The two ships of the line had outmaneuvered the French ships and escaped under the cover of darkness. All of the ships waited at anchor for a few days. Eventually the remaining 3,000 Provincials received orders to go ashore.

An artist's rendering of a battle during the French and Indian Wars.

A copy of the original promotion received by Peter Ward, when he was fighting in the Colonial Militia in Cuba for England during the French and Indian Wars.

The English had established a beachhead northeast of Havana, Cuba. They had been blasting their cannons for over a month at Castle Morro, which guarded the entrance to Havana's harbor. Their attempts to take Morro had been unsuccessful because of a deep ditch around the fortress built on and surrounded by rock. Both disease and casualties had weakened the English forces, so they had been eagerly awaiting the arrival of the Provincials.

After weeks aboard their ship, Peter and Nate were relieved to finally set their feet on land. The English had built breast works to approach Morro but there was no simple way to fill the ditch. Once the breast works had been moved sufficiently close to the ditch, the English commander had his men bore into the rock next to the ditch. When sufficient forces arrived he intended set off to dynamite to fill in the ditch. Then he might be able to take Morro.

English cannon had been battering Morro Castle for over a month. The Spanish had very few cannons remaining that functioned. Without the cannon it was much safer advancing the breast works. Peter was one of the 699 men picked to attack the right bastion of Morro once the dynamite was discharged to fill in the deep ditch.

The blast was set off and the men, both English regulars and Colonial Provincials, immediately attacked Morro Castle. Twelve of the men, Peter among them, breached the right bastion and caught the Spanish by surprise. The fighting was desperate with a number of men on both sides killed or injured. The Spanish commander was one of the ones badly injured. Soon the Spanish in the fort capitulated. The commander of the English forces congratulated Peter for his bravery and told him that he would be recommended for a promotion.

The soldiers dragged cannon up into Morro Castle and aimed upon the city of Havana. The Spanish commander refused to surrender. Soon, over 50 guns were pounding the Spanish fortifications of Havana. It didn't take long after that for the Spanish to surrender.

Less than three weeks after arriving on Cuban soil, the English and their Provincial allies, Peter among them, marched victoriously into Havana. The troops were billeted in Cuba for several months, maintaining order and making sure their positions were secure. It was an interesting period for Peter and Nate who had never experienced anything like the people of Cuba and the environment where they lived.

Only a week or two after marching into Havana a hurricane hit Cuba. Winds even stronger than what they had experienced on the seas blew away their tents and ravaged many of Havana's buildings. Peter never saw such desolation. The soldiers were put to work finding their windblown tents and supplies or coming up with alternatives to protect themselves from rain and mosquitos. The pesky insects seemed to be everywhere.

By the time the battle for Cuba had ended, almost 3,000 of the English and Provincial troops had been killed, wounded or captured. Nearly 1,000 more had died from sickness. Most of the deaths from disease followed a similar pattern. The men had headaches, fever and ached all over. The symptoms went away for a few days before they returned again, often proving fatal. Peter saw friends afflicted with this scourge, some surviving but more dying. He thought to himself, "I will survive."

Peter was shocked, however, when he learned that his youngest brother, Giles, who was only 20, had succumbed to the disease. Nate had contracted what seemed to be the same disease, but had fully recovered. He was one of the lucky ones.

On October 16, 1762, at a special ceremony, several of the Provincials who had exhibited outstanding leadership and heroism, were honored. Peter was a little surprised and very much pleased to be promoted to Sergeant in the Connecticut Provincials. It not only would give him more opportunity for leadership but would provide more money for Lucretia and the children. Nate and the rest of his friends pounded him on the back and congratulated him.

Peter's glory was short-lived when he also developed the sickness in the middle of November. He went through the first symptoms and began to feel better, thinking he was to be one of the survivors. Soon he took a turn for the worse. As Nate was consoling him, he asked him to contact Lucretia and the children to share with them how much Peter loved them and would miss them. He also gave Nate his paper of commission to the rank of Sergeant to take to his family along with a few other of his personal effects. Just before he passed on, he softly whispered to Nate what a wonderful friend he had been.

Nate was saddened not only because he had lost a close friend but also knowing he had to share the sad news with Peter's family. It would be one of the most difficult assignments he had ever had. The sailing trip back to Boston was uneventful as negotiations were underway among England, France and Spain to end the war.

After arriving in Boston, Nate headed to Connecticut. Lucretia saw him come to her door and was bewildered as to why Peter wasn't with him. Nate, with hat in hand and tears forming in his eyes, shared the sad news with Lucretia. Peter Jr., called Pete, who had just turned 11, was speechless and his sister, three years younger started sobbing. There was little reaction from the two younger children who hardly knew their father. Nate offered to help the family anyway he could. Then he continued his difficult mission to share the sad news with Hannah Ward, the widowed mother of Peter and Giles. To Nate's surprise she took the news rather stoically. She had previously lost several other family members as well as her husband, Jacob, and had decided that bad news was inevitable.

Nate finally went home to his family. When he went to bed the first evening home he couldn't get to sleep. His mind kept going back to Lucretia and her four children. How would she survive? What would become of Peter's children?

The next morning Nate made the three mile walk to see Lucretia again. Thoughts were rolling through his mind. She's an attractive woman. She's a good cook and keeps her home neat. She has proven that she is fertile by having four children. She is probably about my age, 30 years old.

Then questions came to his mind. The children need a father but do I want to become the father of four small children? Would she even consider marrying me? Peter died only a few months ago and she has just heard the sad news of his death, is now the right time to ask for her hand in marriage?

He knocked on her door. Five year-old Abner answered the door and without a smile or even a simple good morning turned to his mother and said, "It's the man who was here yesterday. Do you want to see him?" The other children, even Pete, who Nate thought would be the most difficult child to befriend, was courteous.

She greeted him with a warm smile, exclaiming, "Nate it's wonderful to see you. Please stay and have dinner with us. I had no idea when we would see you again." Nate eagerly accepted her invitation, Soon Nate was getting better acquainted with the family. Pete told him that he was attending the winter school session in Somers and having some trouble with his arithmetic. Nate showed him how to add several two digit numbers. Lucretia then asked him if he could repair their table for her.

Dinner was served and the afternoon passed very quickly. Lucretia asked him to stay and have supper with them. All of the family, except Abner, urged him to stay. After a second fine meal, Nate was feeling quite comfortable with Lucretia and her family. He even stayed, after eating the meal, and shared with the family many of the adventures he and Peter had experienced on the Cuba trip. When it was bedtime the children reluctantly went to bed, hating to miss the stories Nate was sharing with the family.

Nate and Lucretia continued to talk late into the evening. It was becoming quite clear to Nate that Lucretia liked him. Finally, Nate summoned all of his courage and asked Lucretia if she would consider marrying again. She responded, "Yes Nate, I would like to marry again but not just to anybody. The children need a father. I have been very lonely these past few years with Peter away. If someone like you were to ask me I wouldn't hesitate a moment!"

Nate immediately rose from his chair, reached down to her and gave her a big hug and kiss! He didn't utter a word. She looked up at him expectantly. After a period of silence, Lucretia thought to herself that Nate might need a little help, She asked, "Nate, was that a proposal of marriage?" Nate again said nothing but reached down and gave her a hug and a kiss that she would never forget. "Well," she said, I believe that settles the deal!"

Nate never went home that evening! The children were surprised to see him in their house when they arose. Lucretia shared the news with them and all were happy except little Abner. Although he never knew his father very well, he admired him and didn't want anyone else to take his place.

The next seven years were happy ones for the new Pinney family. Unfortunately, Abner never warmed up to having someone take the place of his father. Finally, when he was 12 years old, Lucretia and Nate decided that something must be done with Abner because of his deteriorating relationship with the family.

Previously, when the family had visited a farm owned by one of Nate's brothers, Abner had shown an interest in the livestock. He had asked several questions about the farm and was reluctant to leave when it was time to go home. Nate's brother had several sons of his own so had no need of another boy. His wife, however, mentioned that she had a sister and brother-in-law on a farm in Westborough who had no children. They might be interested in a boy to live with them as an apprentice. She agreed to write to her sister and see if they might have an interest in Abner.

Two months later Nate received word from her sister and husband that they were interested in having 12-year-old Abner bound out for six years. He would have the opportunity to experience farming and learn enough so he could operate his own farm. He was to receive food and lodging. He would have the opportunity to attend school and would be treated similarly to a son as long as he fulfilled his responsibilities. If he remained for the six year apprenticeship he would receive 20 pounds sterling at the end of the bounding out years.

Nate and Lucretia asked Abner if he was willing to be bound out. He agreed and both his mother and Nate willingly signed the bounding agreement. Abner reasoned that even though he would miss his mother and siblings he would be better off learning a trade. A date was set to meet George and Ann Phillips, two weeks later, at Sturbridge about half the way to Westborough.

After a few months Abner began to be less cooperative. He objected to having to arise at daylight and work until dark every day. George Phillips gave Abner some time to become adjusted to farm life before he set him in a chair and reminded the boy of the requirements of the agreement. He showed Abner a stout ash branch about four feet long and told him in no uncertain terms that he was willing to use it on Abner the next time he didn't cooperate. Apparently the lecture wasn't completely effective because a few weeks later Abner was taken to the barn and told to stand leaning against a mow full of hay. Mr. Phillips never had to apply the stick to Abner again.

Gradually Abner became accustomed to farm life and was actually enjoying himself. Mr. and Mrs. Phillips treated Abner fairly, but expected much from him. Although Abner didn't realize it, he was not only learning a great deal about farming but also many other life skills that would be helpful to him in later life.

CHAPTER 6
Revolutionary War Years

" Abner, you have completed your bounding out admirably! Don't hesitate leaving us now. I would go myself, but it is a long march and you are in better physical condition. Go!" exclaimed Mr. Phillips. They had been discussing the news that the hated British General was planning to send hundreds of his redcoats to destroy the munitions the militia had been accumulating at Concord. It was rumored that a lady friend of the British General had heard the General discussing troop deployment with one of his colonels. She sympathized with the colonials' plight and had secretly passed on the information.

Ever since the end of the war with the French in 1763, the British had been gradually levying new and higher taxes on the colonies. The war had depleted the King's coffers, which they were now filling at the expense of the colonies. The colonists were also losing some of their rights for self-government. The part that annoyed the colonists the most was that they had no representation in the British government. If this trend continued, the colonists would be nothing more than slaves. So many of the colonists decided that they should stand up for their rights before it was too late.

With his bounding out years completed, Abner could now leave the Phillips. Mr. Philips had presented Abner with the 20 pounds sterling he had promised him, along with another five because of his dedication and extra effort. Abner wanted to buy a farm of his own someday so he asked Mr. Phillips to hold the money for him. He didn't expect to be gone for more than a few weeks. Most people felt that the British would ease their oppressiveness once the colonials made a show of force.

Abner was a member of Westborough's militia, which had been established as soon as the town was formed. The militia was needed to protect the settlers from the Indians. Although it had been several years since there had been an Indian raid, they continued to train because of the strained relationship with England. Word had come from the patriot leaders in Boston that all militia units within two days march of Concord should assemble to demonstrate to the British that the colonists would no longer quietly accept their continued aggression.

On the 15th of April, 1775, Abner set out with about 30 other militia members to Concord. As they passed through Marlborough, Hudson, Maynard and West Concord, militia from each of these communities joined them. By the time they reached Concord there were about 200 men in the group. There was a mind set of, "We'll show those damn British they are not going to push us around anymore!" However, some of the older men who still had some loyalty to England were thinking, "Perhaps we will regret this action!"

Abner saw that there were already about 100 militia men in Concord. John Hancock and John Adams were already in the area. Everyone knew that if captured by the British both of these men would be executed as traitors.

Paul Revere rode out of Boston on the 18th of April with the details of the imminent British attack. Along the way he warned his countrymen that the British were coming. At Lexington other patriots rode through the countryside to Concord to spread the word that the British were planning to attack on the 19th.

It was believed that the British would attempt to capture Hancock and Adams at Lexington and then move on to Concord to destroy the munitions stored there. Both Hancock and Adams were immediately moved north from Lexington to prevent their capture. Word was sent on to Concord to move the munitions to outlying villages and to hide whatever they were unable to move.

The Westborough militia was given the task of hiding whatever munitions that the other militia didn't have time to move. Abner, who was used to tilling the soil as a farmer, saw that a nearby field had recently been plowed, suggested that the smaller munitions could be buried under the furrows and be retrieved after the British left. The militia Captain agreed and the men went to work. By the time word was received that the British had arrived at Lexington and were marching on to Concord all the munitions had been hidden.

Somehow the British learned that cannon had been buried on the property of a local innkeeper. They forced their way into the inn and threatened to kill him if he didn't tell them where the guns were hidden. The British found three huge cannons that fired 24-pound shot. They destroyed the cannons' trunnions and some other gun carriages but found little else.

Abner was with about 400 other militia and minutemen on a hill near the North Bridge in Concord. About 70 Redcoats were near the bridge and seemed to be in a state of confusion. Someone fired a shot and soon the British and the Patriots were exchanging fire at each other. Abner heard a musket ball whizzing by his head and fired his musket. The gunpowder smoke was filling the air. All he could see was an occasional dim view of a redcoat. British reinforcements were arriving as the remaining Redcoats ran for their safety. Soon all of the British were withdrawing, forming in ranks and heading back toward Lexington.

A loud "hooray" went up from the patriots as the British withdrew. The British removed four dead Redcoats and helped several of their injured as they withdrew. The militia were saddened to have lost one of their own along with several others, but they were elated and a bit surprised to see the British retreat. Abner was thinking to himself that the Redcoats weren't as tough as he had heard.

Many of the militia wanted to try to catch up with the Redcoats and finish them off. The Patriot leaders were much wiser and ordered them to assemble into ranks and march back to Concord. The officers knew that there were many more Redcoats in Lexington and it would be suicidal. In addition, war hadn't been declared. Up to this point they had been protecting what was rightly theirs and only had fired when fired upon.

Abner and the rest of the patriots were put to work retrieving the weapons they had hidden. The next morning word came from Lexington that there had been a skirmish there with eight patriots killed. Word also came of patriots, hiding behind the trees, along the route back to Boston, firing on the Redcoats, wounding and killing many.

Some of the militia went back to their villages but many stayed, including the one that Abner was with, to protect Concord in the event that the British were to return.

After waiting three days, word arrived that the British were back in Boston and there had been no sign of another attack. The Westborough militia marched back home without a man injured or killed, feeling justly proud of their success against the British.

Mr. and Mrs. Phillips were overjoyed to see Abner and the rest of the militia safely home. Word arrived that the British were angered and not at all intimidated by the Colonial success at Lexington and Concord. Most of the members of the militia in Westborough had families and jobs so they couldn't be away fighting indefinitely. Abner and a few of the other single men were anxious to take on the British again. They decided to join the army as regulars to be where any engagement with the British occurred. On April 28, Abner signed up and became part of Colonel Timothy Danielson's regiment.

The Colonial army, including the regiment Abner was with, surrounded Boston. In mid-June the colonial forces learned that the British were planning to send troops out from the city to occupy some unfortified hills. Immediately, Abner found himself as one of over 1,000 Patriots occupying Breed's and Bunker Hills. They were put to work fortifying the hills in anticipation of a British attack.

In the early morning of their third day of building fortifications, cannon balls from a British ship in the harbor started bombarding Breed's Hill in an attempt to destroy the Colonial fortifications. Abner and the rest hunkered down into the trenches.

Soon Abner could see the British marching toward Breed's Hill. As the first line of Redcoats marched up the hill, he and the rest of the Colonials were ordered to hold fire until the Redcoats got so close that they could hardly miss. His regiment commander shouted to the men, "Don't shoot until you can see the whites of their eyes!"

At the command, "Fire!", there was a deafening roar as more than 50 muskets fired at the same time. A cloud of black smoke went up in the air and then the second line of Colonials fired while the first line reloaded. Redcoats were falling left and right and soon retreating down the hill. Abner was elated. Already they were on the run! His joy was short lived as a second assault marched against them. Volley after volley was fired and they just kept coming. Soon the Redcoats hesitated and then retreated again. Abner was worried. He was getting low on ammunition.

It wasn't long before there was a third assault against the hill. Abner fired, reloaded and fired again. The Redcoats were getting closer. Ammunition was running low for all of the defenders and the order was given to retreat up the hill. Abner loaded his last charge, fired and then started running up the hill in retreat with the others. He had only taken a couple of steps when he saw one of his buddies stumble and fall as blood gushed from him. Abner passed several other, lying on the ground, two of them moaning. He thought to himself, "Legs get moving now or you'll never move again." Fortunately the musket balls eluded him and he made it over the top of the hill. He realized he had underestimated the British.

Most of the injured Colonials were rescued but a few remained in what was now British lines. Abner's regiment leader exclaimed, "If we only hadn't run out of ammunition we could have held the hill!"

The Colonials reassembled and the commander attempted to get a force together to attack the British but instead retreated to safety over the

Cambridge neck of land that they had crossed when fortifying Breed's Hill. Many thought the Battle of Bunker and Breed's Hills was a British victory. Abner and his fellow patriots thought otherwise. Many more Redcoats than Colonials had been killed and injured in the battle. After retreating from Breed's and Bunker hills, the Colonials joined their fellow soldiers in continuing the siege of Boston.

Abner's term of enlistment, along with many in the army, was to end on December 31. George Washington, who had been named the Commander-in-Chief of the Cononial's army by Congress, was on his way to Boston at the time of the Bunker Hill battle. Until Washington arrived, General Artemus Ward, a cousin of Peter Ward who Abner never knew, was commander of the colonial army. When General Washington arrived at Dorchester Heights he transformed the various militia and army units into a more cohesive fighting force. He was concerned about the number of men whose term of service was ending at the end of the year. The number of Colonial forces had dropped from 20,000 to 13,000 since Bunker Hill.

The Continental Congress, with no money available, set a quota of men that each colony was to meet. Massachusetts provided a bonus to each man that signed up for an additional two years. Abner took advantage of this offer and signed up for another two years. He was going to add this money to what he had accumulated, while bound out on the farm, to buy his own farm after the war.

He had a month between enlistments and decided to take advantage of the time by going back to Westborough to see Mr. and Mrs. Phillips as well as some of his old friends. He especially enjoyed Mrs. Phillips' home cooked meals after surviving the last few months on whatever the army had to offer. While helping Mr. Phillips harvest his squash and potatoes he noticed an attractive young girl hanging clothes on the line to dry, at the neighboring farm. He asked Mrs. Phillips who she was and found that her name was Edna. She was the oldest daughter of their new neighbors. Sensing that Abner had more than a passing interest in Edna, Mrs. Phillips invited Edna to dinner that evening.

Edna was only 16 but she was blossoming into a pretty young lady almost as tall as Abner. The evening was spent in small talk but Edna and Abner seemed to be attracted to each other. When it was time for Edna to leave Abner offered to walk her home. Mr. Phillips interjected that it would not be proper for them to be alone together, since Abner had not been introduced to Edna's father and mother. He would, however, be willing to go along with them as chaperone. Abner wasn't exactly pleased but realized it was only the proper thing to do.

When reaching Edna's home, Mr. Phillips introduced Abner to Edna's parents. He explained that Abner was almost like a son to him and how Abner had been away fighting against the hated British Redcoats who were gradually taking away their freedom. After Abner shared some of his experiences at Concord, he and Mr. Phillips headed back home. When Abner went to Sunday services at the Westborough meeting house a few days later, he saw Edna with her family across the room. She glanced his way and gave a little smile of recognition. That was all the encouragement Abner needed to find a way to see her again.

He must have prayed real hard in church that day because Edna's father came over to him after the service and invited Abner to join them for dinner the following Wednesday. The next couple of days Abner was often heard whistling a happy tune. Mrs. Philips remarked to her husband that it appeared that Abner was in love. The dinner at Edna's went well. She had seven younger brothers and sisters so it was a lively dinner hour without any private opportunity for the couple to talk. Edna's mother took pity on them and after dinner suggested since it was such a beautiful October evening Abner and Edna might like to go out on the porch to enjoy the evening away from all of the children.

They followed her suggestion. It wasn't long before Abner slid his hand around Edna's. Her face turned from a pale white, to pink and then to a bright red. She had never held a man's hand before and it sent shivers up and down her spine. What was happening to her? She heard some giggling and looked around. There were four pairs of eyes staring out window at them. She jumped up, ran to the door and yelled to her mother, "Mother, make them go to bed! They are looking out the window at us!" but the interruption broke the magic spell. They continued to talk a while but it was soon time for Abner to leave. He told her that he had signed up with the Colonial Army for two years but would be back to see her as soon as he completed his time of duty.

The Colonial siege of Boston continued through the remainder of 1775 and most of the winter of 1776. Abner and the rest of the army had heard of the success of Ethan Allen's Green Mountain Boys' attack at Fort Ticonderoga. They had also heard that some of the heavy cannons that had been seized might be headed to Boston. In early February he and about 400 other members of the army were given orders to march west to help haul the heavy cannon that had been captured to Boston. It was more than a 100 mile march. The cannons were huge and very heavy. It was several days before they reached the exhausted members of the Connecticut militia that had already hauled the cannon almost 40 miles.

Fortunately the ground was frozen and covered with snow, making it easier to pull the cannons on sleds. The sleds were made from logs that were split lengthwise. Several slabs were placed side by side and fastened together with wooden pins driven through holes in the cross pieces. The first sleds were worn down so they made new ones, which they hoped would last until they reached Boston.

Each of the large cannons weighed over a ton. Eight men were assigned to each of the 16 sleds carrying the cannon. Two ropes were attached to each sled with four men on each rope. There were two teams of men for each sled so they could change off every hour. Abner was young and well muscled but he had never worked so hard in his life. Going downhill, they also had to attach ropes to the back of the sleds to keep them from running over the men in front. Extra men were needed to pull the sleds up steep hills. Upon reaching an unfrozen river it was necessary to build a large raft to ferry the cannons across.

Five miles a day was excellent progress. Upon reaching the Connecticut Valley scouts were sent out to obtain ox teams from the farmers in the valley. After much searching and some threatening of the oxen owners,

16 teams of oxen with their drivers were obtained. Although the oxen were slow, it was faster and much easier for the men. They could now average eight miles a day. In early March the cannons finally reached Dorchester Heights overlooking the city of Boston. The cannon were aimed at the city of Boston and the British warships in the harbor.

With the large cannons looking down upon them, the British Commander in Chief on March 17 decided to move away from Boston with its hot-headed New Englanders to the much safer port at New York. A loud "Hooray" echoed across the hills of Dorchester Heights as the British ships with all their Redcoats sailed out of the harbor.

After spending several more months at Boston while General Washington waited to hear news of the British Army's location, the Colonial Army marched toward New York City. In route to New York the soldiers learned that the Continental Congress had announced that the several colonies had united and declared themselves to be free and independent from Britain.

Abner completed his two-year tour of duty successfully and without injury. He was stationed near New York at the end of his two-year stretch. The army badly needed members so he was encouraged to sign up again. He wanted to go back home to see Edna but it was a long distance and he was sorely needed where he was. He decided it was his duty to enlist for another two years. After all, he thought, Edna would only be 20 when he completed his next term of duty. It was a long time but he was sure she would be there for him.

Abner continued to move from spot to spot in both New York and New Jersey with his regiment. There were skirmishes with the British and they were even sent out to find the pesky Indians, who with help from the cowardly Loyalists, Colonists loyal to Britain, were attacking settlers in upstate New York. He couldn't understand how some of the settlers could still be loyal to England after so much oppression during the last several years. The Indians and Loyalists would strike and then quickly disappear. It was almost impossible to find them.

IN THE WAR OF THE REVOLUTION.   523

WARD, ABNER, Westfield. Private, in a Westfield co. of Minute-men commanded by Lieut. John Shephard, which marched April 20, 1775, in response to the alarm of April 19, 1775; service, 1 week 1 day; reported enlisted into the army April 28, 1775; *also*, Capt. Warham Parks's co., Col. Timothy Danielson's regt.; muster roll dated Aug. 1, 1775; enlisted April 28, 1775; service, 3 mos., 1 week, 3 days; *also*, company return dated Roxbury [probably Oct., 1775]; *also*, order for money in lieu of bounty coat dated Camp at Roxbury, Dec. 23, 1775; *also*, return of men raised to serve in the Continental Army from Capt. John Kellogg's (Westfield) co.; residence, Westfield; engaged for town of Westfield; joined Capt. Ball's co., Col. William Shepard's regt.; term, during war; *also*, Private, Maj. Lebbeus Ball's co., Col. Sheppard's (3d) regt.; Continental Army pay accounts for service from Jan. 1, 1777, to Dec. 31, 1779; *also*, Capt. Lebbeus Ball's co., Col. Shepard's regt.; return endorsed " Feb'y 3rd 1778;" mustered by State and Continental Muster Masters; *also*, same co. and regt.; muster roll for July and Aug., 1778, dated Camp at Providence; *also*, same co. and regt.; muster roll for Oct., 1778; *also*, Maj. Lebbeus Ball's co., Col. Shepard's regt.; muster rolls for Nov., 1778, March and April, 1779, dated Camp at Providence; enlisted Dec. 4, 1777; enlistment, during war; *also*, Major's co., Col. Shepard's (4th) regt.; Continental Army pay accounts for service from Jan. 1, 1780, to Dec. 31, 1780; *also*, same co. and regt.; return for gratuities, dated Highlands, Feb. 24, 1780; gratuity paid said Ward Feb. 1, 1780; *also*, Capt. George Webb's (Light Infantry) co., Col. Shepard's regt.; return made up for the year 1780, dated West Point; enlisted Jan. 1, 1777; *also*, Corporal, Capt. John Fuller's co., Col. Shepard's regt.; muster rolls for June–Sept., 1781; *also*, muster rolls for Oct., Nov., and Dec., 1781, dated York Hutts; *also*, muster roll for Jan., 1782, dated York Hutts and sworn to in Garrison at West Point; *also*, muster roll for Feb., 1782, sworn to in Garrison at West Point.

Abner Ward's record of service fighting for independence from England during the American Revolutionary War.

An artist's rendering of a battle during the American Revolutionary War.

After Abner's second two-year tour of duty he was determined to make it back to Westborough to see Edna. He set out from the Hudson Valley with a light step, whistling as he went. He went right home to the Philips to clean up before he went to see Edna. The Philips were overjoyed to see him! They had no idea whether he was dead or alive. They had heard nothing for four years!

He asked how Edna was and didn't see Mr. Phillips put a finger to his lips and shake his head as he looked at his wife. "Oh!" Mr. Phillips responded. "Edna is very good. She has blossomed into a beautiful woman. She has moved, however. You will find her three doors down from the meetinghouse where the Stones used to live." After Abner headed on his way to see Edna, Mrs. Phillips scolded her husband for not telling him more.

Abner eagerly set out for the center of town and quickly found the right house. He expected to be met at the door by Edna's mother but was surprised to be met at the door by a beautiful young woman with a baby in her arms. It was Edna! What a beauty she was! Abner's face glowed with joy as he exclaimed, "You look wonderful Edna! You have no idea how I missed you. It's nice that you have a new little sister."

Edna glanced down toward the baby in her arms with a demure look on her face and responded. "Abner, you said you would be back in two years. It's been four years. I had no idea what might have happened to you. I'm married and this is my baby." Abner was speechless. His mouth dropped open and he stepped back.

He gathered his thoughts together. She was right. He had said he would be back two years ago. It wouldn't have been wise to be married and then leave his wife for God knows how long. He might never have made it back. He wished Edna much happiness, then turned with a heavy step and walked down the street.

On his way home he stopped by a little gurgling stream along his path. He thought about what had just transpired and vowed never to be smitten with love again. At least not until after the war was over!

He headed back to West Point where his regiment was stationed. This time he signed up with the army for only a year. The war seemed to be moving to the colonies in the South. For several years he had heard of more victories by the British than by Washington's army. Now, however, it seemed to him like Washington's victories were coming more often.

In November 1781, word reached the colonial soldiers near New York that a huge British army had surrendered in Virginia a month earlier. Perhaps the British would now consider giving the colonies their freedom and leave New York. Unfortunately, however, the British continued to stay. Because of the continued presence of the British in New York City it was necessary to keep a colonial army available nearby. Abner, having no special reason to go home, continued to sign up for short periods of time. Finally in late 1783, word was received that the war was over. The colonies had overcome the British! Abner was overjoyed! Now he could go home and begin a normal life.

He wanted to own a farm but didn't know where. He lived and worked with the Phillips for a while. They offered to sell him their farm but Abner felt it was too stony and hilly to make a good living and continued to look for good farmland in the area.

His search for affordable land was fruitless. Several soldiers whom he had served with during his last tour of duty had told stories of the large areas of rich soil in New York. They reported that back in 1779 they had been part of the forces under General Sullivan that had been sent by General Washington to destroy the Iroquois Indians. The Indians, as allies of the British, had been attacking New York settlers. The soldiers had destroyed large quantities of the Indian's crops and orchards. They had driven most of the Indians from New York. With the Indian menace removed New York offered wonderful opportunities, especially for someone interested in farming.

While Abner was contemplating what he should do, he decided to visit his older brother Peter who lived in nearby Hopkinton. While he was there Peter's wife introduced him to her younger sister Hannah. As soon as Abner saw Hannah his heart skipped a beat. She was only 18 and a real beauty. Abner's next visit to Hopkinton wasn't so much to see his brother but to see Hannah.

During Abner's frequent visits to see Hannah he asked her if she would be willing to go west to the frontier in New York with him. She expressed some concern about going so far away from her family and worried she might never see them again. As they sat together one evening Abner had his arm around her waist. He pulled her close, bent over and gave her a long kiss on her mouth. Then he pulled back a few inches and whispered to her, "Will you marry me?"

For what seemed to Abner to be hours but actually only a couple of minutes Hannah softly responded, "Abner, I love you very much. I would give an immediate yes if we were to stay in this area but I cannot bring myself to go into the wilderness of New York. Please understand."

Abner continued to hold her close as he replied, "I want you to be my wife! Would you consider going with me if we found a place only a few days travel away, where we could come back to see your family at least once a year?"

After many more hugs and kisses, interspersed with conversation, it was decided that they would marry as soon as Abner was able to locate a suitable piece of farm land.

Hannah said that her sister and Peter would stand with them when they took their vows. Since it was now the middle of May, Abner estimated that he could find an appropriate spot and return in about a month. He told Hannah about his trip to help with the cannon several years earlier and the good land he had seen west of Massachusetts.

Abner borrowed a horse from Mr. Phillips and set out the next morning in a northwesterly direction. He made good time his first day because he was traveling through countryside with occasional villages and farms scattered along the highway. On his second day out he stopped in western Massachusetts to inquire about the availability of farmland. He heard the price of farmland in that area was discouraging.. He was told that he needed to go further west into Vermont, in relatively unsettled forest land, and he would find land readily available at little cost.

He continued on to Rupert, Vermont, a small four-corners settlement with only a general store and a blacksmith shop. There wasn't even a church or school in the little settlement. He entered the general store to inquire about land that might be available. He was told that if he were to go North about 20 miles to Rutland, he might be able to receive 100 acres at no cost provided he homesteaded. He would be required to improve the property with a home and remain there for a minimum of ten years. Thoughts immediately passed through his mind. Would Hannah be willing to start life with him in this wilderness? Would it be too far from her home in Hopkinton?

He decided to travel the 20 miles to Rutland and see what was available. The first half of his ride was a bit difficult as there was only a narrow trail through the forest. Several times he had to ride around a large tree lying across the trail and one stream was so deep that he was challenged to get his horse to swim across it. The last ten miles were much easier because of a well used road leading into Rutland.

Rutland was just a small village so it was easy to locate the county offices. He was pleased to find that he could obtain 100 acres at no cost provided he met the homesteading requirements. There was, however, a fee of ten dollars that had to be paid to have the land surveyed and another fee of five dollars to pay for having the survey filed. They told him there had been too many problems in the past with squatters settling on property that other people actually owned resulting in conflicting claims. After considerable thought and more questions Abner decided to pay the fees and hoped that Hannah would approve.

A difficult part of his decision came when he was required to choose his land from a map without any possibility of seeing the property until after it had been surveyed. The official showed him a map and he decided upon a property that appeared to be about a mile north of Rupert. He also told Abner that if he stayed over a day he could go with the surveyor to help him mark the property.

A night at the local Inn and two good meals appealed to Abner so he happily spent the night in Rutland. The next morning he met the surveyor and the two of them headed back toward Rupert on horseback. The surveyor knew exactly where they were going as he had surveyed land just south of the 100 acres Abner had chosen. The surveying was made much simpler because of the markings on the trees from that survey. They had to measure the correct distance for the ends at right angles from the already surveyed plot and connect the two points. There were trees to go around and a small brook to cross but this was all accomplished in one day. They used an axe to mark the trees on each corner and then marked a tree along each side about every 100 feet.

There were some large maple trees on the property so Abner knew that the soil underneath was fertile and capable of growing a good crop. He smiled as he thought about collecting sap from these trees the following spring to make maple sugar. He thought about the great amount of work it would take to clear some of the land for crops. He remembered the stories that had been passed down through the family of his grandparents who had cleared the forests to grow crops. It gave him a warm feeling to think he'd experience something similar. He thought to himself, this is even better than buying land that has already been cleared with its worn out soil from growing crops year after year.

Abner spent an extra day deciding where to situate his future home. He located a wet spot on the land with a small flow of water coming from it. He would dig a shallow well on this spot to furnish his family with water. A ridge not too far from the trail passing in front of his property, not too far from where the well was going to be, was chosen.

He decided to stay an extra few days to clear the site for his cabin and to make a small lean-to for he and Hannah to sleep while they were building their cabin. It was early summer and they would only need protection from the rain for the next three months. They should complete the cabin before November.

Abner was able to purchase some extra food at the general store in Rupert to supplement what he had brought with him. He also learned that there was a single young army veteran who was living nearby who might be willing to help him build his cabin. The man also owned a team of oxen that would be invaluable in pulling the cabin's logs into place. Arrangements were made to have the man help him three weeks later after Abner completed cutting the logs for the cabin.

Hannah was overjoyed to see Abner return from his trip. He went into great detail of all his experiences and told Hannah he hoped she would be happy with the decision he had made. He related about the temporary lean-to and picking a cabin site. Hannah either enjoyed adventure or her eyes were clouded with stars of love because she responded, "Honey, I know whatever decisions you made were perfect. I will be at your side supporting you wherever we go! I can't wait. Let's get married tomorrow!"

The wedding took place as planned. The newlyweds set out for Rupert the next day. They developed the farm during the next 16 years. Hannah bore eight of her children before they moved a little further west to Schuylerville, NY where they spent about 10 more years and had four more children. In the winter of 1811 the entire family moved further west again, to Scipio, NY where Abner died in 1838.

CHAPTER 7

The Continuation of the Family's Westward Movement

Ever since William Ward of the first generation made the decision to leave England to settle in New England in 1638, almost every generation of the family continued moving to the west. Some generations, such as Abner's, even moved in a westerly direction three times. William Ward of the seventh generation continued the western movement. There seemed to be a continuing urge in the family to tackle the unknown or to better themselves.

William Ward of the seventh generation, who we will be referring to in this chapter was born in Rupert, VT in 1788. When he was about 12 his parents, Abner and Hannah, moved to Schuylerville, NY where, for the next 10 years he lived while his father developed their farm. William has reached the age of 23 as this chapter begins.

Abner and Hannah made the decision to leave Schuylerville because of the stories, shared by some of Abner's Revolutionary soldier acquaintances, about the rich land in the Cayuga Indian country. All 11 of their living children, including William, moved with them. Within a year after their arrival in the town of Scipio in Cayuga County the war of 1812 broke out between England and the United States.

England could easily invade New York from many points on Lake Ontario so the US military decided it was necessary to prevent England from becoming the powerhouse on the lake. Men were recruited from all over the state to go to a little village along the eastern shore of Lake Ontario called Sackets Harbor. It had a large sheltered harbor capable of mooring many boats. There was also an abundance of timber in nearby forests to supply the lumber needed to construct ships. Labor of all kinds was not only necessary to build the ships but a substantial military force was needed to prevent the British from attacking. Ships being constructed along the shore would be sitting ducks. Once the British gained a foothold Redcoats would soon be marching through New York and the other states.

William soon answered the call to join the NY militia and was assigned to a unit from the Cayuga area. After a two-week training period the unit received orders to report to Sackets Harbor. It was only about 100 miles and took them four days to reach. William enjoyed seeing great areas of forested land as they marched along. When they crossed the Seneca River into Lysander on their path west of Oswego he mused that this area might be a good place for him to settle some day after the was was over.

Sackets Harbor was a bustling village. There were men working on several ships along the harbor's edge. The number of men that had arrived in the village to build ships had taken every sleeping spot around. Even the village residents were required to house as many workers as they had room. The army was busy building barracks for the men but none had been completed yet. Hopefully some would be ready before winter!

William and about 30 others in his regiment were assigned to sleep in a barn at the edge of the village. It served them well when they arrived in early September but one day when a cold windy storm came across Lake Ontario the chill from the water made him wonder what winter would be like. The barn was empty now, except for hay and straw, but during the winter they might be sharing the barn with livestock.

William's first duties were to help transport cut blocks of stone from a nearby quarry to the masons constructing the barracks. Wagons were not available so the blocks were loaded on a large flat sled and hauled by a team of oxen to the masons. William had driven oxen many times back on the farm so he was assigned the job of loading the stone, hauling it and then unloading it. As soon as he had made one trip he started on another. It was hard work but no worse than when he had helped his father cut trees, dig out stumps and clear the land back at Schuylerville.

He had never seen so many men working. It was a race against time to build enough ships to prevent the British from invading New York. Each day he could see the progress being made. Some of the barracks had roofs, more were being started and several ships had been launched. Guns were being fitted on these ships. All the men hoped the British wouldn't attack before the Americans were prepared.

Summer quickly turned to fall. William marveled at the beauty of the area. The leaves on the trees had turned into all shades of color and now the leaves were floating gently to the ground. An early fall snowfall gave imminent warning that the weather would soon be different.

Hopes for the completion of a sufficient number of barracks to house the Cayuga militia were soon dashed when newly arrived militia units from other parts of the state were assigned to all available barracks. The men in William's regiment were destined to spend the winter in the barn. When William brought the team of oxen back to the barn one night in early November, the sled they were pulling was loaded with pieces of lumber too small to use in the ship construction. He had also confiscated a sufficient number of nails to hold the pieces of lumber in place. He and some of the other men went to work patching holes and spaces in the barn's siding that let the wind whistle through. The extra ventilation during the summer had been pleasant but the cold drafts of late fall were not desirable.

Work constructing the barracks continued right through the winter. The snow was a nuisance but it didn't seem to be any worse than what William had experienced back home. The bitter cold wind off the lake is what bothered them the most. Some of the men that had volunteered from New York City and New Jersey were experiencing a real winter and weren't especially enjoying themselves.

Six mornings a week all the soldiers were required to report for review followed by a period of exercise to keep them in shape and to warm them up before they began their various work assignments. One Thursday morning the large warning bell started ringing. They were notified that five British ships had been sighted as the sun rose in the eastern sky. The men were assigned to their battle stations and work on the ships and the barracks ceased. The cannons were manned and the large frigate, the USS Oneida, moored in the harbor but ready for battle, turned to face the enemy ships. When within range, but before the British fired a shot, the batteries on shore sent off a barrage of cannon shots at the ships. Most missed their target but one shot took down the main sail of an English ship. The other four continued to move toward land but soon another barrage from the shore batteries sent them on their way. During this battle William, with his oxen and sled, was assigned to keep a supply of gunpowder and cannon balls available to one of the shore batteries.

The oxen were ideally suited to this duty as they seemed to totally ignore the loud blasts and smoke coming from the guns. William thought to himself how differently horses would have reacted. By now horses would have been tearing in some direction away from the noise with William hanging on to the reins. He wondered if maybe the blasts from the gunpowder used to break layers of rock loose in the stone quarry had accustomed them to the loud noises and smoke. They didn't even seem to be bothered when one of the British cannonballs went whisking over their heads.

At parade the following morning their commander warned the men not to become complacent as the British were most likely to attack again. He ordered the men to renewed efforts in completing more ships so their navy would be strong enough to sail out and defeat the British. If the American fleet was unable to stop them the Redcoats would be marching ashore by the thousands.

The winter hadn't been as difficult to withstand as William feared. He would curl up at night between his ox team that gave off enough heat to ease the bitter cold of the unheated barn. His fellow militia that were billeted in the barn kidded him about how much he smelled like a cow. William just smiled at them because he knew they were jealous and they actually smelled as badly as he because of sleeping in the same barn.

Finally in early May 1813, the British again attacked Sackets Harbor. This time they secretly sent men ashore in a secluded area near the harbor. The British diverted attention away from their landing force by directing their shots at the American ships in the harbor and against the shore batteries. By the time the Americans discovered the invasion, the British had a good foothold and were only a few miles from Sackets Harbor.

The Americans redirected their militia against the oncoming British but left the shore batteries fully manned to continue firing at the British ships. William continued to supply American cannons with gunpowder but knew that if his gunpowder loaded sled happened to be hit by a stray shot his life was over.

Fortunately one of the artillery commanders received word that the Redcoats had come within three of his cannons. He immediately ordered his soldiers to give the Redcoats a good American reception. The British advance came to a standstill as they tried to regroup and by that time the American militia was upon them.

Soon the British decided to withdraw, not realizing their superiority in numbers over the Americans. Good timing, along with some accurate artillery, saved the day for the Americans.

The shipbuilding race between England and the Americans continued during the next year and a half. Spies kept track of the additional new ships constructed by the opposing forces. Each country hoped to outbuild the other in order to win control of Lake Ontario. William continued to use the oxen and sleigh to keep the stonemasons supplied as they constructed more barracks for the troops. There was hope that all of the troops could be housed in the barracks during the coming winter. There never seemed to be enough room in military housing for the Cayuga militia so William and the rest of the regiment continued to spend their nights in the barn.

There was little military action at Sackets Harbor the rest of the year. In late September word came of a successful battle by the Americans on Lake Erie where the Americans had gained control of the lake. There was hope that the war might end soon. To almost everyone's dismay the war continued. There had been two successful invasions of Canada with York pillaged and burned by the Americans. There was talk that the army might also be sent to invade Montreal.

William and the rest of the Cayuga militia anxiously awaited June 1814 when their two year enlistment would be complete. Two more winters in Sackets Harbor with no available women and no home cooking was too long. There were some women in Sackets Harbor but they were either older married women or were ones that followed the army waiting to relieve the soldiers of whatever money they had. All of the families with young daughters made sure they were sent to a relative's home away from the woman-crazed workers and military at Sackets Harbor.

In June, action beyond the continued building of ships was occurring around Sackets Harbor. William said a sad farewell to his faithful team of oxen and his regiment headed back to Cayuga County. They had been very fortunate. One man had been killed by an exploding cannon and two had slight injuries that had healed. Nineteen men were happy to be heading home to join their families.

William was amazed to see how much his brothers had grown. Four of his brothers were strapping young men and a sister who had turned 17 made the neighbor boys' eyes turn. Abner's farm was looking more like a farm than a wilderness. William wondered if he shouldn't purchase some land in the same area. He had saved some of militia his pay and could use that to purchase land.

There was a problem, however. He had been thinking these past two years of a young lady, named Hannah, back in Schuylerville. He had become acquainted with her at the community's Congregational

Church. There had been no dating as she was only 17 and came from a well-to-do family. William had been afraid that her father might not approve of him because he was only a laborer on his father's farm. Before he left with his father's family, almost three years earlier, they had talked quite extensively about each other's plans for the future. He had told her he wanted to clear his own land and turn it into a productive farm. She wished to have a family and would enjoy pioneering in undeveloped country.

Mailing a letter was difficult and costly so he had written to her only twice. The first time he told her about the magnificent country he had passed through coming to Scipio. The second letter had told her some of his experiences at Sackets Harbor. He received one letter from her that expressed the hope he would be coming back to Schuylerville when he was discharged.

Soon after he arrived home he approached his mother and asked what she thought were his chances for Mr. Finch's approval of his calling on Hannah. William's mother and Mrs. Finch had been good friends when they had lived in Schuylerville so he needed her opinion. His mother told him that if he could stand and face 1,000 Redcoats he certainly should have no fear of approaching Hannah's father!

Soon he was retracing his steps of three years earlier but now with even more anticipation. Little had changed except now he was meeting numerous settlers heading to Western New York rather than being part of a family that was heading West. East of Cazenovia he was offered a ride with a man driving a four-horse team pulling tandem wagons loaded with wheat heading for the Hudson River at Albany. He would be able to ride and be paid in exchange for driving the horses. The driver had been kicked in the arm by one of the horses and it was difficult for him to hold the reins for very long at a time.

He explained to William that the hills of the last 20 miles had been very difficult. They were huge and he had been forced to hire a teamster because it was too difficult for his horses to pull both wagons over the hills. The horses didn't speed William's travels any but it gave him a break from walking all the way and the opportunity to earn a little money. Once in Albany, William helped the driver unload the sacks of wheat, then headed north along the Hudson River to Schuylerville.

He paid for one night's lodging at the local inn. He didn't have any idea if he would be there more than one night. After washing up and eating supper, William nervously set out toward Hannah's home. Once he almost turned around and headed back but then remembered how lonely he had been the last two years and continued on. As he walked up the steps to the Finch's front door, he was actually shaking. He hesitated a few minutes before knocking, hoping his shaking would not be noticeable. Mr. Finch came to the door, took one look at him and said "You look like you might be one of Abner Ward's boys."

William responded that he was, that his name was William and that he had been away the past two years fighting the British. Mr. Finch immediately invited William to come in and sit down. He told him that he had heard that the local militia had also returned. He was pleased that William's generation was protecting the freedoms that he and Abner had won at the cost of many lives. He then quizzed William about his experiences during those two years. Finally he said, "You must have come here for something. I've been busy asking you questions without giving you a chance to say why you came."

William hesitated and finally said that he would like to see Hannah if she was willing to see him. Mr. Finch immediately called out to Hannah, who unknown to both of them, had been in the next room with her mother listening to every word that was said. She immediately appeared with a big smile on her face. Mr Finch remarked, "Hannah, by the size of that smile on your face I believe you have given William a very clear answer. Introduce William to your mother. Take him into the parlor where the two of you can talk without interruption."

After further conversation among the four of them, Hannah and William moved to the parlor. They spent the next two hours sharing what had happened during the past three years. Near the end of the evening Hannah told William that she had several potential suitors come to her door but she waited for him to return. William told Hannah of his father's move to Cayuga Indian country in New York and the fine farm that he had developed. He would also like to farm in the West but he would stay in Schuylerville if that was what she wanted. After a warm embrace and a passionate kiss Hannah invited William to join the family for supper the next evening.

William decided it was best not to pursue at this time where they might live if they married but to give Hannah time to consider all possibilities. Although he had been warmly received by both of Hannah's parents he wasn't yet sure if they would approve of him as a son-in-law. Before he had left Scipio he used some money he had saved and most of his militia pay for the last two years to purchase 43 acres of land. He had taken a chance that Hannah might return to Scipio with him. The land was near his father's farm along the shore of Owasco Lake. Although he had to pay $215 for the land he was quite sure that if he didn't settle there that he could sell it some day for a good profit.

The next evening William was warmly received by both of Hannah's parents. During the meal Mr. Finch asked William what his future plans were. William responded that he would like to clear land for a farm in New York near where his family had moved, but he really wanted to do whatever Hannah desired if they were to be married. Mr. Finch replied, "Talk to Hannah but if the two of you decide to marry, her mother would like to have you both nearby. You might provide us with grandchildren. It would be wonderful to have them living close to us. In addition, I need a young man like you to clear some of my land near here."

The young couple again retired to the parlor. Immediately William took Hannah into his arms and gave her a long but gentle kiss. He then, asked her to be his wife. He never received a verbal answer. There was no need of one after Hannah immediately threw her arms around his neck and kissed him like there was no tomorrow!

They settled down on the loveseat in the parlor and began to discuss their future. It became obvious to William that Hannah would like to stay in Schuylerville near her family and friends. William and Hannah then went back into the room where her parents were sitting and announced their good news. Hannah's mother beamed with joy when she heard that they were going to stay in Schuylerville. Apparently her parents had discussed the various possibilities and were ready with a proposition for the young couple. Their home was too large. Hannah was the only child left at home. They would divide their home into a two-family home if they were willing to live next to them. To Hannah and William it seemed to be a perfect solution to their housing needs.

Mr. Finch then said that he had something else for them to consider. If William was willing, he had 300 acres of land nearby. Much of it was hilly but there was about a fifth of it that would make good farmland. If William was willing to clear that land he would either give him the land he had cleared at the end of ten years or loan him $1,000 to buy land near his family in western New York. During the ten years all the lumber and ashes from the timberland were to be William's.

It didn't take William and Hannah long to discuss the offer. William had helped his father clear land at both Schuylerville and also Cayuga. He enjoyed the sound of the axe echoing in the woods as it bit into a tree and to see the wood chips flying from the tree as his axe took a hearty bite from its trunk. Logs were plentiful but would provide him with a nice income as a reward for his efforts.

William spent the next several days dividing the large home into two separate living areas. He didn't need to stay at the local inn more than his first two nights in Schuylerville as he was able to sleep in a bedroom in the part of the Finch home where he and Hannah would be living. Living in the same home as his bride-to-be, he had the opportunity to interact with her and her parents for about a month before the wedding. He never had any second thoughts. He became a welcomed family member and loved Hannah more each day. Daily proximity to his betrothed without any conjugal union was most difficult but long days cutting timber made sleep come easily at night.

October 9, 1814 was the day of the wedding. It was a simple event. Hannah's dress was blue and she wore a white veil. William wore his Sunday best. The local Congregational minister performed a brief ceremony in Hannah's home with only her parents present. After a fine dinner in the evening to celebrate the occasion William and Hannah retired to their side of the house and consummated their marriage.

William and Hannah settled into their new home. During the next eight years they were blessed with the births of three boys and a girl. Soon the westward wanderlust that seemed to have been a part of the Ward family for several generations hit William. He had heard glowing reports from his father and brothers of the fertile soils in the West. William and Hannah had talked of eventually heading West since before they were married. Although Nancy Jane was only two years old, Nathan nine, Willie six and Hiram four they decided that it was time to make the move. Mrs. Finch had passed away the year before. Mr. Finch was going to move to Glens Falls to be closer to his business interests and near where his oldest son lived. William had completed clearing the timber from the best farmland and had turned the property into a salable farm. Mr Finch had provided him with a $1,000 loan as had been promised.

During the winter of 1824 they set out. The rivers and streams were frozen over and a covering of snow on the ground made it much easier for the oxen to pull a sled loaded with their goods. Abner had urged William to come west and to stay with them while he found a place for his family. With a trip of a little over 200 miles they felt that they could average 10 miles a day and make the trip in about three weeks. William remembered it had taken his father's family less than a month during the trip 10 years earlier. Now that the snow was on the ground they ought to make the trip more quickly.

Goodbye dinners were held with close friends and the family set out in early February in anticipation of their new future. William was a bit surprised and pleased that Hannah was eager to tackle this significant move with four young children. Although she had had a comfortable childhood she seemed to thrive on adversity. He had thought that

A photo of men digging the Erie Canal. The canal opened trade to almost all of the world for people living near it or near access to it.

Changing mules on a boat on the Erie Canal. The mule going on to the canal boat could now eat and rest for a few hours while another mule pulled the boat.

she might resist leaving her family and friends but instead she was even more enthusiastic about their new adventure than he was. They planned to travel south along the Hudson River, cross it near Troy and then follow the Mohawk Valley west to Salina and then turn south again toward Scipio. William remembered that when he had gone west earlier they had gone to Albany and followed the Cherry Valley Turnpike but that route had been very hilly and hard on the oxen.

During the eight years since Abner and his family had moved, William had heard about the beginning of the construction of Clinton's Ditch. Word had come that the eastern half had been completed more than a year earlier. It would, of course, be closed at this time of year but people said it was a much easier route to travel.

Early in February the family started out. A second sleigh had been attached to the rear of the first that had a spot for Nancy Jane and the younger boys to ride when they were tired. Below where they would lie or sit was a pile of hay for the oxen to eat during the middle of the day along with some oats to give them an extra treat from time to time and additional energy. It was comfortable for the children to ride on top of the hay. When the hay ran low they would need to purchase more along the way.

With a light tap on the backs of the oxen with his whip and the words, "On Sam, on Mike," the William Ward family was on its way. William had trained Sam and Mike to work together since they were six-months-old. They were now five years old and each weighed over 1,000 pounds. They hadn't plowed or done other heavy work until they were two but had worked together almost daily since then. By the time they were doing heavy work William almost never needed to use his light whip to direct them. Each understood his name and the words 'on, whoa, gee and haw' were all that was needed to direct them. They responded best to William, who cared for them daily, but Nathan and even Willie were able to drive them when necessary. The boys learned that they would be severely punished if one of them said any of those four words unless they had been given the responsibility of driving the oxen. Sam and Mike had become almost like members of the Ward family because of their importance.

Everyone except Nancy Jane walked along behind the sleds. Hiram boasted that he was going to walk the entire distance to Scipio but soon discovered it was much further than his little mind imagined and after a few miles eagerly decided to ride.

Two miles an hour was a good average pace for the oxen. They also needed about an hour of rest during the middle of the day to eat their hay and chew their cud. William knew it was going to be a long trip and he wanted to keep Sam and Mike in top shape. If he had to replace one of them it would not only be expensive but two oxen that are not used to working together are much harder to guide. The first day the family covered 14 miles, all the way to Mechanicsville. Hannah had an uncle that lived there. They were pleased to see Hannah and her family and happily put the family up for the night. The next day after a big breakfast for both the family and the oxen, they headed through Waterford where they found refuge for the night with a family that had moved from Schuylerville a few years earlier. After this stop they knew they would be on their own since they wouldn't know anybody until they reached Scipio.

In Albany they stayed at an inn that William and his family had stopped at ten years earlier. It had been in business ever since a veteran of the Revolutionary War had opened it in the 1780s. The innkeeper suggested inns that were inexpensive and clean in both Schenectady and Amsterdam. They were making wonderful time but decided to stay over a second day in Amsterdam to give the oxen a well-earned rest. William and Hannah marveled at the number of people in both Schenectady and Amsterdam. Schenectady already boasted a large cotton mill. Clinton's Ditch was bringing people to those villages because of both trade and water power for manufacturing. They knew that Albany would be large because it was an old city and the capitol of New York.

Early the next day the family headed toward Palatine Bridge where there had been a German settlement for many years. In the afternoon, several miles from Palatine Bridge, a blinding snowstorm hit them. The children and Hannah huddled under a cover on the second sleigh while William walked ahead trying to find the road for the oxen to follow. All of a sudden, Sam fell to the ground. It took a minute for William to realize that the oxen weren't following him. He hastily retreated back to where the oxen stopped and saw Sam lying on the ground. He urged Sam to get up and though he tried he couldn't raise himself.

Sam had a broken front leg! He lay where he had fallen in obvious pain. This was one of the worst things that could have happened. With Sam permanently injured they didn't have an ox team. They were stranded in the country away from any village. The entire family was caught out in a late winter storm. Hannah came forward to see what was wrong, concerned about why they had stopped. She told William that the children were all shivering with cold. They decided that all they could do was to put some hay in front of the oxen and the whole family huddle together on the sleigh while they waited for the storm to pass so William could go to find help.

Suddenly William thought he heard some sleigh bells. Perhaps there was someone else traveling in the storm. He ran out to hail them. "Whoa," the driver yelled to his horse. "It looks like you are having some trouble! Can I help you?" William immediately explained their situation. The unknown man offered his and told William to have Hannah and the children join him in the cutter. His name was Hans Kuntz. He lived just a mile up the road and would return with an ox team to pull the sleds to his farm.

After the family had left with Mr. Kuntz, William freed Sam from the yoke. Sam was then able to move a few feet but immediately fell right back down in obvious pain. William examined the situation and found that the oxen had wandered off the road and that Sam had stepped into a woodchuck hole. That is what had broken his leg. William put his face down next to Sam's ear and whispered to him. "Sam it hurts me to do this to you but I can't bear to see you suffer. You have been a good friend!" He then took his musket and fired a ball between Sam's eyes rendering Sam unconscious. He then took a butcher knife from their household goods and cut a deep slash across Sam's throat. Tears were running from William's eyes as blood gushed from Sam's throat. Putting Sam out of his misery was harder than anything he had to do while in the militia. He would have to explain to the children that Sam had been badly injured and died.

As William stood pondering the family's fate, Hans returned with an ox team. He immediately fastened them to the sleighs and moved them out of the way. He then went back and helped William fasten a rope around Sam's stiffening body and hooked Mike to the other end of the rope. Hans went ahead with the sleighs and William followed along behind in the sleigh tracks directing Mike as he dragged the unfortunate Sam along on top of the snow.

Upon arriving on the Kuntz farm, Hans and William discussed the situation and agreed on a trade. Hans grew and trained oxen. He was willing to swap the team of oxen that had just pulled the sleigh in trade for Mike, Sam's carcass and twenty-five dollars. Sam would be put to work in a new way: providing food for the Kuntz family.

The men went inside where William found his children playing with the Kuntz children while Hannah helped Mrs. Kuntz prepare supper. It was the best meal they had eaten since leaving Waterford. Hans explained that his family had cleared the land where they lived over 100 years earlier. He also told them about the difficult times with the Indians during the war for independence.

The snowstorm had abated during the night and the Wards were able to start out on their travels again the next morning. The new oxen were Jim and Joe. They were more difficult to drive because the commands they were used to were German but with the use of a light touch with the ox whip William was able to direct them satisfactorily.

The remainder of the trip, fortunately, was less eventful. There had been one other bad scare a week later when they passed through Salina. They had stopped to rest the oxen and have some lunch. There was a busy salt industry in Salina but not much else. They watched big iron kettles, with wood fires underneath being filled with salt water. Other kettles were being emptied of the salt that remained, which was being put in wooden barrels. When they were ready to leave they couldn't find four-year-old Hiram. He had disappeared! They asked everyone if they had seen a little boy but none had. There were dozens of older boys hauling wood to the fires, but no sign of Hiram. Nathan suddenly exclaimed, "There he is!" Hiram came toward them munching a potato.

After a barrage of questions and some stiff raps across Hiram's bottom the story came out. Hiram had wandered along the salt kettles fascinated with the entire process. A kind man was munching on a potato and had invited Hiram to have one. Hiram talked with the man while the potato was cooling enough to eat. Hiram said it was the best potato he had ever eaten. The man had cooked his lunch of potatoes in the boiling salt water, which gave the potato a nice salty taste.

On their eighteenth day of travel they crossed the outlet of Owasco Lake and had hopes of making it to Abner's in two more days. They crossed the outlet a little south of the village of Auburn, a growing manufacturing center and the Cayuga County seat. As they were traveling down the side of the lake they noticed a robin, a sign that spring would soon arrive. Twelve miles further down the lake they found an inn and decided to finish the final leg of the trip the next day. None of the children had ever seen their grandfather and grandmother or their aunts and uncles so they were filled with anticipation.

After an uneventful night at the inn they started out. They found Abner's home, a log cabin within 100 feet of the lake. It was a joyous reunion for Abner and William after nearly a decade separation. William was surprised at how much Abner had aged. He was now 67-years-old and somewhat bent from his many years of hard work. Only the youngest two children were living at home so there was plenty of room for William's family.

Abner and William discussed where there might be opportunities for William to purchase land. William said that he wanted to have his children have the same experience that he and the previous generations of the Wards had enjoyed. Life held a special meaning when you started your farm with nature's gift to man: undeveloped forest. A man's muscle and sweat that went into taming the land was one of man's greatest joys. The sound of the axe, the pulling of stumps from the ground and then using the land to provide sustenance for your family and others gave life real meaning. After doing all this, the land he cared for, when it became productive, seemed to become a part of him, much like the blood flowing through his body.

One of the men in Salina had mentioned that about a day's travel north from Salina in a town called Lysander a great deal of forest was being cleared to furnish fuel for boiling the salt water. The wood was being floated down the Seneca River from Lysander. There still might exist in this area the opportunity to purchase land that was forested. He told William once he reached a small village called Baldwin's Bridge to head north a few miles and he would find forested land.

William hugged Hannah and his children, said goodbye to his parents and headed out on foot toward Baldwin's Bridge. He could walk almost twice as fast as the oxen and didn't need such long stops, so he was able to cover a longer distance each day. He had to walk to Auburn over paths but just a little north of Auburn he picked up the Seneca Turnpike to Onondaga Hill and there traveled north on a road that took him to Baldwin's Bridge. At Baldwin's Bridge he was obliged to pay a four-cent toll to walk across the bridge.

At the bridge he asked the toll collector who would be a good person to talk with regarding purchasing forested land. He was told to go to Otis Bigelow's store as Mr. Bigelow knew everybody and could point him in the right direction. It was a short walk to the store where he found Mr. Bigelow selling a customer some fabrics. As soon as Mr. Bigelow was available William explained that he wanted to purchase some forested land to clear for a farm. Mr. Bigelow told him to see a Mr. Voorhees about five miles northwest near a little hamlet called Wilson's Corners.

He said that Mr. Voorhees owned a large farm that was located on top of the largest hill on the road. It took William a little over an hour to reach the big hill. He soon was able to locate Mr. Voorhees, who couldn't have been more than 30-years-old.

After William shared his request for land Mr. Voorhees responded, "I believe I have exactly what you need. I buy timbered land, clear it and then build a barn on it. On this map you will see several of the properties I have recently purchased. Pick out whichever one you are interested in and I am sure we can make a deal." William located a tract of 50 acres on the map and set out to examine it. He was pleased to see an increasing amount of forested land as he went north and was able to locate the timbered parcel, totally surrounded by other timber land.

He walked back to Wilson's Corners and located Mr. Voorhees. William indicated his interest in the property, but Mr. Voorhees offered him some other land with an existing log cabin and 20 acres that had already been cleared. The price was satisfactory but the pioneer blood in William's body made its presence felt and he declined the offer. Instead they struck a deal for 50 acres of forested land.

William knew that he couldn't bring Hannah and the children to the property without a place to live but hated to be away from them long enough to build a satisfactory cabin by himself. He also wanted his boys to have the experience of being a part in developing a farm from the raw forest. He decided to see if he could lease a cabin within two or three miles of the newly purchased land so they could live nearby while the cabin was being constructed.

He took an extra day to visit the hamlets of Betts Corners and Palmertown. Near Palmertown he found a farm where the prosperous owner had just constructed a frame house and was abandoning the log cabin where his family had been living. He talked with the owner who told him that he was welcome to live in the cabin until fall when he intended to use it for some of his livestock. It was the solution to William's problem.

William returned to Scipio anxious to share the news that he had found a piece of property that seemed suitable for their new home. He told them that they would be living in a temporary spot for a few months until he had completed their own cabin. He was pleased when his brother, Sidney, volunteered to go to Lysander with the family for a month or two to help construct the cabin.

The William Ward family again packed their belongings on the sled and headed to Lysander, which was the final step in the family's westward migration of almost 200 years. Jim and Joe, who had proven themselves to be worthy replacements for Sam and Mike had now learned English and with the words, "On Jim, on Joe," leaned into their yoke and the family was on its way.

CHAPTER 8

Ward Family Life in Plainville Prior to the Civil War

After ten years in northern Lysander struggling to grow a decent crop, William finally came to the conclusion that wet ground and early frosts were more than he could overcome. He didn't want to have his sons continue to fight a losing battle like he had. Each year he had to draw from his little pool of savings to subsidize the small income he received from the crops he had harvested. The cost of cutting wood and getting it to the Salina salt industry was more than he received for it. Logs were bringing almost nothing. It was time to throw in the towel!

Hannah had been amazing. She never complained about their poverty but he knew that underneath she missed many of the extras that they had enjoyed in Schuylerville and it hurt to have both of them struggle each year. She had offered to ask her father if they could borrow some more money. William absolutely refused. "I haven't completely paid him back for the money he loaned me earlier and I refuse to ask him for more until that is all paid!"

Nineteen-year-old Nathan and sixteen-year-old Willie had observed the superior crops that were being grown only a few miles to the south. He knew that within a couple of years both Nathan and Willie would be heading to greener pastures if things didn't improve.

One winter day William hitched their horse to the wagon and went to have his axes and wedges sharpened and tempered. The blacksmith in Plainville had a reputation for being the best blacksmith in the area. While watching the blacksmith sharpening one of his axes he mentioned how poor his farm was and how much he wanted better land but that he had almost no money to pay for it. The blacksmith suggested that he see a wealthy local farmer by the name of Jeb Smith who had a 72 acre farm for sale that had good soil and might be willing to take a large mortgage.

William immediately left the blacksmith, agreeing to pick up his axes later in the day, and set off to find Jeb. It took him less than an hour to find Jeb's home and they were soon discussing the possibility of an agreement. Jeb said there was a log cabin and a small log barn on the property. About 30 acres had been cleared and was being used to grow excellent crops. William said he wanted to bring Hannah and his children to look over the farm. Would Jeb give him a few days to decide and then determine if they could work out a satisfactory method of paying for the farm? Jeb replied that he would give him a week but didn't want to wait longer as there was also another buyer trying to come up with the money.

After stopping back at the blacksmith shop William was eager to return home and share the potential good news with his family. William excitedly asked Hannah, "Remember the field of wheat south of Plainville that we both admired last summer? We may be able to buy that farm. If the weather is good tomorrow I want to take you and the children there."

The boys and Nancy Jane were excited when they heard they were going to look at a farm. Early the next morning Hiram gobbled down his breakfast and had their horse Betsy harnessed and hitched to the wagon before Hannah was able to finish preparing a lunch to take with them. It was a cold, crisp February morning but between the joy of anticipation and two buffalo robes the family kept warm.

It took them only an hour to reach the Plainville four-corners and then another ten minutes to reach the farm. William pointed out the blacksmith shop, general store and the log schoolhouse. Just south of Plainville they passed a prosperous farm owned by a Mr. Wilson and a little later came to the farm that Jeb Smith was selling. The log cabin sat on a small rise of ground and the log barn sat about 100 yards to its left. Each looked like it had been constructed about ten years earlier. The house and barn were both empty so Hannah explored the house while William and the boys followed the rough map Jeb had given them showing the farm boundaries.

They discovered that the land that had been cleared was near the buildings and couldn't have been more than 15 acres. About half of the farm was hilly and if cleared would only be usable for sheep and cattle pasture. There was, however another 15 acres that would be tillable when they found time to clear it. The 15 acres that was already cleared was more than they would have time to work for the next few years.

Upon returning to the cabin, Hannah reported it was adequate but needed some work on the roof before they moved in. It had a dirt floor but a wood floor could be put in during the summer. The family decided that if they could work out an agreement with Mr. Smith the farm would meet their needs.

They set Betsy off on a trot, as they were anxious to see Mr. Smith. After only 20 minutes they reached the Smith home. It was a fine frame home covered with clapboards, very similar to the one the Finchs had owned back in Schuylerville. William cautioned the children and Hannah to stay on the wagon while he went inside to see Jeb. If either Mr. or Mrs. Smith asked them to come in it would be fine. Many men didn't want a woman and children around when they were discussing business.

Soon William returned, followed by Jeb who told them that they wanted the family to come inside. Hannah was surprised to see that the home had a cast iron stove rather than a fireplace in the living room. Hannah and Nancy Jane stayed in the living room with Mrs. Smith. Jeb invited William and the boys into the kitchen. He then started to ask the boys questions like how old they were, if they had gone to school and how they liked farming. He motioned to several chairs for the boys to sit in and then he and William sat on chairs by a kitchen table to discuss their business.

He asked William what he and his family thought about the farm. William replied that they liked it but estimated only 15 acres had been cleared and that half of it was quite hilly. Jeb admitted that he had estimated the cleared acreage too high and that part of the farm was hilly but each year the cleared land had produced excellent crops. When Mr. Smith told William that he had to have $1,600 for the farm, William was speechless. Finally he said that all the money he had available was $500. and would pay the remainder at the end of each year in annual installments. Mr. Smith thought a minute and finally said that he would have to think it over and would decide within a week. He needed to give the other interested buyer a few days to determine if he could come up with the money.

After a little more talk about what the price of wheat might be the following year and the possibilities of making butter for sale, William thanked Mr. Smith. The family, now a bit dejected that the farm might be sold to someone else, headed back home.

The next few days passed quite slowly, especially because of another snowstorm that might delay Mr. Smith from getting word to them about whether the other buyer had purchased the farm. A week went by with no word. William came to the conclusion that the other person had purchased the farm. He hated to spend another year where they were but there appeared to be no other choice. The following day Hannah was surprised when a horse and cutter drove up next to their home. Mr. Smith got out. Immediately Hannah came to the door and invited him in. She and Nancy Jane were in the house alone as the men were out cutting wood to burn in their fireplace. She sent Nancy Jane, who excitedly ran all the way to the woodlot, to tell her father that Mr. Smith was there.

William hastened back to their home not knowing what to expect. Was Mr. Smith going to tell him the farm had been sold to the other buyer or was it possible that he would be able to purchase the farm? If this didn't work out he might not have a decent farm before his boys all moved away because of a lack of opportunity for them.

Mr. Smith apologized for taking so long to see William. He did have an offer from the other man but both he and Mrs. Smith had been favorably impressed when they met Hannah and the boys. They could tell that, barring some extremes in weather or prices, the Wards would make a success of the farm. He didn't want to take a mortgage, however, but would sell it to them with a land contract where they would pay him $500 now and $135 a year for ten years. The farm would be theirs at the end of 10 years but, if they missed the payment any year all the equity they had in the farm would immediately be Mr. Smith's and the farm would revert back to him.

William thought for a minute. "These are very strict terms," he told Mr. Smith. He didn't think that it was fair if he missed payment he would then lose everything they had invested in the farm. Mr. Smith agreed and said that he could temper those terms under certain conditions. If William should happen to default after he had built a permanent building on the farm and had made his first two years of payments in a timely manner he would return the $500 initial payment.

William asked for time to talk with Hannah. The couple conferred, then agreed to the revised terms. The $500 was counted out, the papers were signed and the Wards could now take possession of their new farm.

After Mr. Smith had gone on his way ,Hannah remarked that it was obvious why Jeb Smith was successful. He made sure he would never come out on the short end of a deal! Plans were made for William and Nathan to take Betsy and the wagon loaded with some supplies to Plainville the next day. They could make the barn ready to house the livestock and start making the log cabin livable. Willie was to bring the oxen pulling a sled filled with dry wood for the fireplace. Hiram was to stay at home and take care of the sheep, pigs and chickens. The family would try to move within a week so as to be at the new farm in plenty of time to prepare for spring work. Everyone was looking forward to moving to their new home.

Hiram went out to care for their five sheep, two pigs and small flock of chickens. The sheep furnished wool that Hannah used for spinning into yarn for weaving cloth. One of the pigs had been bred to a neighbor's boar to produce little pigs in about a month. About the same time the other pig was to be butchered as food for the family. The chickens were mostly hens and in April would hopefully start nesting and laying eggs. Any chickens that didn't produce eggs would end up, along with the two roosters, in Hannah's kettle hanging over the fireplace. The animals they grew were extremely important for the family's welfare.

In the evening, after a busy day, Hiram went to bed early, soon followed by his mother and sister. Hiram usually slept soundly during the night. However, with the move to the new farm on his mind, he woke in the middle of the night to the chickens making a ruckus out in their shelter. Something was wrong! He got up, slipped on a coat and grabbed the musket that was hanging on the cabin wall. It was the one his father had carried during the war and fortunately his father hadn't taken it with him to Plainville. He quickly put in the gunpowder, wadding and ball. His mother had awakened and warned him to be both careful and silent. They had no idea whether it was a person, animal or false alarm scaring the chickens.

Hiram silently opened the door of the cabin and since it was a moonlit night, could clearly see the chickens' shelter. In front of him he could make out the cause of the problem. A large animal was munching on one of their chickens. Hiram was shaking with excitement. He knew he couldn't hit the animal unless he stopped shaking. He rested the gun on a log extending from the corner of the cabin, cocked the gun and carefully pulled the trigger. He knew that he wouldn't get more than one shot. The gun kicked like a mule and almost knocked him down. Whatever was eating the chickens had disappeared by the time he straightened up to look.

He slipped on his boots, reloaded the gun just in case he might need it and, followed by his mother, carefully made his way to the chicken shelter. There were feathers scattered all over but now the chickens had quieted down. It looked like at least two had been killed. Somehow an animal had forced its way between two of the posts surrounding the pen and one of them, apparently rotted, had broken off making an opening large enough for the animal to enter. Fortunately the animal had moved outside the pen where Hiram was able to see it. He had no idea if he had hit it or not. He temporarily fixed the break in the fence and went back to bed. Sleep didn't come easily, though, because of all of the excitement.

As soon as he awakened, Hiram slipped on his clothes and headed to the chicken shelter. The remaining chickens seemed to have recovered because the roosters' crowing had served as his alarm clock. He found the remains of the chicken the animal had been eating outside the pen and one partially eaten carcass inside the pen. Hopefully, later in the spring, the remaining chickens would still lay eggs. He then went to the small barn which usually housed the oxen and Betsy as well as the pigs and sheep. Everything seemed to be in order..

As he came from the barn he searched the snow for possible animal footprints. All of a sudden he found the footprints of what appeared to be a large dog. Could it have been a wolf? He continued to look and came upon another set of tracks with signs of blood in the snow next to them. He had hit his target!

He ran to the house to tell his mother and to get the gun. Following the tracks he soon noticed more blood and a shorter distance between the animal's tracks. Hiram's heart was beating rapidly. Would he find it? Was it still alive? Was it a wolf?

Ahead he could see a large animal lying on the snow. He cautiously approached but there was no sign of movement. He nudged the animal with the barrel of his gun, but it obviously was already dead. It was a wolf!

He had to show the wolf to his mother, and to his father and brothers when they returned! None of them had ever shot a wolf. He had heard many tales of wolves terrorizing the earlier settlers. With the gun in his left hand he took hold of the wolf's tail with the other hand and slowly made his way back home. It was hard work dragging the wolf through the snow. It must have weighed 60 pounds. Halfway home he decided to leave the wolf, take the gun home and then come back to get it.

Finally dragging the wolf to the backyard, he ran into the cabin and excitedly called to his mother and sister to come outside and see what he had shot. Nancy Jane examined it from a distance, not willing to accept that it wasn't alive. Hannah gave Hiram a big hug and said, "Son, I am very proud of you!" Hiram beamed with joy. He had been disappointed that he was unable to go to Plainville with his father and brothers, but this more than made up for it.

As the day progressed Hiram kept looking down the road to see if his brothers were returning. He mused that maybe they wouldn't refer to him as their helpless little brother any more. In the late afternoon Willie returned with the oxen and a little later his father and Nathan arrived on the wagon behind Betsy. As they drove up, Hiram ran out to greet them and told them of his adventure. William couldn't believe it, thinking that it probably was just a wild dog. When Hiram took him over to show him, William was shocked. It really was a wolf! "Hiram," he exclaimed, "There is still a $50 bounty on any wolf killed in the town. You are going to be a rich young man!"

William and the boys had lots to report about their last two days at Plainville. They had fixed the roof, cleaned out the fireplace and chimney (which had apparently previously been home to some owls or other large birds) and worked to get the barn ready to house their animals. William said that it would take about three more trips before they were completely moved. Hiram's encounter with the wolf, however, was truly the center of the family's attention.

William knew that the kill had to be verified with a town assessor so the next day they loaded the wolf on the wagon and went to the nearest assessor's home. He too, was surprised to see a wolf. He cut off its tail and ears so it would be impossible for anyone else to collect the bounty on the animal and told Hiram that he would be getting paid in a month after the town board had authorized the payment.

Over the next several days and several trips with loaded sled and wagon, the move to Plainville was completed. The William Ward family began a new chapter in their lives. Their crops were excellent and they made the annual payment on the farm without difficulty. With three able-bodied sons, more of the acreage had been cleared and they now had three milking cows. Hannah, with assistance from Nancy Jane, made butter from their milk and sold some of it at the Plainville General Store. Life was the best it had been for the family.

Some sad news arrived in October 1838. Abner had died at the ripe old age of 81. He had named William as administrator of his estate. To settle the estate, William had to make an inventory of his father's assets and dispose of them, which required two trips to Scipio. These were both sad and happy visits as William renewed friendships with his siblings and a multitude of nieces and nephews.

Now that the ownership of their farm at Plainville was secure, William and Hannah decided it was time to replace their log cabin with a frame home. Ten acres of the original 72 were left as a perennial woodlot. It would provide, indefinitely, all of the fuel the family would ever need for heating their home and cooking. The woodlot would also provide logs for lumber to build any buildings they might need. As they cleared the other remaining forested land to use for growing crops, they saved some of those logs to use in the construction of their new house. They had already used some lumber to build a new and larger barn.

Nathan was now 23, Willie 20, Hiram 18 and Nancy Jane 16. There was plenty of family labor to operate the farm and construct a new home during their spare time. Logs had been hauled by the oxen to the Voorhees sawmill, which was located just a short distance from their farm.

One thing that was missing was a well close to the house. The previous three years they had carried their water from a spring 200 feet south of their new home. A shallow hole about three feet both in diameter and depth had been dug. Stones had been laid around its perimeter. Some boards were placed across the top and every time they needed water the top had to be uncovered, the water dipped out and then carried 200 feet to the house. In the summer it sometimes ran dry and they had to go much further to obtain their water. William vowed that after the hay and wheat were harvested that summer they were going to dig a well much closer to the house.

Digging a well was not a job for an inexperienced person. Anyone could dig a hole but laying up the stones in a well took a great deal of skill. Enoch Ellsworth, who lived about three miles away in the Town of Cato, was known to be an expert at this job. William was acquainted with him because both his family and the Wards attended the community church in Plainville.

William hired Mr. Ellsworth and began making preparations. Stones from about the size of a person's head up to twelve inches in diameter had been saved the past two years as they had picked them from the fields before planting their crops. There was a good sized pile waiting to be used. Prior to saving the stones, William had cut a crotch stick from one of their apple trees and 'witched' for water. Only a few people possessed the ability to do this. Each arm of the crotch stick was about ten inches long and about the diameter of William's little finger. He held a branch of the Y in each hand with the third branch extending upward. Then he walked slowly near where the house was to be located. Each time he passed over an underground vein of water the branch pointing upward would be forced down by some mysterious invisible pull. There were several places near the home's future location where the stick went down but William chose a spot where the water appeared to be about fifteen feet deep and also gave a strong pull on the stick. It was about twenty feet from there that the stones were piled in anticipation of using them for the well.

Nathan, Willie and Hiram were assigned to help Mr. Ellsworth. The previous week, as they had been instructed by Mr. Ellsworth, they dug a perfectly round hole six feet in diameter, where the well was to be located. It was the driest time of the year and the earth was stable all around the hole. It was dangerous work, however, when the depth of the hole was greater than a man's height. There were stories of the sides of wells being dug caving in and burying the men digging in the well.

As the hole got deeper Nathan and Hiram had to climb down a ladder into the hole. The top three feet had dug quite easily because the soil was a sandy loam but as they got deeper the sandy soil changed to clay and they had to use a pickaxe to loosen the earth before they could shovel it out. The soil from the top three feet had been left near the hole to use for a gentle crown around the top of the well to prevent any surface water from entering it. The clay soil was being loaded on a sled and hauled away as fill for a tool shed they hoped to build some day.

When the hole was too deep to throw the dirt out with a shovel a tall three-legged tripod with a pulley in the center was placed over the hole. The dirt had to be put in pail and pulled up, dumped and the empty pail returned to the bottom of the hole. This was a slow process. Nathan and Hiram took turns loosening the soil and filling the pail. Willie had been assigned the job of pulling the pails of dirt up and dumping them. Some choice words came out of the well from Nathan and Hiram whenever Willie got a little careless and spilled dirt back down into the well.

Digging the well was a dirty job and hard work, but the cool temperature down in the hole made the working temperature bearable. Willie complained because it was so hot in the sun at the top of the hole but since he was deathly afraid of closely contained spaces his complaining was mild. When the hole reached 13 feet deep a little water began showing in a thin layer of sand. At this point Mr. Ellsworth took charge and began the job of a master craftsman laying up the stones around the sides of the well. He instructed the boys to deepen the center of the hole a little further. After going only six inches a vein of fine gravel with water appeared. The boys were elated to have found water and not have to dig the hole any deeper. Now it was a race against time to lay the stones before the water covered them. Stones were placed in the bucket one at a time and lowered into the well. Water was scooped up and sent back up in the pail that had delivered the stone. Before the day ended Mr. Ellsworth was working in water above his knees. It was either fortunate or well planned that several layers of stone

A man cutting oats with a grain cradle similar to one used by Abner Ward, his son William Ward and his grandson Hiram Ward.

had been laid before the boys were instructed to deepen the hole in the center.

The stones were laid from the bottom to the top of the well in circular fashion. The stone for each spot was chosen for both its size and shape. The back of each stone rested against the dirt wall with the greatest width next to the dirt so that once the circle was complete it was impossible for any stone to move toward the center of the well. The stones on each successive layer rested on two stones in the layer below. In this manner the stones were laid to the top of the well.

After the stones reached a height of four feet, a platform of plank was made to stand on. This had to be raised each time it became difficult to lift the stones into place. Often a stone of inappropriate shape or size came down in the bucket and had to be sent back in exchange for another. Mr. Ellsworth would call out the shape and size of the next stone he needed to eliminate many of the size errors.

After the well had been completely stoned, a four foot square box was built over the well and a well sweep installed. A bucket was fastened to the long end of the pole so it could be dropped into the water and easily bring a pail of water to the top of the well.

All of the families were elated to have a good well close to their home. But Nathan and Hiram both told their father that this was the last and only well they would ever dig. It was a job, however, that they reminisced about to each other as long as they lived!

Continued improvements were made to the farm over the next three years but the major improvement was the new frame house next to the well. William and Hannah had chosen the site for their new home when they had first moved to the farm. It was only 100 feet north of their log cabin and was sitting on the same little hill. As soon as the frost was completely out of the ground in April 1839 one of the oxen was hooked to a slip scoop and an area of about 30 feet square was dug to a depth of four feet for the cellar and exterior wall of the two story portion of their new home. The living room and the parlor were on the first floor with three bedrooms on the second floor. A one story wing without a cellar was attached on the east side. This held the woodhouse, kitchen, pantry and wash area. There was no cellar under the wing but there was a low ceilinged, attic storeroom above. There were no fireplaces in their new home. The house was heated with an iron stove in the living room and an iron cook stove in the kitchen. The cellar had a dirt floor and made an ideal root cellar to store potatoes, apples and squash.

Hannah was elated to have a new house with more room and the convenience of stoves instead of the one fireplace. The root cellar was far more convenient than the one they previously used. It was a covered hole in the ground away from the log cabin, which she sometimes had to shovel snow off the top of.

While the new house was being constructed, the family continued to live in the original log cabin. Finally, in the early summer of 1840 the house was completed and the family moved in except for Nathan and Willie. They went across the driveway to have meals with the family but enjoyed the freedom of living in the old cabin by themselves. Nathan was now 25 and had been enjoying the social companionship of some of the young ladies in the community. He began to especially enjoy spending time with Samantha Tillotson who lived on a farm about a mile south of the Ward farm. Her father David had operated a tannery near Warners for about ten years and continued to operate a tannery at the farm when they moved there in 1836.

Since the Ward farm was now well established, there was not as much labor needed. One day when Nathan was visiting Samantha, Mr. Tillotson mentioned that he could use help in the tannery if Nathan's father could spare him. Mr. Tillotson explained the process of hide tanning and showed Nathan how it was done. Nathan decided to join Mr. Tillotson because it looked like a better opportunity than he would have on the farm with two younger brothers, one of whom would likely take over the farm. The fact that he would be near Samantha made his decision easy. Apparently it was also a good decision as he and Samatha were married in January 1841.

Willie, who was now 21, also decided to look for new opportunities. When he had traveled with his father on a trip to Scipio a year earlier he had taken a liking to one of his uncles' farm and voiced his admiration. His uncle told Willie that he would enjoy having him come and help him. Willie decided to do just that.

Now with both Nathan and Willie gone, Hiram and his father were responsible for all the farm work. Hannah and Nancy Jane helped too. They milked the cows, which now numbered five, made the butter and cared for the garden in addition to doing all the household chores.

Since the log cabin stood empty they decided to use it as a hog house. Hannah wasn't very pleased to have the hog house so close to their home but the pigs were convenient for disposing of table scraps and the buttermilk. They didn't have to feed the pigs very much corn by disposing of the waste food in this manner. The pigs provided inexpensive food for the family and the sale of two or three generated extra income.

The farm's livestock had now increased to four oxen, one horse, five cows, one bull, three heifer calves, eight sheep and five pigs. William and Hannah were pleased with the success that had come to them and their Plainville farm. They owed just three more payments of $135 for the farm and then it would be totally theirs. In 1841, William had even been able to donate $20 and a week's free labor in replacing the old log schoolhouse in Plainville with a new frame one. Life was good to the family!

Three years later, Nancy Jane left the family home to marry Sanford Tillotson, her brother Nathan's brother-in-law. She moved a mile south to a separate home on the same farm where Nathan now operated the tannery for his father-in-law. Hannah was pleased to have her two married children only a mile away. She could see them often and also visit her new grandchild. With the close relationships that existed between the Wards and the Tillotsons, the families helped each other regularly during such labor intensive jobs as haying, harvesting wheat and butchering.

Willie came back to join his family when Nancy Jane married, helping fill the labor void created by her absence. Now Willie and Hiram took over the chore of milking the cows and also did all of the planting and weeding in the garden.

Although Willie, 30, and Hiram had both taken an interest in girls for the last decade, they were either too bashful to ask a girl to marry them or felt that they were not financially capable of supporting a family. Hiram had shown an interest in Polly Ellsworth, the daughter of Enoch who had laid up the stones in the Ward's well. When Willie had returned from Scipio, he seemed to be attracted to Polly's sister Celestia, The two brothers took the sisters on picnics and sleigh rides. It appeared that two marriages were forthcoming but nothing happened.

One day Polly and Celestia were bemoaning the fact that the Ward brothers were so shy that they would probably never ask to marry either of them. Celestia suggested that they might use the time proven method of baiting each of the brothers so that in a state of passion, each might get pregnant and the boys would be forced to marry them. Polly absolutely refused to do this. What would her parents think of her if she did that? Finally Polly firmly stated to her sister, "Tonight I am going to ask Hiram to marry me! He is so shy that he would probably be afraid to say no!"

Celestia was shocked. She had never heard of a woman directly confronting a prospective husband in this manner. It was usually far more subtle, with the man thinking he had asked the woman when actually she had maneuvered the situation so cleverly that he never knew how it happened. Finally Celestia responded, "I'll see how you make out. If it works I may do it. If it doesn't I'll use my method!"

After a church social that evening, Hiram offered to take Polly and Celestia home with the horse and wagon. Celestia made a fake excuse because she knew Polly would want her hide if she were to tag along and mess up her plans. Little did Hiram realize the trap that was being set for him! It was a beautiful spring evening. It was a little cool but the grass was beginning to turn a dark green, daffodils were blossoming, the geese were honking overhead on their way north and the moon was out.

Polly mentioned that she was a little cool and reached for Hiram's arm and placed it around her back. He could drive the horse as well with one hand as two. She reached up and gave him a kiss. She let the effect settle in for a few moments and then said to him, "Let's get married on June 15. The crops will be mostly planted and it is before you start haying. It will give us five weeks to make our plans, which is plenty of time!" Then she reached over and gave him a really big kiss! Hiram was speechless but a big smile came on his face and he reached down to kiss her back. The deal was sealed!

The marriage was held in the Plainville Community Church, where they were both members, with just the immediate family present. Hiram and Polly moved into the frame house with his parents. The old log cabin was still being used for the pigs and with the rest of the family gone there was plenty of room.

Apparently whatever method Celestia used had the desired effect because just two weeks later she announced that she and Willie were to be married the following December. Willie had enjoyed the time he spent on his uncle's farm in Scipio but had inherited the old family urge of wanting to move to new country in the west. Following their marriage the couple moved to Fayette, Ohio.

Polly quickly became a valuable member of the Ward family. She took over the milking and even the butter making giving Hiram more time to spend tending the livestock and crops. The farm continued to prosper and the two families developed a close bond while living under the same roof. In addition, all the payments had been made on the farm. The Wards were debt free.

The family had only received two or three letters from Willie since he had married and moved to Ohio but during early fall of 1851 a letter arrived that shocked them. Celestia was very sick and unable to care for the couple's first child, a baby girl. The bleeding associated with the birth would not stop. The doctor had told them that if she lived it would take her at least a year to recover her strength. Willie had written wondering if Hiram and Polly would be willing to take the baby. He had no way to raise her as there were no family members in Ohio and he had would be busy caring for Celestia.

William, Hannah, Polly and Hiram discussed the situation. Polly quickly offered to adopt her little niece and bring her up as one of the family. She and Hiram had been married for three years with no children of their own. Hiram happily approved of the plan and William and Hannah added that they would love to have a child in their home. A letter was written to Willie sharing Hiram and Polly's eagerness to take the child. They could come to Ohio to bring the little girl back to Plainville in late October, after the corn had been put into shocks and before the Erie Canal closed for the winter. Two weeks later a letter came from Willie gratefully accepting the offer and saying that the little girl now had a name. It was Ida.

Nathan and Samantha agreed to help Hannah and William while Hiram and Polly traveled to bring Ida home. The trip would take about two weeks since Fayette was located in northwestern Ohio about 20 miles west of Toledo. They would take the Erie Canal from Syracuse to Lake Erie and then a Lake Erie steamer to Toledo. They would have to travel from Toledo to Fayette by stagecoach.

Traveling on the Erie Canal was a real learning experience for both of them. They were on the move 24 hours a day. They were amazed to see the mules go up and down from the boat to the towpath every four hours as they took their turn pulling the packet boat. At Rochester four fresh mules replaced the four that had hauled the boat since leaving Syracuse. Because they were on a passenger packet, it had priority over the freight packets and moved along at an average speed of more than three miles an hour. At night curtains were hung on each side of the large center cabin with the men on one side and the women on the other. Bunks to sleep on were dropped down from the wall. Some of the passengers sat up all night or slept on the floor but Hiram decided they should have bunks considering the length of their trip. Polly remarked that she had never heard snoring like she experienced her two nights on the packet boat.

Hiram was amazed at the villages scattered along the canal and all the activity going on. Upon reaching Buffalo he was overwhelmed at the size of the city and the amount of grain coming in from the west on large boats. His grandfather had told him of the tales from his fellow soldiers of nothing but wilderness and Indians west of Syracuse. Soon, after their arrival in Buffalo, they booked passage on a steamer traveling on Lake Erie to Toledo. How fast it went! It was an amazing invention. Hiram thought to himself, that with such innovations as the Erie Canal, steamships and railroads, soon there wouldn't be anything new to invent!

Willie had sent directions from Toledo to Fayette in his last letter. It was not hard to find because it seemed to be even smaller than Baldwinsville. The brothers and sisters had a joyful reunion. Soon Polly was happily holding baby Ida in her arms. Since Celestia was unable to nurse Ida, a neighbor who had lost a baby had been wet nursing her. The last 10 days they had gradually moved her over to other food in anticipation of Hiram and Polly's arrival. Willie and Celestia both shed some tears at saying goodbye to little Ida but were most thankful that Hiram and Polly would adopt her as their own daughter. In their minds, each was wondering if Celestia would live and if Ida would ever see her birth parents again.

The return trip was uneventful except it was a little slower. The Erie Canal seemed filled with boats. It would be closing for the winter soon so everyone was trying to get as much shipped as possible before then. It would be several times more expensive to ship grain and other items by wagon once the canal closed. Shipping by railroad was becoming more common but with each railroad company traveling only short distances it often required the freight to be transferred to more then one railroad. For long distance shipping, rail wasn't practical.

As they traveled back toward home, there was a frost almost every night and a chill in the air during the day. Hiram was pleased they hadn't made the trip any later. Ida was a good baby and weathered the trip well. Hiram often looked over at Polly with admiration and thought to himself, she is not only a great wife but she is going to be a wonderful mother!

They had been able to connect with the Syracuse and Oswego Railroad from Syracuse to Baldwinsville and then took a stage to Plainville. From Plainville they walked the final half-mile to their home. What a joyous reunion it was! William and Hannah hadn't expected them back for several more days. Almost immediately, two-month-old Ida was in Hannah's arms.

Thirty- five acres of the farm was planted in crops each year. Over half of that was used to grow corn, oats and hay as feed for their livestock. The remaining was planted in wheat and potatoes, which were sold as cash crops. Wheat had been their major source of income but a few years earlier all the wheat in the area had been hit by the midge and the last four years the yields had been disastrous.

Their neighbor, Billy Wilson, had started growing tobacco the past three years and was happy with the return he received. Some farmers near Marcellus had been growing it successfully for five years. There was one big drawback. A special barn was necessary to dry the tobacco when it was harvested. If the Wards grew it this next year, they would have to have the barn completed before September 1.

Sanford, Hiram's brother-in-law, was also considering growing tobacco and they had given it a great deal of discussion. Finally, they decided to partner in growing two acres. Sanford would help Hiram build a tobacco shed and also to grow and harvest the crop. They would split whatever profit it produced.

They immediately made arrangements to visit Billy Wilson. He showed them his shed, which had long narrow hinged doors on its sides to control ventilation as the tobacco dried. Billy offered to sell them some tobacco seed to be sown in a special bed during the middle of May after the last frost. Question after question was fired at Billy, which he responded to with in-depth answers. They had no idea how complicated and labor intensive growing tobacco would be!

Once the tobacco bed had been sown, it seemed to Hiram that every spare minute he had was spent in weeding, setting, cultivating, hoeing or some other task associated with the crop. Polly even helped when the tobacco worms started appearing. If they weren't removed, they would chew big holes in the leaves and take away most of the value of the crop. It was a tedious and messy chore to examine each plant for those dark green worms, which were the same color as the leaves, pick them off and then squeeze them to death. She began to think that growing tobacco wasn't a very good idea!

The tobacco shed was finished in late August and the harvest began in early September. Timeliness in harvest was important so even Nathan and Samantha helped out. It took four people to pass the lathes, filled with the harvested stalks, from person to person when they were put on the hangars in the peak of the shed. They hoped they had made the tobacco shed large enough to hold their crop. There was a sigh of relief when the last lathe, loaded with tobacco stalks, was hung.

On a foggy morning in December, after the tobacco was thoroughly dry, they removed the lathes filled with tobacco plants from the barn. The tobacco had lost over half of its weight during the drying process. They took it down on a foggy morning so the leaves wouldn't be brittle and fall from the stalks or shatter. Now, during the next month in their spare time, they would remove the leaves and pack them into bundles for sale.

Hiram didn't know in advance what price he'd receive for his tobacco until he sold it. The price varied depending upon the supply and demand. He was elated to learn that Billy Wilson would pay him eight cents a pound this year. That was more than he anticipated. Other than the seed and the cost of materials for the tobacco shed, there were no expenses other than their many hours of labor. When Hiram showed Polly how much their half of the profit was, she decided that she wouldn't mind picking the tobacco worms off the plants the next summer! They earned more from their half of the two acres of tobacco than they had earned from the eight acres of wheat they had grown. Tobacco became one of the crops the Wards now grew every year.

In the summer of 1852 a violent thunderstorm brought tragedy to the community. The church had been struck by lightning. Hiram had taken shelter in the barn after he had felt the first raindrops. He knew that lightning had hit within a mile of the farm three different times because his mother had taught him, while he was still a child, to count from 1,000 to 1,007 between the time he saw the lightning flash and heard the thunder from it. If he didn't reach 1,007 he would know that the lightning had hit within a mile. That afternoon he had only reached 1,003 one of the times.

When the rain ended, Hiram went outside, looking around to see if everything was alright and was shocked to see what appeared to be a large building burning to the northwest. He hurriedly harnessed a horse and headed to Plainville. As he was going up the hill into Plainville he could see that the Community church was on fire. By the time he turned west at the four-corners and reached the church, the steeple had fallen in. Nothing could be done to save it. Two men were pouring pails of water on the shingle roof of a nearby house. The church was a total loss.

Services were held in the frame schoolhouse the following Sunday. Planning for a new church began immediately. There was no insurance on the burned church so donations would have to come from church members before it could be rebuilt. Pews were sold to the members that could afford to buy them with the cost set at $45. The sale of 16 pews would bring $720, more than half of what was needed to rebuild the church. Dinners and dances were held during the following year to raise additional money. The Wards, Ellsworths and Tillotsons all worked tirelessly to replace the church.

Plans were made to build a brick church and it was to be located at the top of a small rise just to the west of the previous church and adjacent to the church burying ground. Money continued to come in and in the summer enough had been raised to begin construction. A year later the church was completed. It had a tall white steeple that could be seen from all four directions as people came into the little hamlet of Plainville. There was a large bell placed in the steeple that tolled each Sunday morning to beckon all within listening range to come and worship within its walls. A joyous dinner of thankfulness was held for the entire community after the first Sunday in the new church.

Life on the Ward farm continued to be busy but enjoyable. There were challenges, such as in 1854 when a summer hailstorm almost destroyed their tobacco crop. But, then a joyful event took place in October: Polly gave birth to a son whom they named Ira. Two years later another son, William, named after his grandfather, was born. Hannah and Polly were kept very busy with five year old Ida, two year old Ira and now baby William. Their house rang with the sound of a crying baby mingled with the joyful laughter of little children.

Sadness came to the family the following February when Hannah died at age 62. William's close friend and partner of 43 years left a void in his life. William continued to help Hiram with the farm work but at the age of 69 he was doing much less. William had always been a lover of flowers. Most homes in the Plainville area had a front lawn of grass that was mowed by either tying animals to stakes in the yard or putting a fence around it and letting some of their animals use it for pasture. William planted the entire front lawn in flowers. He had made a path from the road to their front door through the middle of the flower bed. Now William had more time to enjoy his flowers. Travelers admired the flowers but Hiram had other thoughts. He had spent more time than *he* enjoyed, helping his father with his huge flower bed.

William's greatest joy was his three grandchildren, especially his namesake. Watching little William brought back pleasant memories of his own childhood back in Vermont. He mused about the changes he had seen and was thankful for the many ways both he and his family had been blessed. Since moving to their farm at Plainville life had been good!

CHAPTER 9

Ward Family in Plainville from the Civil War to 1918

In April 1861, word came that Fort Sumter in South Carolina was fired upon by southern confederate forces. They were anticipating the new president, Abraham Lincoln and his Republican party, were going to abolish slavery in the United States. The coming war, that was to last over four years, was about to drastically change the lives of all Americans. The Ward family, like most of the northern farm families, hated to have war come but were opposed to slavery.

William, who was now 73, wasn't able to help Hiram very much. Ira was only seven and William E. was only four, so they too were of minimal help on the farm. The past four years Hiram had employed a young man who lived in Plainville to work for him, and also had hired a man to work by the day during harvest time. It looked like there would be war and it was possible that these young men soon would not be available.

Billy Wilson and some of the other larger farmers in the area had been using a steel plow for several years. They had been able to plow twice as much land and do a better job than Hiram had been able to do with his wooden plow with an iron plow point, in the same amount of time. Hiram decided it was time for him to buy one of those new plows! He also decided to buy a peg tooth harrow with steel pegs placed in a heavy wooden frame. With his old harrow he had to replace its wooden teeth at least twice a year because they wore out so rapidly. He also had to replace the wooden pegs whenever one of them hit a large rock. He had received a good price for his tobacco earlier in the year and would use that money to purchase these new tools. When he started using them he could hardly believe what a difference they made. He wished he had made those purchases several years sooner.

Within a year, as Hiram had anticipated, both of the young men who had been working for him signed up with the Union forces. Ira, William E. and even Ida, who was now ten, helped fill the void. Polly was also able to assist more now that the children were older. Beginning at the age of six, all three children attended the winter school session at the Plainville school, but were home to help their parents the rest of the year. Ida was now milking two of the cows, helping to churn the butter and taking care of the chickens. Ira took care of the pigs, William E. took care of the sheep and both helped their father with many tasks.

In 1864, the Ward farm mechanization took another giant step forward. Hiram purchased a reaper. The reaper not only cut the wheat and oats but left the stalks in neat piles that could be easily bound into bundles. He was now able to cut and bind almost two acres in a day by himself. He hitched his team of horses to the binder in the morning and in less than three hours had cut all he could bind and shock in the afternoon. William was astonished to see Hiram harvest more grain in one day than both he and Hiram could do together in a day only ten years earlier.

Hiram also wanted to purchase a mowing machine to cut his hay. But his farm was small and he realized that a mowing machine would be an unnecessary expense. He decided that he would try using the reaper to cut the hay. He was pleased to find that it worked very well. By leaving the hay in small piles, he didn't have to use a rake nearly as much and that also saved time and work. He missed the young men that had helped him before the war, but with these labor-saving farm tools he was doing quite well.

In early 1865, the family mourned the death of 77-year-old William. He had seen many changes in his lifetime. He was just a baby when George Washington became president and now, in his last years, William was saddened to see the country torn apart with thousands of young men giving their lives in an attempt to keep the states together. William was buried in the Plainville Cemetery and now, once again, was resting next to Hannah who he had sorely missed during his last few years.

William's will left his estate in equal portions to each of his four children. The farm was appraised for $6,000, much more than it would have been worth five years earlier. The high prices that farmers were receiving, because of the war, had about doubled the farm's value. Hiram contacted his uncle, James L. Finch, to arrange a mortgage on the farm of $2,000 at 7% interest to help pay his brothers and sister their shares.

Polly and Hiram had been discussing what they should do ever since William had died. The farm was valued at twice what it would have been worth at the beginning of the war. Now that the war was over, tobacco and other crops would be coming from the South. Would the good prices continue? Would they be able to make the payments? The $2,500 needed, in addition to the mortgage, had taken almost every penny that Hiram and Polly had saved during the previous five years. Finally Hiram said, "We should purchase the farm. It has been good to us. We have profited every year including the year that hail almost destroyed our tobacco. The children are helping more and more every year. We will succeed!"

William E., now referred to as Will, especially missed his grandfather. They had often sat together and discussed the war, farming, what life had been like for William as a boy and later when he was in the militia. A close bond had developed between them.

Will had been intrigued to hear about how his father and uncles had constructed the well by the house, and admired their bravery in digging a hole that extended six feet above their heads while wondering if it might cave in and bury them alive. He also told Will about all of the ditches they had dug by hand to drain wet spots in the fields. He explained that before clay tile were made, they had laid field stone in the bottom of the ditch and then laid flat stone on top to form an underground channel for the excess water to flow from the fields making them more productive.

Hiram and Polly were very pleased that the price of tobacco remained strong for several years after the war. They were especially proud of their three children who had joyfully accepted their responsibilities on the farm. Now that the war was over and help for the farm could be found, it wasn't needed because Ida, Ira and Will were such good help.

After the war ended, cotton quickly arrived from the South to supply the northern mills and the price of wool took a big drop. Everyone was pleased not to have to wear the heavy wool garments during the summer anymore but it was no longer profitable for the Wards to keep sheep. Polly remembered that her mother used to make their summer clothes of linen from the flax, but in recent years, up until the war, cotton had become more common and was more comfortable.

Tragedy struck the Ward family when on his 20th birthday, Ira complained of not feeling well. Dr. Schenck, who lived in Plainville, came but there was nothing he could do. Ira had a high fever and only eight days later he passed away. He was a personable, kind, and hard-working young man who would be greatly missed. Will had been very close to Ira and found the loss of his brother most difficult.

The family had always attended the Christian Church and Society of Plainville, NY, commonly called the Plainville Christian Church, from the time the children were very small. Will was unable to accept that a loving God could take his brother, who had never sinned, at such an early age. He refused to have any association with the church for a number of years. Will's parents and sister Ida tried to understand how he could change his beliefs so quickly, but without success.

Ida was now 23 years old and there were no indications she would ever marry. She was somewhat heavy for her height and the young men in the community seemed to have no interest in her, and she showed no interest in any of them. She continued to care for the cows and make the butter which was recognized as the best in the community. She used her own special butter marker, which left the print of a sheaf of wheat on the butter. Customers at the general store always looked to purchase butter with this print.

Will, now 18, was busy learning all aspects of farming from his father. His father had recently purchased a grain drill to sow their wheat and oats. They had a much better stand of grain with the drill than when they had scattered the seeds on the ground by hand and harrowed them in. The yields were so improved that the drill paid for itself in two years.

The oxen, which his grandfather had loved and driven all of his life, were now gone. They had been replaced by two teams of horses. Having two teams was a bit of a luxury but if a horse got lame or sick they would be unable to complete their work in a timely manner. One of the teams was lighter than the other so it was always used to pull their wagon when they went to Baldwinsville to obtain supplies. They normally walked to Plainville because it was only a half mile.

There was a huge hotel in Plainville where special dinners and dances were held. Sometimes the dances would continue into the wee hours of the morning. Will loved to go, dancing with the young girls in the community but showing no special interest in any one girl. He had persuaded Ida to go with him one time but she didn't enjoy it and never went again.

One of his memories that often came back was of a beautiful young maiden that he had danced with at several of the dances. She went by the name of Liz even though her real name was Elizabeth. She used to come with her uncle and aunt who lived in the nearby hamlet of Lysander. One warm summer night she suggested they take a break and go outside to cool off. When they had gone down the stairs and were outside she took his hand and led him around to the back of the hotel. They kissed a few times and before he hardly realized it she had placed his hand inside her dress on her bosom. Will's face began to flush and he noticed a decided change in his anatomy. How wonderful it felt inside Liz's dress. He was in ecstasy!

Soon Liz suggested that Will put his hand on another spot that he might even enjoy even more. This was a new experience for Will and he decided that, as much as he hated to stop, he had better before things got out of hand. He took Liz's hand and forcibly led her around to the front of the hotel and told her it was later than he thought and had to head home. Liz had a few choice words to say as he left but he knew he was getting into uncharted waters.

When the next dance came to Plainville Polly wondered why Will didn't want to go. It was another year before he went dancing at the Plainville Hotel. When he went the next year, one of his friends remarked that Liz had married and had a little girl. Will thought himself fortunate to have walked away from temptation.

Every 4th of July there was a big celebration in Plainville. There was a parade with a local band, costumes, fireworks and a dance. One of the day's high points was when the local blacksmith blew the anvil. A large anvil was placed out in the middle of the road and the hardie hole in the top was filled with black gunpowder. A wick was placed in the gunpowder and then another large anvil weighing over 100 pounds was placed on top of the first anvil. The wick was lighted and everyone quickly got out of the way as the gunpowder gave a loud explosion and sent the top anvil flying into the air. Afterward there was always a lot of cheering for the blacksmith and a few free drinks awaited him at the hotel.

The late 1870s and early 1880s brought some difficult years due to lower farm prices. Some years it hardly paid to grow tobacco because the price was so low. A cheese factory began operation in Plainville in the early 1870s but a fire in 1877 destroyed it and with it went a market for milk. Hiram and Will decided to increase their production of potatoes. Syracuse had become a large city and there was great demand for potatoes. Previously they had grown potatoes only for their own use and occasional sale at the general store or to some neighbors. In 1882, they increased their production to an acre.

Extra potatoes were stored in the root cellar under their house. When it was time to plant the potatoes, they left some of the small ones whole but the larger ones were cut into two or more pieces, each with an eye so it would grow.

The ground was plowed and fitted. Then they made a shallow furrow with a plow and placed a piece of potato every six inches in the furrow. Next they covered the potatoes with a hoe. It took Hiram and Will almost two days to plant the potatoes. As the potatoes grew they used a hoe to remove the weeds and to bring fresh soil around each hill of potatoes. When the potato vines started to spread into the row they used a cultivator to loosen the soil in between the rows. Next they used a hoe to pull more dirt up and around each hill.

Earlier in the year they had made some bushel crates out of a basswood log to hold the potatoes. The potatoes would be dug up and placed in the crates, which were taken to the root cellar. The potatoes would be dumped into the cellar and the crates taken back to the fields for refilling. One Friday evening Will loaded 30 bushels of potatoes on the wagon, hooked the large team of horses to it and set out for the Syracuse Public Market. He left at 10:00 Friday evening to arrive at the market before it opened at 5:00 the next morning.

It was a long hard pull for the horses over the Voorhees Hill east of Plainville but since the horses were fresh and the ground was quite level the rest of the way it wasn't too difficult for the horses. Will crossed the Seneca River in Baldwinsville, passed through Warners, Fairmount and into Syracuse. The market was next to the Erie Canal in the center of Syracuse. He was pleased that he had started when he did because some of the hucksters were already arriving to buy the produce they needed for peddling that day. He drove his horses to the watering trough, hung a feed bag with oats over each horses head and prepared to offer his potatoes for sale.

He checked with some other farmers as to what they were charging for their potatoes. One of the farmers was Ansel Gates, who lived in the Town of Van Buren just across the Seneca River from Will. He was there with both potatoes and squash. Ansel told him that most of the farmers were asking $1.10 a bushel this year because there was not a large crop. If the buyer had his own container he would only charge $1.05. He also warned Will that the buyers always offered less and not to fall for that trick. Will was surprised to see a fine looking young lady with Ansel and discovered her name was Lilly. Will thanked him and turned to Lilly and said he hoped he would see her again sometime.

The market was a bustling place. Since it was Saturday all of the hucksters were filling their wagons with produce in anticipation of a busy day. It was the best day of the week for the storekeepers too. They came with their horses and wagons to buy produce for their stores. Will estimated that there were at least 200 horses hauling wagons or carts at the market. The odor of horse manure mixed with the foul odors coming from the canal was a new experience for Will's nose.

As he was warned by Ansel, almost all the buyers asked the price of his potatoes and then went on their way saying it was too much. He became a little concerned until one of them came back and told him he would take two bushels. Soon others were coming back and he knew that they must like the looks of his potatoes and his price was right. As they purchased his potatoes he had to carry them to their wagons and usually dumped them into their containers. At first he was a little worried to leave his stall with no one there but soon learned that the farmers always looked out for each other and nothing was ever taken.

He was pleased that all of his potatoes were sold by 8:00 a.m. so he spent a little time walking around the market to see what was for sale. He also hoped that he might see Lilly again but was out of luck because Ansel's wagon was not there. He noticed that there were farmers selling a great variety of items including butter, cheese, apples, prunes, cauliflower, squash and potatoes. He noticed that the farmers who still had potatoes for sale were asking only a dollar a bushel but their potatoes didn't look very good.

The Erie Canal was very interesting. Will was fascinated by the boats meeting and passing each other. What was especially intriguing was the building where the boats passed through to be weighed. The fees they paid were determined by the load they were carrying.

Will watered his horses and set out for home. It was now 9:00 a.m. and he hoped to be home in six hours. The horses always walked faster when they were headed toward home. He was very pleased to have $32 to take home from his first sale of potatoes at the Syracuse Public Market. There were enough potatoes in the cellar for one more trip on the following Saturday. Maybe Lilly would be there.

The week seemed to go slowly for Will. He couldn't wait to take the potatoes to market again and see Lilly. The first thing he did on arriving was to see if Ansel was there and if Lilly was with him. Ansel was there and he greeted him warmly. Will asked about Lilly but was told it was only a coincidence that she was there the previous week. Will asked if he could come to see her sometime. Ansel replied that it would be fine but to come on a Sunday afternoon. He also added that Lilly had mentioned to him that she hoped to see Will again. Will said he would plan on stopping to see her the following Sunday. The potatoes sold well again this time. Maybe they were something he could continue to grow in future years.

The following Sunday, after the Wards had dinner, Will harnessed the horses to the wagon and set out to the Ansel Gates farm, in an area of Van Buren called Satan's Kingdom. He noticed as he approached that it was a well-kept farm. Everything was neat and where it should be. No tools were in the yard and three sheep were in the front yard keeping the grass well manicured.

He was met at the door by a young man named Ralph, who he later learned was Lilly's brother. Ralph took him into the living room where he met Ruth, Lilly's mother. She chatted with Will a few minutes and then called Lilly and told her she had a visitor. Lilly knew because she had kept peering out the window in anticipation of Will's visit. Ruth asked him about his family and how long they had lived there. She mentioned that she grew up on a farm near Homer that her grandfather had settled on in 1802. Soon she excused herself and Will and Lilly were left alone to get acquainted.

Lilly mentioned that she enjoyed playing the piano and was studying music at a new school, Syracuse University. She would be performing in a Christmas concert in Jordan in early December and wondered if Will

Photographs of Hiram and Polly Ward who lived on the farm at Plainville from 1835 until their deaths.

Ira, Ida and William Ward, the children of Hiram and Polly Ward.

Our Farm in 1864

70 acres – of which 50 were improved and 20 unimproved

25 acres plowed, 11 pasture and 9 meadowland

Production:

Wheat	8 acres	250 bushel
Barley	8 acres	105 bushel
Indian corn	6 acres	75 bushel
Tobacco	1 acre	500 pounds
Oats	4 acres	116 bushel
Buckwheat	½ acre	8 bushel
Potatoes	½ acre	70 bushel
Apples	52 trees	150 bushel and 4 barrels of cider
Cows	4	300# butter and 100# cheese
Chickens	value was $20.	Sold $6. of eggs
Pigs	3	Produced 800# pork
Sheep	19	Produced 70# wool

Had 3 horses.
One sheep was killed by dogs.
Purchased $3 of fertilizer.

Farm value was $4,000.
Stock value $300
Tools and implements were valued at $75.

A copy of the information from the United States Census of Agriculture taken in 1864. At this time William Ward was still living but Hiram Ward was doing most of the work on the farm. The total farm acreage was 72, which included about 27 acres of woodlot and unused land. Notice that tobacco was one of the crops and that the milk from the four cows was used to make butter and cheese on the farm, which would have been sold locally.

A huge hotel at the Plainville four-corners circa 1880. Travelers could house their horses in the hotel's stable at the far end of the building.

A general store in Plainville. Plainville had a general store from shortly after it was founded around 1810 until the last one closed around 1980. Residents from nearby, including the Ward family, could buy most of the items they needed like salt, sugar, nails, gun powder, shovels and molasses. Farmers, like the Wards, often traded butter, eggs and cheese for items they needed.

would like to come to hear her. He asked if she would be willing to play for him some that afternoon. They moved to the parlor and Lilly began to play. Will was enamored by her talent and almost before he realized it he was humming along with the music. Suddenly his hand rested lightly on her shoulder as she played. When she had finished she asked Will to sit next to her on the piano bench so they could sing the next song together. Will bashfully replied that he was not a good singer but would try. The time flew by as they sang several songs together.

Soon Ruth appeared and asked Will to stay and have supper with them. There were a variety of topics discussed during the meal including Lilly's studies at Syracuse, the price of tobacco and farming in general. After eating, Will thanked Ruth for the fine meal and said he should be heading home. Because of having to go to Jack's Reef to cross the Seneca River, it was about eight miles back home. Ruth invited Will to join them for dinner next Sunday so he could meet the rest of the family. He said he would be pleased to come and might row across the river at Turner's making the trip less than two miles.

As Will began his Sunday trip to Lilly's home, the river was so low he might have been able to walk across it. But not wanting to take the chance of getting wet, Will borrowed a boat from Sam Turner. After crossing the river he walked across some fields where the corn had been cut and shocked and in less than a half hour was at the Gates farm. Lilly came out to greet him, then introduced him to her four brothers. After a fine chicken dinner Lilly suggested they go for a walk to help settle the big meal.

As they strolled along the road Will reached over and took Lilly's hand. There was no resistance but just a gentle squeeze of approval. Will asked Lilly what her future plans were since she was going to school to study piano. She replied that she would be completing her school the following June and hoped to marry some fine young man. Will impulsively bent over and gave her a kiss on the lips. Then he whispered to her, "Would I have any chance of being that young man?" She gave a smug smile and responded that only time would tell.

Will told her of his plans to build a new house near his father's the following year. He said that they had cut some extra logs the year before, which he would have sawed at the Voorhees sawmill near their farm. He and his father would not have sufficient time to build it that year but he might hire a carpenter to do much of the work. Lilly suggested Will might want to hire her brother Emory, who was a master carpenter. Will spoke with Emery, who was interested in the job if he could get one of his brothers to assist.

Before leaving Lilly invited Will to come to hear her play at the Jordan concert the first week in December. Will thanked Ruth again for the fine dinner. Lily walked along with him for the first part of his trip home. Half way across the family's corn field Will led her behind a corn shock to kiss her. She responded with a long wet kiss of her own. She told him, "I think you are going to be that fine young man I have been looking for, but I am not quite ready to say yes at this time." Will held her close and after another long kiss each headed home.

The courtship continued with growing passion. There was no question in anyone's mind, including Lilly's, that soon she and Will would be married. Will put his house building plans into action. The newlyweds' home would be two stories with a bay window in the living room, which would be an ideal spot for their Christmas tree and for plants during the remainder of the year. Four upstairs bedrooms guaranteed room for several children. The couple would marry as soon as the house was finished.

Their lives kept them busy as they eagerly awaited the day they would marry. Until June, Lilly lived near Syracuse University to study piano. Her mother needed her help on the farm in the summer and during the fall. Any spare moment Lily found was spent preparing items for her new home. Will had his farm work and also helped with the construction of the house.

Finally, December 5, their wedding date, arrived. The couple were married in Homer, Ruth's hometown which is where the Gates family lived until moving to Van Buren. Will hitched his horse to his new cutter early in the morning and traveled to Homer the day of the wedding. It was almost 40 miles and had taken most of the day.

Arrangements had been made with the minister of the local church to come to Lilly's grandmother's house to perform the wedding early that evening. After the ceremony there was a family dinner before the bride and groom retired for the night. Early the next morning Will hitched the horse to the cutter and they headed to Plainville and their new home.

The new house was less than 100 feet from Hiram's and Polly's so there was frequent interaction between the families. Lilly and Polly developed a close mother-daughter relationship and usually worked together canning their fruits and some of their vegetables. There had always been a large orchard on the farm but Hiram took a special interest in it during his senior years. Originally the orchard's main use had been for the production of apples to make cider. Several barrels were filled and stored in the cellar so they could enjoy a glass of cider anytime during the year.

There had been a religious oriented movement through the area in the first half of the century opposing the use of alcohol, including hard cider. Like many other church oriented families, barrels of hard cider in the Ward cellar became a thing of the past. But apples were still an important part of their diet, enjoyed fresh and in applesauce and pies. Apples were stored in the root cellar as well as dried to ensure the fruit was always available to enjoy. There were also two prune trees, three cherry trees and three pear trees, which the family enjoyed fresh from the trees and from glass canning jars other times of the year.

Hiram, in his senior years, derived pleasure from both the orchard and the garden. He had learned to graft apple trees and by grafting three different varieties of apples to one tree he now had a tree that produced four kinds of apples. He also had a patch of raspberries that ripened into sweet juicy morsels that they all enjoyed.

Another generation of Wards began to appear on the farm beginning with Edith in 1885, Ruth in 1889 and Marcia in 1890. Both Will and Lilly enjoyed their three girls but still hoped for a boy.

When she was about four years old, Will and Lilly became concerned about Edith. One day she fell to the floor and began making erratic motions with her arms and legs. In a few minutes she got up and appeared as if nothing had happened. They had no idea what was wrong. In a few weeks she became unconscious when the same thing happened again. They decided to take her to see Dr. Schenck in Plainville to find out what was wrong. If this happened when she was on a stairway she could be seriously hurt, or if she was outside playing during cold weather and lay unconscious very long she might freeze.

Dr. Schenck had no answers. Since these spells happened without warning there seemed to be nothing he could do to help. He mentioned to them that when he had helped deliver Edith she had been a blue-baby and that perhaps the initial lack of oxygen to her lungs might have affected her. All he could suggest was that they watch her closely to see if she showed any signals of a forthcoming attack.

In 1892, Hiram went to join his son Ira in the family plot at the Plainville cemetery. Now Polly and Ida were left alone in the old family home. Their days were brightened by daily visits from little Edith, Ruth and Marcia. It was almost like the girls had three loving mothers.

Surprisingly, shortly after Hiram died, Will contacted a neighbor and bought 20 acres of land near his farm. He borrowed $900 from another neighbor, Billy Wilson, to purchase the land. He then bought an additional four acres adjoining his first purchase from another neighbor. Lilly wondered why he bought the extra land when he already had all he could do especially since they didn't have any boys. Will responded that he had to hire a full-time man anyway and the extra land would provide enough additional income to pay him. Besides, with the continuing improvements in machinery one man could now do as much as two could 50 years ago.

In 1896, Will and Lilly decided to have another child. Maybe this time it would be a boy. On November 17 another child came into the world but again it was a girl. They named her Metta but Will decided to give her the nickname of Mike. The other girls were already starting to do useful chores on the farm and as soon as Metta could help she was out with them.

When Will had married Lilly, she told him that once they had children she wanted him go to church with her and to take their children. Will was gradually beginning to realize that bad things happened to both good and bad people so he shouldn't let the untimely death of his brother turn him against the church. He knew, even though he didn't believe everything the Bible said, that many of its teachings would be beneficial for his children. Since Edith turned four the family had been attending the Plainville Christian Church each Sunday. He was pleased that he had returned because he was enjoying the fellowship of his friends and neighbors.

When the Plainville Rural Cemetery Association was formed in 1897 Will became its first secretary-treasurer. Previously part of the cemetery had been owned by the church and part had been a private cemetery started by the Norton family about 80 years earlier. The new cemetery included both of the older sections and about another acre of unsold lots. Since there was no money in the treasury, the cemetery sold these lots to people and then if the purchasers wanted to have their lots mowed they had to pay additional fees. Hiram had purchased a large lot after Ira had died and that lot, where Ira and Hiram were buried became part of the new cemetery. William had earlier purchased a lot from the Norton's which had also become part of the new cemetery.

Ida passed away in 1899 and was followed by Polly in 1901. The Ward family now consisted of Will, Lilly and four little girls. The old homestead didn't stay empty for long, however, because it was soon occupied by the hired man and his family.

The farm continued to prosper. An addition was added to the tobacco shed providing room to hang three acres of tobacco. Potatoes were

William E. Ward cutting and binding wheat into bundles on his farm at Plainville. Circa 1910. His father and grandfather had cut their wheat with a grain cradle. Their parents had used a scythe to cut grain and before that a sickle had been used by farmers for centuries. Using the grain binder William was able to cut and bind as much wheat in an hour as his father could have done in six hours. Because of the invention of the binder and other labor saving equipment William could farm twice as many acres of land as his father or grandfather.

Metta Ward (Bitz) and William E. Ward weeding a tobacco bed. Circa 1920. In the background is the house that William's grandfather William had constructed in 1840. On the far left a pump is visible on the well that Hiram and his brothers had dug more than 80 years earlier.

William E. Ward standing in a field of tobacco about ready to be harvested on his farm at Plainville. Circa 1910. Tobacco was a cash crop that had been grown on the farm since about 1850.

A copy of the original invoice dated October 25, 1884 for furniture to equip the new house of William and Lilly Ward on their farm at Plainville.

A photo taken in 2007 of the table purchased by W.E. Ward in 1884 for his new home in Plainville. It is the ext. table listed in the invoice for $6.80. The six cane chairs, listed in the invoice for $5.50, are also shown in the photo. This is the table upon which W. E. Ward's appendix was removed in about 1918. Susan Dettbarn Bonaiuto, great-granddaughter of W. E. Ward is the current owner of the table. Her mother's and her Uncle Bob's families have enjoyed eating together at the table several times since she inherited it.

selling very well because the growing population of Syracuse provided a market for them. There seemed to be no end to the amount of potatoes some families could eat. Potatoes were also a cost effective food for low income families.

With Ida gone, Will decided to sell his milk to the creamery in Plainville. Over the years the sales of Ida's butter had increased so they had been milking as many as ten cows during the summer. Plainville was nearby so he could deliver his milk each day to the creamery in less than an hour. Lilly's brother Ralph lived on a nearby farm and often picked up Will's milk and took it to the creamery with his.

A problem surfaced, though, when Will started taking his milk to the creamery. The cows had to be milked twice a day and the creamery only took milk in the morning. He had to build an ice house next to the cow barn, to store ice for cooling each night's milking. Every winter Will and Ralph Gates helped each other cut ice from the river to fill their icehouses. After the cakes of ice were packed in the icehouse, sawdust from the Voorhees sawmill was packed around it to help keep it from melting. By putting a cake of ice in the tank with the cans of milk each evening, the ice would cool the milk sufficiently so it could be taken to the creamery the following morning.

The barn where Will kept his horses and heifers was getting old and was too small for the farm's needs. For years he had wanted a larger barn to provide more room for his dairy heifers and to store potatoes and hay for the livestock. In the winter of 1905 he drew up plans for the barn and cut logs that winter to provide the lumber for the barn.

It was to be a tall gambrel roof barn, 36 feet wide by 60 feet long. The basement of the barn would be divided to use one-half for horses and heifers while the other half would have the potato cellar and a place to store a large wagon. On the top floor there were to be two mows for hay and a mow to store bundles of wheat or oats. Under the haymow was a granary with 10 bins where he could store wheat and oats after they had been threshed. There would be trap doors in the floor of the granary so that potatoes could be dumped from the crates from the fields into the potato cellar below. A master carpenter was scheduled to construct the barn in the spring of 1907 so it would be completed for use in the late summer. Aside from his wedding day, this was the most excited Will had ever been.

A day had been arranged for the neighbors to come and help with the barn raising. The master carpenter had all the timbers cut and fitted together so one section could be raised at a time. Each section was 30 feet high and 36 feet wide so it took a dozen men to put each one in place. Long pike poles were used by some of the men to push a section up, while others used ropes and pulled from the other side. Each section was placed 12 feet away from the previous one. When a section was in place, 12 foot timbers connected the two sections, which were held in place by wooden pegs.

The barn raising was an exciting event. Lilly had been busy preparing food for several days. The neighbors' wives also brought food when they came. The men had a good lunch while taking a break but the big dinner was saved for the evening after all of the sections had been placed and pegged together. One of the high points of the day was when one of the men climbed to the very peak of the barn and stood on his head while waving to the gasping audience on the ground. He always did this whenever he was at a barn raising and everyone looked forward to his performance. This time he added more excitement for the crowd by walking on his hands, on top of the ridge, the length of the barn. Ten-year-old Metta along with her sisters, started watching but soon covered her eyes in fear that he might fall.

At dinnertime great quantities of cider flowed and a fiddler played some lively tunes to add to the festivities. Even though the Wards didn't drink hard cider, it was an essential part of a barn raising for some of the men. The floor of the barn was swept clean and soon all the young couples were square dancing on it. Ruth and Marcia were out on the floor dancing but Will when noticed Metta longingly watching from the sidelines, he asked her to dance with him.

The new barn was sided and completed for use in August. It was too late to store the hay, but in time to hold the oats and store the potatoes. With more room for potatoes, Will had increased production to three acres. The yields had increased to 150 bushels an acre but they didn't even half fill the new storage area. This year he would have to go to the Syracuse market more than ten times to sell all of his potatoes.

As a young man Will had helped Hiram thresh his oats and wheat with a flail. A few bundles of grain at a time were removed from the mow, placed on the barn floor and then hit numerous times with a flail to separate the kernels of grain from the grain heads. It was a tedious job that took about a month to complete. For the last 20 years a threshing machine, powered by a horse treadmill, had been used to thresh the grain. It cut the time it took to thresh his grain down to four days, which was a great improvement. Now, with the new barn, he could hire a man with a steam engine and a large threshing machine to thresh his grain in less than a day.

The threshing machine was backed onto the new barn floor and a long leather endless belt connected it to the pulley on the steam engine that was parked outside the barn. Two men had come with the thresher. One man kept the boiler supplied with wood and water and the other fed the bundles of grain into the threshing machine. Will had helped the Gates and the Tillotsons thresh their grain and now two men came from each farm to return the favor. The threshed oats were carried into the new granary by one man while two others formed the straw as it came out of the thresher into a neat stack in the barnyard. The straw was to be used the following fall and winter to bed the cows and horses. Three other men pitched the bundles of oats out of the mow to supply the man feeding the threshing machine.

Lilly had been busy all morning as well as the previous day preparing a big dinner for the eight men. They all worked hard and were not only dirty but very hungry by noontime. They enjoyed chicken, biscuits and gravy with plenty of mashed potatoes. Lily had made several apple pies the previous day and each man was served a quarter of a pie with a good chunk of cheese. It was a jolly time around the table as the men joked, told stories and filled their stomachs.

The threshing was completed by mid-afternoon and the thresher owner and his machinery traveled down the road to another farm. Will looked up at his new barn and smiled with satisfaction. Threshing the grain had been much easier; he had a place to store more potatoes and now had more room for his livestock. Life was good!

A photograph of the Plainville Christian Church, constructed in 1854, attended by six generations of the Ward family. One of the stained glass windows was given by the Wards and the baptismal font was given in memory of William E. Ward.

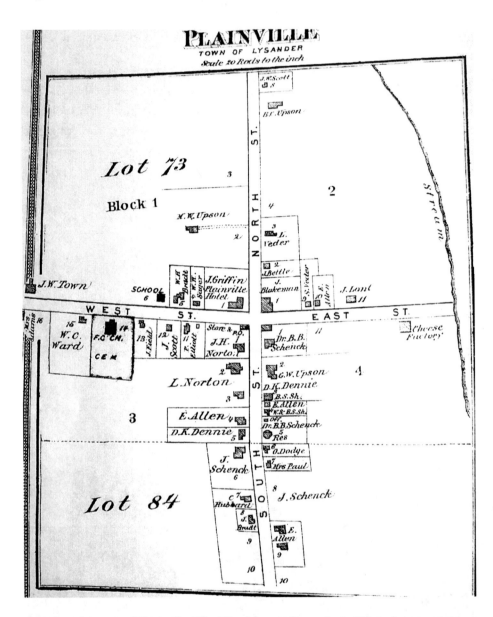

An *1870 drawing of Plainville. The Ward farm adjoins the J. Schenck property on the South. Notice the 1854 church with cemetery behind it on West Street. The Plainville school that four generations of Wards attended is on the north side of West Street.*

An 1898 photograph of the William E. & Lilly G. Ward family. From left to right are Ruth, Lilly, Edith, Metta, William and Marcia.

A circa 1908 photograph of the teachers and pupils that were attending the Plainville School. Second from the left in the back row is Ruth Ward, one of the school teachers. The fourth person from the left in the third row is Metta Ward.

The four daughters of William and Lilly Ward. From left to right are Edith, Marcia, Metta and Ruth.

The house constructed by William E. Ward in 1884. It was the house where Metta and her three sisters were born and raised. It is also the house where Ruth Bitz Dettbarn was born and the house where she and her brother Robert Ward Bitz grew up.

An 1899 photograph of Maude, Harry and Nellie Bitz. It was common for little boys to be dressed in girl's clothes at age four during this period of time.

CHAPTER 10
Ward-Bitz Family 1918 to 1948

R uth and Marcia both left home and became schoolteachers while
Metta stayed on the farm helping her father and her mother. She
was needed to help her mother care for her sister, Edith, who had been
diagnosed with epilepsy, and to help her father on the farm. There
was a great demand for food during World War I that resulted in the
highest prices Will had ever seen for his milk, wheat, tobacco and
potatoes. He decided that he would use some of those profits to build
an addition to their home. He hired his brother-in-law Emory Gates,
who had constructed the house for him 35 years earlier, to build the new
addition.

Will was surprised to find that the two-room addition cost him more
than the entire cost of the original house. Even so he was glad he
had it added on because he didn't want Edith to go up and down the
stairs anymore. He and Lilly could now have a downstairs bedroom
while Edith slept in the room next to them. He didn't tell Metta this
but he secretly hoped that she would find the right man to marry and
eventually continue the farm.

About 1918 the Ward family had a bad scare that turned into a close
call. Will, who was normally quite healthy developed a sharp pain in his
abdomen that wouldn't go away. First he thought it might be indigestion
but the pain persisted. When Lilly thought he was getting a fever
she became worried. Metta went to Plainville and called Dr. Hawley
who lived in Baldwinsville. After describing the symptoms to him he
thought it might be a ruptured appendix. Dr. Hawley told her to have
Will lie perfectly still and he would be there as quickly as possible.

In about an hour Dr. Hawley arrived. Because of the symptoms he brought another doctor to Plainville with him. After a quick examination the doctor determined that there would be no way to save Will's life unless they operated immediately. Dr. Hawley instructed Lilly to clear the dining room table, the one they had purchased when they were married, because they were going to use that as the operating table. The doctor had come prepared with anesthetic and surgeon's tools.

Will was stretched out on the top of the table, given some anesthetic and the doctors went to work. As anticipated, the appendix had burst. Fortunately, it was well contained and they hoped that none of the infection had spread beyond what they removed. After the operation, they moved Will to a couch where he gradually gained consciousness. The doctor told Lilly that he did the best he could under the circumstances. He said he would stop back in two days to examine the wound and see how Will was progressing. Will was to remain still until then to help prevent the spread of infection. Upon the doctor's return, he looked at the wound and told Lilly that he was pleased with Will's progress. When Dr. Hawley saw Will a month later he confided to Will that when he had performed the operation he had given Will less than a fifty percent chance to survive.

Will continued to sell most of his potatoes at the Syracuse Public Market. Metta would sometimes go with him to help even though they had to start out with the horses and wagon at 11:00 the night before to arrive by 5:00 the next morning when the market opened. Both Will and Metta had gone to the market on November 11, 1918 with their potatoes, which were selling rather slowly that day.

All of a sudden, shortly after 11:00 a.m., church bells started ringing, firecrackers were set off and trucks and automobiles started blowing their horns. What a racket it was! The horses, which usually peacefully munched their hay, went wild with fear. Some horses ran away with their wagons hitched behind them, bumping into trucks and other wagons. Both Will and Metta ran to the horses and took hold of their halters. They had all they could do to restrain their horses. Rapidly the news was spreading that the armistice had been signed ending World War I!

In 1919, a concrete road had been constructed between Baldwinsville and Plainville. What an improvement it was compared to the dirt and gravel road Will had traveled on all his life! There had also been a plank road along the river near Baldwinsville that long before had deteriorated. He decided with a new road it was now time to invest in a truck. The road to Plainville was still dirt but it was only a half-mile and it was all concrete road the rest of the way to Syracuse. The new truck was a Ford and it would haul a load weighing up to 4,000 pounds! That was twice as large a load as he could draw with the wagon and horses. Meaning he could cut the numbers of trips to the market in half. Now he wouldn't have to leave the farm until 3:30 a.m. and would be able to be back by the middle of the afternoon. The new barn he had built a decade earlier had extra room in its potato storage area so, with the new truck, he could now grow more potatoes.

During the winter a man came from Onondaga County and told Will that the county wanted to purchase a chunk of his land, to avoid a hill, where they were building a new concrete road from Plainville to Jacks Reefs. The man told him it was less than an acre and that they would pay him $300. Will replied that the new road was needed and he wanted to give the land to the county because the new road would be a benefit to him.

The county notified the farmers on Plainville Road and others nearby farms that great quantities of stones would be needed to build the new road. Ever since the land had been cleared for farms, over 100 years earlier, farmers had removed stones from their fields before the fields were planted with crops. The stones were used to build stone fences or simply put into large piles in the fields. Since barbed wire had now been invented, stone fences were no longer used and the stone piles were in the way of larger farm equipment. It was an opportunity for farmers to get rid of these stones and make a little money by delivering them to the county's stone crusher. It seemed to the farmers that no matter how many stones they removed each year there were as many more waiting in the fields to be picked up the next year. These stones appeared as if by magic. Will discovered what was happening. Each winter the frost went into the ground two or three feet. When the frost came out of the ground the following spring some of the stones that were hidden the year before moved up a few inches, so when the ground was plowed they came to the top.

A young man who lived in Plainville by the name of Harry Bitz had been renting some land near Plainville in an effort to earn money with the hope of buying a farm of his own sometime in the future. During the winter and whenever he had spare time, he worked for other farmers who needed extra help. He owned his own team of horses, a wagon and a few other small pieces of farm equipment. He contacted one of the local farmers who wanted to rid himself of some stone piles but couldn't do it himself. Harry was told he could have all of this farmer's stones if he would draw them with his horses and wagon.

The county set up its stone crusher near the end of Gates Road, across from Will Ward's farm. The stone crusher was powered by a steam engine that burned soft coal. When the engine was working hard it belched clouds of black smoke that sometimes could be seen from a mile away. The coarse crushed stones were being used as a base for the new road and the finer crushed stones were being mixed with sand, cement and water to form the surface of the road. The road was 16 feet wide and had eight inches of concrete over its six inch stone base. It was constructed to last a long time. The concrete mixer was set up in the middle of the road with the crushed stone, sand, cement and water each brought to the road in front of the concrete mixer where men shoveled the materials into it. The mixed concrete was dumped directly on to the road where men leveled it for the highway.

Harry had to draw the stones to the crusher from a half-mile away. He had to load the stones by lifting them on to the wagon and unload them the same way. He was able to haul about a ton of stones with each load and was able to draw about 10 loads a day. He received 50 cents for each load, which was big money for him. That amounted to five dollars for the team, wagon and his labor each day. He had never earned more than two dollars a day when he worked for farmers.

Will Ward was also drawing stones to the crusher and noticed that Harry was making a trip more quickly than he was even though Will didn't have as far to go. After watching Harry continue at the same pace for several weeks, Will was impressed. One day, when they were both unloading stones at the same time, he turned to Harry and said, "Harry, on April 1 my hired man is going back to Camillus to take over his father's farm. Would you consider working for me? I will pay you ten dollars a week and if you continue to work like I have seen you work this winter I will increase it to $12 a week."

Harry thought a minute and responded that he didn't think it would work out because he had his own team of horses and wanted to keep them. Since Will didn't want to lose the opportunity to hire Harry, he told Harry he could keep his horses at Will's farm, he would furnish the feed for them and pay Harry two dollars a week for their use. Harry said that he needed a week to think it over and then he would let Will know one way or the other.

When Harry returned to his home in Plainville he discussed the offer with his father. Irving responded that Will had a good reputation, was a man of his word, active in the local church and involved in a number of other community activities. Harry remembered that one of Will's daughters had been his teacher for one year in the Plainville school and had been an excellent teacher. He also fondly recalled that Will's youngest daughter, Metta, had been in his class for several years.

Two days later, when Will and Harry were again unloading stones at the same time, Harry told Will that if the offer was still good he would accept it. Will smiled and told him to plan on bringing his horses to start work April 1. The two men shook hands but unknown to them, their deal would affect both families for many years.

Ruth and Marcia were planning to take a trip to Newfoundland the following summer and asked their sister, Metta, to join them. Will and

Lilly encouraged her to join them. They made arrangements for a cousin to come and stay to help care for Edith while Metta was away.

The three Ward sisters packed their suitcases, took a trolley to Syracuse and then went by train to Boston. Metta was especially excited because she had never been more than 50 miles away from home or on such a large ship out in the ocean. The ship was a freighter designed to carry about 50 passengers in addition to freight. None of the girls had been to Boston before and other than Ruth, who lived in New York City, had never seen a city larger than Syracuse. It was an exciting time for them!

To minimize the cost, the sisters had booked the cheapest cabin possible with all three sharing the same room. There was one small chair and little else in the room except for the two bunk beds. The rest room and shower, serving all of the passengers, was down the hall.

A magnificent sight greeted the sisters gathered on the deck watching their ship make its way out of the Boston harbor. There were many ships in the harbor; some were passenger ships but most were carrying freight to and from all corners of the world. The tall buildings in the background were amazing to Metta who had never seen a building more than six stories high.

As their ship moved out into the Atlantic Ocean the waters were calm and the sky was beautiful with only an occasional puffy little cloud. Seagulls floated gracefully by and occasionally they could see a fish jump out of the water. It was paradise!

After an enjoyable dinner in the ship's dining section they returned to the deck to gaze at the evening sky before returning to their cabin for the night. What an exciting and enjoyable day it had been! After much talking and reminiscing about their childhood together they drifted off to sleep. Towards morning, Metta was awakened by a sudden jolt and found herself on the floor. The ship was pitching up and down, back and forth and in all directions.

What was wrong with her head and stomach! She felt like she was going to be sick. Although she never had experienced a feeling like this before, she had heard stories of how some people got seasick when the water got rough. Metta threw on her robe and ran down the hall to the restroom. There was already someone in the rest room and she could hear them heaving up their dinner from the night before. She could hardly stand up as the ship rolled back and forth in the water. She held her hand over her mouth and wondered if she could contain herself until the rest room was available. Fortunately the door opened just in time! Others were ill in the hall, filling it with a sour odder. She got down on her knees and heaved until she thought her stomach would come up to join its former contents. There was rapping on the door and she exited as quickly as she could but one person had already thrown up on the floor in the hallway. How awful it smelled! When she got back to her room she found her sister Ruth sick, but Marcia was fine.

In the evening the boat's rocking and pitching gradually decreased. Marcia ventured out to get something to eat and bring her sisters some water. There were only about half as many people in the dining room as the night before. She returned to the cabin with water and a few cookies. Both of her sisters were lying in their beds still suffering from motion sickness.

By morning the ship had stopped its erratic motions as it entered the harbor at St. John's. Marcia was on the deck enjoying the sights but both Ruth and Metta refused to leave their beds until the ship had docked. Finally they got cleaned up and went up on the deck to disembark. Ruth whimpered to Marcia, "Is there any possible way to return home without going by boat? I don't think I could survive another trip like that one."

The fresh air gradually rejuvenated them and they enjoyed looking at the sights in St. Johns. They marveled at the extreme changes in the harbor's water level as the tide went in and out. It was amazing to see small boats several feet above the water that a few hours earlier had been surrounded by water.

Later they returned to the ship in preparation for their voyage back to Boston. All of them were able to enjoy some dinner that evening although Ruth and Metta ate very little in case they hit rough seas. The next day the seas were much calmer and they were able to see the taller buildings of Halifax in the distance as they passed by Nova Scotia. The return trip turned out to be enjoyable. Upon reaching, home they shared some information with their family and friends about their trip experience, with their motion sickness at the top of their list.

Harry had been working a year for Will and their relationship had turned into that of a father-son rather than an employer-employee. Some months earlier Lilly had invited Harry to have dinner with the family and from then on he joined the family at their noontime meal. More than a friendship seemed to be developing between Metta and Harry. Both had been in the same class at the Plainville School and both had gone on to Baldwinsville Academy for their high school education. Metta had boarded with a family friend while going to school in Baldwinsville while Harry had earned his room and board working for the school janitor. During all of those years they seemed to almost completely ignore each other.

Harry and Metta were active in both the Plainville Christian Church and the Charter Oak Lodge. At dances they occasionally danced with each other. In Plainville there were a number of young men and women involved in these activities who they also danced and interacted with, so very few had any thoughts that a romance might be budding between the two. In fact, since Metta had just turned 26 many people thought she might grow up to be an old maid like her three older sisters.

With the opportunity to talk each day during and after dinner a romance was indeed beginning to grow. Soon Harry was invited to occasionally eat supper with them. It provided Harry the opportunity to be with Metta in the family parlor that had been added a few years earlier. Metta stressed that she couldn't live anyplace else because her mother needed her to help care for Edith, a situation that might not be acceptable to Harry. Metta was ecstatic when Harry replied that he realized the situation and would be very comfortable living in the same house with her family; Metta's father and mother were like a second set of parents to him. In addition, his mother had recently been sick with cancer and one of his older sisters had left teaching for an entire year to care for her until she had passed on.

Harry had a history of playing pranks on his friends. He had even been an instigator of a prank to take a bride in one direction in a buggy and the groom in another direction following the wedding ceremony. Because of his pranks, Harry knew that there would be problems for him if any of his friends found out that he was getting married. So the possibility of a marriage was kept under wraps.

The couple planned to marry on February 1, 1923. After they had been sworn to secrecy, the immediate families were apprised of the pending nuptials at Christmas. Ruth was a schoolteacher in Yonkers but had an apartment in New York City. She offered the prospective bride and groom the use of her apartment for their honeymoon.

It was not uncommon for the local minister to earn a little extra money during the winter by helping Will sort potatoes or strip tobacco. On February 1, the minister came to Will's house in his work clothes, the same as he always did when he was helping Will. This time he stayed in the house a little longer and performed Harry and Metta's wedding ceremony with only Will, Lilly and Edith as witnesses. After the ceremony Will harnessed a horse to the cutter, brought it to the house and the bride and groom were quickly on their way to catch the trolley in Baldwinsville, with no one the wiser. They left the horse and cutter at the livery stable to be picked up and taken back to the farm the next day. The trolly took them to Syracuse where they stayed overnight at a hotel before getting on the train to New York City.

Harry's sister Maude was as much of a practical joker as Harry. She lived in an apartment in Syracuse and somehow discovered where the bride and groom were staying. Late in the evening, when she was sure they were in bed, she called their room with her telephone. Disguising her voice she said to them, "This is the hotel management calling and we don't want to unnecessarily alarm you but a fire has broken out in the hotel. We believe we can bring the fire under control but suggest you get dressed to quickly evacuate the hotel if it becomes necessary." Then, unfortunately, she couldn't restrain herself any longer and burst out with a big laugh! It was something that Maude teased Harry and Metta about for many years.

After a few days enjoying New York City, the bride and groom settled into a familiar pattern of work, but now they had a bedroom of their own upstairs in the family home. Their friends were both surprised at the marriage and disappointed that they had missed the opportunity to get even with Harry for his practical jokes.

Potatoes were still one of the crops they continued to grow but now Harry usually drove the truck to take them to market. By going to the market every year, housewives had become familiar with the quality of their potatoes and often purchased their entire winter's supply from Harry. The number of bushels they wanted, usually between five and fifteen, were saved and delivered to their houses after the remainder had been sold at the market. Usually Harry had to park the truck on the street in front of customers' house and then carry the potatoes around to the back door of the house. After that, the housewife wanted the potatoes carried down the cellar stairs and dumped into her potato bin at the front of the house. It was a good bit of work to make the trip over and over with a sixty pound bushel of potatoes on your back. Because of this, since Will was now 67 years old, Harry often went to market.

The day before Thanksgiving both Harry and Will were in the market selling their potatoes. Farmers from north of Watertown quite often grew a small flock of turkeys and brought their live turkeys to the Syracuse market for sale prior to Thanksgiving. One of these farmers had eight live turkeys left when the market closed. If he had lived close to Syracuse he would have taken them home and come back before Christmas to sell them. In 1923, more often than not the roads from Watertown to Syracuse were closed because of snow and this farmer wanted to sell his turkeys now.

He offered them at a reasonable price to Harry and Will who initally had no intention of buying them. After a short discussion they decided to buy the turkeys, take them home, fatten them up and bring them back for sale at Christmastime. They would be bringing some of their potatoes so it wouldn't be an extra trip. They also reasoned that since turkey was more popular at Christmas than at Thanksgiving they might make a nice profit on them.

Neither Will or Harry had any previous experience with turkeys but they had chickens so it was not difficult for them. They made a pen in one corner of the tobacco shed and fed them corn to fatten them. While they were at the market they noticed that anyone with turkeys that had been killed and had the feathers removed seemed to easily sell. They also noticed that these farmers received more for their dressed turkeys. With their experience slaughtering chickens, they reasoned slaughtering the turkeys shouldn't be difficult.

A few days before Christmas they sharpened a knife, hung each turkey by its feet, used the knife to cut the arteries in its neck and then removed its feathers. They found that the feathers were harder to pull on a turkey than a chicken and resolved that if they ever dressed any more they would find a better method.

Three days before Christmas they took some potatoes and their turkeys to the market. If they were unable to sell all of the turkeys they would now be able to return to market the next day to sell the rest. Happily, all eight sold that morning and they received more than twice what they had paid for them. On the way home from the market they agreed that they would like to purchase some live turkeys and dress them for sale the next year.

Soon after the end of World War I, the prices for farm products had substantially dropped. Milk prices were lower and it had hardly paid to grow tobacco the past three years. Harry suggested that it might be a good idea for them to diversify a little and if they could grow turkeys successfully they might discontinue growing tobacco. Most farmers that grew turkeys didn't have more than a dozen and there was no one that grew more than 20 or 30.

A circa 1925 photograph of William E. Ward and Harry C. Bitz. This photo was taken in the home where the two families lived together and where Ruth and Robert Bitz grew up.

A circa 1935 photograph of the Ward/Bitz farm where turkeys had been added, in 1924, to the other farm products of milk, tobacco, wheat corn and oats that were grown on the farm.

A circa 1935 photograph of bronze turkeys, in and adjacent to the farm's tobacco shed, being finished for the Christmas market.

A circa 1936 photograph of Harry Bitz explaining, to visiting New York State turkey growers, how turkeys are dressed and prepared for market.

A circa 1931 photograph of Lilly and William Ward with their grandson Robert Bitz.

A circa 1937 photograph of Harry and Robert Bitz on a farm Harry was renting, across from their farm.

A circa 1938 photograph of a threshing machine and straw baler working on a rented farm near Plainville. Increased efficiency created by labor-saving farm equipment allowed Harry Bitz to farm a greater number of acres. Robert Bitz is one of the boys sitting on top of the threshing machine operating its straw blower.

The Plainville Schoolhouse that Ruth and Robert both attended for eight years. It was a two room school that offered grades one through eight. It replaced the brick three room school, which Harry Bitz and Metta Ward Bitz attended, that burned in about 1920. Harry and Metta received ten years of education here and then boarded two years in Baldwinsville to receive their high school diploma.

9

BILLS PAYABLE WEEKLY IN ADVANCE

SYRACUSE, N. Y.,   9/24   19 30

Mrs. Metta Bitz

To SYRACUSE MEMORIAL HOSPITAL, Dr.
736 IRVING AVENUE

BOARD AND ATTENDANCE (Pri.) (Pri. Wd.) (Comp. Wd.) (Ward Ser.) FROM 9/19 TO 9/26 @ $ 5.50	38	50		
OPERATING ROOM FEE				
DELIVERY AND DRESSINGS	10	00		
LABORATORY FEE	1	0		
X-RAY FEE	10	00		
CYSTOSCOPIC FEE				
BOARD OF SPECIAL NURSE DAYS NIGHTS @$1.50				
MEDICINES—DRESSINGS	75			
EXTRA MEALS—COTS				
AMBULANCE				
ELECTRO—CARDIOGRAPH	40			
Tolls TELEPHONE			60	65

No. 1890   Date 9/26   19 30

RECEIVED from Mrs. M Bitz

Sixty + 65 ————————— Dollars
100

For Bill   100

$ 60.65   **SYRACUSE MEMORIAL HOSPITAL.**

PSC

Invoice from Memorial Hospital in Syracuse showing the charges for a full week's hospital stay for Metta Ward Bitz and the delivery charge for the birth of her son Robert Ward Bitz in 1930. Until the birth of Robert, many generations of Ward babies had been born in the home. This invoice is shown as evidence to the change in cost of healthcare.

At the time they purchased the live turkeys, they had asked the man selling them where he had gotten his turkeys when they were small. He told them he kept several hens and a tom each winter to use as breeders. But he said he knew where they could purchase some turkey eggs and gave them the person's address. Harry wrote to that man and arranged to purchase 50 turkey eggs in March.

But how to get those turkey eggs under four broody chickens while removing the chicken eggs? Fortunately the chickens didn't realize their own eggs had been replaced and set on the eggs just as if they had been their own. The setting hens showed great patience; it takes turkey eggs four weeks to hatch whereas it only takes three weeks for chicken eggs. The little turkeys, called poults, thought the chickens were their mothers and the chickens thought the baby poults were their chicks. When the poults reached 10 weeks of age and about twice as big as a chicken it was a laughable sight to see them following the smaller hens.

Metta made sure that the turkeys had plenty of corn and oats to eat and supplemented that with some whole milk because milk was so cheap. After two of the small turkeys disappeared one night, Harry decided to build a fence around an acre of pasture to keep the turkeys confined and safe from foxes. He also started taking care of the turkeys because on May 11 Metta presented him with a baby daughter who they named Ruth Charlotte.

As Thanksgiving approached, 16 hen turkeys and 12 tom turkeys had survived. Since they had found a farmer who would do custom hatching, they decided to save 12 of the hens and two of the toms to use as breeding stock. The remaining turkeys were to be sold on the market for Thanksgiving and Christmas.

After dry picking half of the remaining turkeys for Thanksgiving, they decided at Christmas time to scald the turkeys to make feather removal easier. A double boiler of water was heated on the wood stove in the kitchen. After it had been bled, one turkey at a time was dunked in the water for about 15 seconds. It was amazing how much easier the feathers were removed after scalding! They had to very careful when they removed the feathers, however, as the skin could be easily blemished and spoil the looks of the bird.

The dressed turkeys sold very well again and they realized they could easily have sold more if they had them. They were pleased that they saved 12 hens to use as breeders.

They soon learned there were disease problems with turkeys if they were grown on the same farm as chickens. Chickens carried a disease that didn't affect them but was deadly to turkeys. They had been lucky their first year, but decided to discontinue keeping chickens once they decided to raise turkeys. They would also be able to use the old hen house for starting their turkey poults. Later, before moving the turkeys to pasture they could house the young turkeys in one end of the tobacco shed since they wouldn't need that for tobacco until September.

The turkey hens started laying eggs in early March. Each day the eggs were collected and placed in the cellar of the house. If the eggs had stayed under the hen turkey, she would have used her feet several times a day to turn the eggs. It is natural for a bird to do this to keep the bird that is developing in the center of the egg, so it can eventually hatch. To compensate for this movement, the eggs were placed on a large table that had a small lip around the edge to keep the eggs from rolling off. Each morning and night all of the eggs were turned until enough eggs had been accumulated to take to the hatchery.

The first four weeks they averaged 50 eggs a week from the 12 hens. At the end of four weeks they had accumulated 200 eggs and delivered them to the hatchery. The incubator at the hatchery turned the eggs automatically every four hours. Since they were removing the eggs from the hens every day, the hens continued to lay eggs for a longer time. Hens realize they need about a dozen eggs under them before it is time to try to hatch them. Four weeks later, they again took the eggs, only 180 this time, to the hatchery. On their return trip the car was very noisy as a chorus of 160 poults peeped all the way home.

A kerosene brooding stove had been lighted in the old henhouse to bring the temperature inside up over 90 degrees to simulate the temperature under the mother hen's feathers. Peat moss had been spread on the floor to make a comfortable bed for the poults. A special turkey feed purchased from a local mill was placed in several small feeders and special jars of water were placed in the turkey pen.

Twenty-eight days later 140 poults were picked up at the hatchery and 130 eggs left for hatching. The hens were about through laying and by the time they went back to pick up the poults it would be early June. The turkeys wouldn't reach maturity by Christmas if they were hatched any later.

Harry and Will had been busy building a brooding house for the turkeys to start the second flock because they knew the day old poults couldn't be mixed in with the older ones. They also fenced three acres of pasture to put them in when they reached nine weeks of age. It was also necessary to build a shelter on the pasture to protect the turkeys from the hot sun and from rains.

When Thanksgiving arrived they found they had a total of 220 turkeys but of three different ages. Forty were kept for breeding and the remainder were sold for Thanksgiving and Christmas. It was a big job removing the feathers from all of the turkeys, but some neighbors volunteered to help. They felt fortunate to have grown 220 turkeys from 510 eggs. Three hundred forty had hatched but they had lost over 100 due to a variety of causes.

In retrospect they realized they might have done better if they hadn't increased the number so much. Hereafter, they decided to increase the number they grew gradually until they gained more experience. Each increase required more brooding space, a larger pasture and more help to prepare them for market. So far they had made a nice profit but that might not always be the case. Growing turkeys was similar to growing tobacco in that they spent money and labor for almost a year before they got any back.

They decided to discontinue growing tobacco the next year because of its low price and how much time it took. Fortunately the dressed turkeys were still selling well and several store owners had expressed an interest in buying some for their customers the next year.

Arthur Hudson, a cousin and a good friend, asked Harry and Will if they might like to have him as a partner to help with the labor and spread the risk a little more. They talked it over and decided taking Arthur on as a partner would make it possible for them to grow more turkeys. One of Arthur's reasons for the request was that he had several boys who he would like to keep busy and gain some farm experience. With Arthur as a partner, they increased the number they grew each year to almost 2,000 by 1930. They needed a name for their turkeys and since the farm was near Plainville they decided to call it Plainville Turkey Farm.

In September 1930, a second child arrived for Harry and Metta. They named him Robert Ward to provide a partial continuance of the Ward name. Metta had some health issues and was unable to have a second child until she had an operation the previous year. She decided to have this child in a Syracuse hospital because of her health issues. It turned out to be a wise move because Robert was a 'big one' and she needed help from her doctor.

Turkey production and turkey sales continued to increase. The three partners were fortunate, however, because the retail price of farm products continued to be low. Farmers by the thousands all across the country were losing their farms because of the many years that their costs exceeded their income.

Harry's latest hired man owned his own house across the road from the farm. He also had a grown son who worked for Harry. Now the original Ward homestead wasn't needed to be used for a hired man and was turned into a general purpose building. Sacks of feed were stored in the living room and baby turkeys were started in battery brooders in the kitchen. At Christmas time dressed turkeys were hung overnight in the cellar to keep them from freezing. What would great grandmother Ward have thought if she had lived another 50 years to see her beautiful home used like a barn with live turkeys in it!

Robert had awakened the morning of December 28, 1934, gotten dressed and gone downstairs to find that the Christmas tree and decorations had disappeared during the night. There were two strange men in the house and he had no idea what they were doing. Robert's mother told him that his Grandfather Ward had passed away during the night so they had taken down all of the Christmas decorations. She said that many neighbors and relatives would be coming, his grandfather was going to be placed in a big box, and then he would be going to the Plainville cemetery to join Robert's grandmother who had gone there two years earlier.

Will had lived a full life, witnessing many changes in agriculture. All power on farms had been supplied by horses and oxen in his youth. He had seen steam engines come and go, being gradually replaced by gasoline powered tractors. Transportation on land had been by horse or train. The trolley and bicycle had come and gone. Now automobiles, trucks, buses and even airplanes were becoming common. When he and Harry had started growing turkeys it was only a sideline on farms. Fifty turkeys were considered a large flock, but now Plainville Turkey Farm was growing about 4,000. Will died happy knowing that the Ward farm, now in its 100th year, had survived and even prospered.

Will left the farm and his other assets in equal portions to his four daughters. Harry and Metta bought the farm but now had to take out a mortgage since they only owned a quarter of it. It put substantial financial pressure on Harry and Metta; they were now responsible for paying one-half of the cost of growing the turkeys as well as making mortgage payments.

Harry now had two hired men and Arthur had five sons, three of whom were old enough to help on weekends and when school wasn't in session. By 1938, the farm was producing 5,000 turkeys. Arthur was a partner only in the turkey portion of the farm. Harry wasn't depending on turkeys alone to provide the family's income. He milked 11 cows and grew peas, potatoes, corn, oats and wheat. There were five horses to furnish the farm's power since he still hadn't purchased a tractor.

Arthur had a strong work ethic and wanted to keep his sons busy. He had gone into the trucking business and also farm equipment. He had been able to keep his boys busy helping in the moving business, putting the farm machinery together and helping with the turkeys, but he wanted to have them live on a farm. He and his family lived in Baldwinsville for 14 years, but in 1940 bought a large farm in Camillus where he milked cows, grew beef cattle, and a variety of crops as well as turkeys.

Harry and Arthur each took half of the turkey growing equipment and half of the customers. It was an amicable separation and each one agreed to grow half as many turkeys as they had been growing. This proved to be a satisfactory arrangement because money was in short supply for both of them. Each summer Harry borrowed against a life insurance policy, and each year after the turkeys were sold at Christmas, he paid the loan back.

The following year Harry bought a tractor. He loved his horses and still used them a great deal but over the next several years the tractor began to be used more and more. The price of tobacco had increased. It was now profitable again so he decided to diversify a little more by growing two acres of tobacco. Harry had been renting a farm about two miles away to use for both growing crops and for turkey pasture. It had a large barn with a basement that was used for turkey breeders and a hay loft where he stored extra hay and straw. It also had an empty tobacco shed.

The farm's tobacco shed was no longer available to use for hanging tobacco. The tobacco stripping room, which had a stove, was now where the turkeys feathers were removed and where the turkeys were prepared for sale in the fall. Outside the tobacco shed but near the stripping room, the turkeys were killed. They were hung by their legs one at a time from the end of a long pole that was set at an angle to make its end about six feet above the ground. A narrow knife was inserted in its mouth and the arteries at the back of the neck were cut to quickly bleed the turkey. They died with very little pain by doing this. Next, a boy carried the turkey into the stripping room to dry pick the feathers on the legs because if these feathers were picked after it was scalded there would be permanent ugly blemishes.

The turkeys were then scalded in a tank of hot water on the stove, and their remaining feathers removed. The ones that were not to be sold New York dressed, with head and feet on and intestines inside, had those parts removed in the stripping room. They were then carried into the tobacco shed and hung from tobacco hangers to cool. Once cooled, a large red tag was tied around a leg of each turkey with the name, address and phone number of the farm. Each tag also carried these words, "If satisfied tell others, if not tell us!" It was an early form of brand identification that more and more people began to ask for.

The methods for processing turkeys were very primitive, but it was similar to the way most poultry and livestock were prepared for market. It was a new industry; previously poultry was commonly slaughtered and processed in the home or in the basement of the corner market.

The threshing machine continued to visit the farm each year to thresh the wheat and oats, but now it was powered by a tractor with a gasoline engine rather than by a steam engine. One summer Harry had a small combine come to the farm to harvest the oats. It was a forerunner of the modernization that would be coming to the farm in a few years.

Robert was with his father on the farm most of the time and was a busy farmhand by age 11. He helped milk the cows by hand each night, care for the turkeys, drive the horse on the horse fork and pull weeds out of the crops. He helped do everything but seemed to enjoy working with the turkeys the most. He liked going to the farmer's market with his father to sell the dressed turkeys at holiday time and selling to the retail customers at the farm.

Ruth Charlotte also helped on the farm. She quite often used the tractor to rake hay and straw. Before Robert was old enough, she drove the horse on the horse fork. When she turned 16 she got her driver's license and was soon driving the truck on farm errands. Robert often went with her as her helper. At that time manufactured feed for the turkeys and cows was purchased at Beacon Milling Company, 30 miles from the farm. Ruth drove the truck and Robert oversaw the loading of the bags of feed and covered them with a canvas to keep them dry whenever it rained. They made quite a team!

Because of the extra land and lack of help from Arthur's boys, Harry hired a man who boarded with the family. Turkeys on range were enticing for foxes, owls, dogs and sometimes even human beings. To limit the losses, a man was assigned to sleep with the turkeys. Harry and Arthur had often taken turns doing this. The hired man boarding with the family often received this assignment during the months of July to December when the turkeys were on pasture. A small building on runners was placed in the field near the turkey roosts. It was equipped with a bed, a chair and a kerosene lamp. The man was provided with a shotgun and expected to use it if necessary. A dog, attached to one end of a chain with the other end fastened to dog house, was also provided. The dog barked to wake up the watchman if there was an intruder.

From the beginning of World War II in December 1941, there was increased demand for farm products and their prices rose. Many items, such as red meat, gasoline and tires, were rationed. The price at which many things, including turkeys, could be sold was regulated by the government. There was additional demand for poultry because of the rationing of red meat. Harry was selling all the turkeys he could produce without any problem, so he increased his annual production to 3,500. Even though the price he received was limited by price controls, the government-set price provided a greater profit than had been normal.

Two small farms totaling 130 acres were purchased, more than doubling the size of the original farm. This extra land permitted additional diversification. Harry began growing cabbage and red kidney beans in addition to the crops already being grown. A distant cousin who couldn't go into military service was also employed making three full-time hired men. Occasionally, an older man in the community would also work part-time. Ruth Charlotte went off to college but Robert, still in school, was able to help evenings, weekends and during summer vacation.

By 1944, German prisoners, who were housed about 20 miles away, became available and helped harvest the potatoes and red kidney beans. Harry or Metta had to pick them up each morning and return them in the evening. The first year an armed guard came with them but the second year they came without a guard. They were happy to be American prisoners and not fighting in the war.

Farm equipment manufacturers converted to the production of war armaments at the beginning of the war, so by the end of the war there was a huge pent up demand for farm machinery. Harry had put his name on an equipment waiting list for a hay baler, a small grain combine and another tractor because he could see that mechanization was becoming essential to farming.

The arrival of this equipment brought a drastic change to the farm's production of crops. There was no more loose hay to handle because it was now baled in the hay field. There was no more use of the grain binder because the oats and wheat were harvested in the fields. Another tractor meant that the horses weren't used as much and more work was done faster. The few years following the war brought more changes to the Ward farm than had been made in the previous 100 years.

Ruth Charlotte graduated from college, started teaching, got married and moved away. Robert was now the only one of their generation left on the farm. He enjoyed farming so it seemed quite possible that the farm might continue to stay in the family for another generation.

CHAPTER 11
Ward-Bitz Family 1948 to 1985

Robert, who we will refer to now on as Bob, didn't want to go to college. He just wanted to be a farmer. His family all encouraged him to go to college, but he wanted to begin an immediate career as a farmer. School had always been easy for him and he had probably never been challenged. His parents convinced him to apply to the College of Agriculture at Cornell, which was only 60 miles away. He was accepted and soon learned that they not only offered a bachelor's degree, but also offered a two-year agricultural program and agreed to give that a try.

His mother packed his things and his parents took him to Cornell in September 1948. College opened up a whole new world for Bob but he seemed unable to break his close ties to the farm. Almost every weekend he caught a ride or hitch-hiked back home to help his dad on the farm. He even skipped school the three days before Thanksgiving to help prepare the turkeys for Thanksgiving sale.

Bob may have had a second reason for wanting to come home weekends. The year before he had met a girl from another farm in the community and visited her every weekend that he was home. She was going to another college nearby where she was training to become a teacher, and also came home every weekend.

After Bob's first year of college he decided that college wasn't as bad as he had thought, so he decided to continue and graduate. He was learning a lot from his classes but also was enjoying his life at Cornell.

When he was at home helping at Thanksgiving 1949, his father received a totally unexpected official letter from the NY State

Department of Agriculture and Markets. It stated that the buildings and methods used by Plainville Turkey Farm to process turkeys were totally unsatisfactory and must be discontinued at once. Nothing had ever been said previously so both Harry and Metta were shocked. They didn't know what to do! The Thanksgiving sales had been completed but the busy Christmas season was only four weeks away.

Metta and Harry consulted with their county agricultural agent who called the state and made arrangements for a representative to come to the farm to advise them what they needed to do. He was reasonable and they were able to make the necessary changes in time to prepare turkeys for Christmas sale. Apparently a state representative had visited the farm and made an inspection without their knowledge. The message was clear: if Plainville Turkey Farm was going to continue to grow and process turkeys for sale, greater changes needed to be made within a very few years.

Harry had to decide whether to discontinue growing turkeys or build a new turkey processing facility. It looked like Bob would be coming back to the farm so he decided to build a new building. Bob thought he would like to keep turkey breeders when he returned, so Harry made it a little larger to provide space for an incubator. Construction began in the summer of 1950. Because of a moratorium on the construction of commercial buildings caused by the Korean conflict, it had to be called a garage. To meet this requirement, two overhead garage doors were installed. It was a simple building and satisfied the state's requirements.

Two improvements in the building that had been needed for years were the addition of running hot water and a refrigerated walk-in cooler. Previously, cooling the dressed turkeys depended entirely on the outside air temperature. Apparently the mason who did the work thought water ran uphill, but otherwise the building was a big step forward.

That summer, Phil, the son of a local minister, worked on the farm during his vacation from bible school in Minneapolis. He, like most of the summer help, had his noon time dinner with the family. Somehow he always managed to keep the whole family laughing. Harry and Metta didn't think it was safe for Bob to hitch-hike home from college and wanted to get him a car. Phil related to them how much cheaper cars were in Minneapolis and that he would be glad to have Bob ride back with him to buy one. Bob, of course, liked the idea and asked his college friend, Bill Carr, to go with him to keep him company on the return trip.

In late August they started out at 7:00 a.m. in Phil's little car. They took turns driving all day and all night to arrive there the next day. During the night, Bob and Bill sat in the small back seat because Phil had another person riding with him back to school. There was no such thing as a seatbelt at that time. It rained hard all night with very poor visibility. It didn't bother Phil, who kept up the same speed. Bob and Bill's teeth were chattering and it wasn't because they were cold!

Bob was able to find a Ford demonstrator that he liked and Harry wired the money to him so he could pay for it. Bob and Bill, who had never been in the Midwest, had their eyes opened as they traveled through Minnesota, Iowa, Indiana, Virginia and Pennsylvania on their way home. They visited a turkey farm in Minnesota and a hatchery in Iowa. They marveled at all the chicken houses, hogs and beef cattle, in addition to miles and miles of beautiful farmland, they passed through.

Bob's most notable experience at Cornell was when he was rushed by Alpha Zeta an honorary, social, agricultural fraternity. One of the things that appealed to Bob was that it was a "dry" house. No alcohol was permitted to be consumed in the house but members could bring in as much as they wished in their stomachs, which a few of them did. He lived in the house for three semesters and developed lifelong friendships. Many of the house's members enjoyed successful agricultural careers.

When baby poults came to the farm, half were hens and half toms. The hens were just the right size for most of the customers but not as many customers wanted a tom that weighed over 20 pounds. Harry sold some of these large toms to restaurants but almost always had a few hundred left in January, in what had been a pasture but now was a field covered with snow. These toms, out in the cold weather, ate a lot of feed and didn't gain much weight. Each day they remained alive cost Harry money. There were limited places to sell them and all at a price below the cost of growing.

In January 1952, Harry had dressed 100 of these large toms and sold them to a distributor. The day he happened to deliver them was the day Bob had finished his exams and packed his belongings in the car to return to the farm. Bob met him at the distributor's place of business in Ithaca to help Harry unload the turkeys. Bob vowed to himself that when he returned to the farm he was going to do his best to never sell any turkeys for less than the cost of production.

Now that Bob was back on the farm, consideration was given to purchasing another farm to increase production and become more efficient. It also looked like Bob might be getting married some day and would need a house. He was still dating the same girl he had dated when he was in high school. There was a farm on the market just two miles away with both good buildings and fine soil. There was also another one bordering the home farm that could be purchased. The big problem with this farm was the poor conditions of its barns and large house. One barn had already fallen down and two more could at anytime. Because of the proximity to the existing family farm, the farm with the buildings in poor shape was purchased.

The entire farm was a mess but the soil was excellent. Two men were hired for almost a year to repair the better barns. Bob and the farm workers tore down the other barns and part of the house and had several large bonfires. One of the barns had been a tobacco warehouse and was constructed to hold heavy loads. It was reinforced and turned into a large grain storage building. The building was altered so a special truck, of Bob's design, could be used to feed the turkeys in bulk. It eliminated the need to carry hundreds of 100 pound bags of feed to the turkeys. Bob was constantly trying to improve the efficiency and the profitability of the farm.

One of the barns was remodeled to house turkey breeders. After Bob had examined the pros and cons of keeping turkey breeders, he decided that it wouldn't be in the farm's best interest to do so. The lack of market potential and the extra costs associated with New York's cold snowy winters made it undesirable. He remarked several times after making this decision, that often the best decisions he made were to *not* do something or to quit early when he could see things wasn't working out.

In July, he presented the girl he had been dating for over four years with an engagement ring. They decided to marry the following year. Now it was time to think about where they might live. One possibility was in the house on the farm Harry had just purchased. The other choice was to fix up the 110 year old family home located in the center of the farm's major activities. They decided it would be best to fix up the family home that was less than 100 feet from the house where Harry and Metta lived.

Building repair work, added to the farm work, kept everyone well occupied. The year sped by swiftly and the following July 4th Bob and Janice were married. The wedding took place in the Baldwinsville Presbyterian Church with a reception of ice cream and cake afterwards at Janice's family's farm near Baldwinsville. For a short time though, it looked like the bride might be going on the honeymoon without the groom.

Bob always enjoyed playing practical jokes on others so some of his friends decided it was time they played one on him. Bob had parked his car in Syracuse to keep it away from these friends and had asked his best man to take he and his bride in his car to the airport in North Syracuse. The bride and groom got in the best man's car. He put the car in reverse to back it away from a tree in front of it and nothing happened. The car had been jacked up and the wheels just spun! After jacking up the car and removing the blocks under it the car still couldn't be moved because it was chained to a tree! Bob wasn't bothered at all but Janice was visibly upset. She ran into her family's home, took one of the keys to the family car and backed it out of their garage. Being upset, she backed out of the garage as fast as a man flies out of the cannon at a circus! All of the wedding guests were standing around and luckily she didn't hit anyone. Not wanting to have anyone catch her, she went flying down the road with Bob running after her.

Janice soon calmed down, but Bob and all the wedding guests never forgot it. The escape was followed by a one-week trip to New England where some of the bride's and the groom's ancestors had settled after leaving England in the early 1600s. Upon their return, Bob was busy on the farm and Janice was getting their new home settled before heading back to her job as a schoolteacher.

The facilities for processing the turkeys had been replaced and improved three years earlier, but there had been no significant changes in the turkey growing methods or equipment since Harry had started growing turkeys in 1924. Bob knew that it was important that changes be made to improve efficiency and to lower costs. Bob's parents were adverse to borrowing money so it was necessary that expenses for any improvements be minimal. Bob had read of a Cornell-designed building constructed with poles set in the ground that cost much less than the traditional concrete base and wood stud construction. He did some more research and decided that this type of building might serve to keep the cost manageable.

In the winter of 1954, Bob and the two hired men started work on an 8,000-square-foot pole frame brooder house. All of the little brooding buildings that they had been using for the past 30 years would have easily fit in one end of the new brooder house. They worked on the building all winter and spring in their spare time, to complete it by June, the time to brood turkeys. Although constructed with minimal cost it, was a fine building. It was even equipped with an automatic feeder and automatic waterers. Certainly even better turkeys would be produced!

Several thousand day-old turkey poults were soon running in the building, happily eating, drinking and peeping away. The building was wonderful! But, after a week the little poults started to die for no apparent reason. Experts were called in and they couldn't discover why the poults were dying. Over 1,000 died during their first two weeks and then the dying stopped and the rest grew normally. What caused the problem? It was a real disappointment to build this new state of the art building and have this happen.

After the turkeys were moved from the building to pasture another 2,000 day-old poults were started in the new building. The same thing happened. Over 500 died during the first two weeks and then the rest grew as normal. This time, the answer to why so many poults died was found. The water for the poults came from a deep well that had always been slightly salty. Somehow, just at the time the poults were placed in the new building, the well water's salinity had increased sufficiently to make the water toxic for the little turkeys. Some of them overcame the toxicity but others could not. The well was abandoned and future poults were fine.

On April 25, 1956 the first of a new generation came to the family farm. Bob and Janice were the proud parents of Cynthia Irene! Janice had resigned from her teaching position and was now a full-time mother and farm wife. The wisdom of choosing the old family homestead next door to Harry and Metta for the young couples's home soon became apparent. From the beginning, there was close interaction between the children and their grandparents. All the children had a second home with their grandma and grandpa.

Also in 1956, Bob started construction of a second pole barn. Once cold weather and snow arrived in late November it was hard on the turkeys that were still outside on pasture. They were uncomfortable and as a result didn't grow well. The turkeys, now grown, had broader breasts and couldn't fly up on the roosts like they had years earlier, so they sat all night on the cold frozen ground. Bob would have liked more pole barns to get all of the turkeys inside earlier, but this barn at least enabled him to house the birds that were outside after Christmas.

Bob decided to sell to more restaurants, hotels, hospitals and colleges to move the extra large toms during the year rather than sell them below cost at the end of the year. A walk-in freezer was constructed to hold these turkeys when they were dressed. They were then sold to the regular customers during the year. The farm's turkey production was increased by five to ten percent each year and another pole barn was constructed about every year.

An aerial view of Plainville taken in about 1948. The Plainville Christian Church with the Plainville Rural Cemetery are in the foreground. Four generations of the Ward family are buried in this cemetery. The Plainville School with its playground is in the lower left and the Plainville general store is four doors beyond. The village blacksmith is located diagonally across the street from the store.

A *1951 aerial view of the Bitz/Ward farm. The gambrel roof barn built in 1907, which is described being constructed in Chapter 7, is in the lower left with the circa 1939 silo next to it. The long gable roof barn with the window in the center is the tobacco shed, which later had 25 years' use for turkey processing. The nearest house, which was constructed in 1840 by William Ward, was remodeled in 1953 to serve as the home for Robert and Janice Bitz. The house just behind it was constructed in 1884 by William E. Ward for he and his bride Lilly Gates. Robert and Janice razed that house in 1989 when it was determined that none of their children would be living in it.*

Photo of Ruth Bitz Dettbarn, Harry Bitz, Metta Bitz and Robert Bitz taken in 1963 at a celebration honoring Harry and Metta's 40th wedding anniversary.

A 1954 photo of Harry Bitz holding a baby turkey in the farm's new turkey brooding building.

A 1954 photo of the farm with the new turkey brooding building under construction in the middle-left background.

Circa 1950 photograph of Harry Bitz leading two of his work horses from the barn to the pasture. On the left is the tobacco shed which was later used for turkey processing.

It was obvious to Bob that the market for turkeys was going to change. Almost everyone wanted to buy their turkey in a more convenient form. Bob had never boned a fresh turkey but he knew that it could be done and was determined to learn.

This knowledge came to good use when he called upon a large whole turkey user who told him he wanted to buy boneless turkey breasts rather than whole turkeys. A turkey was boned, tied similarly to a boneless beef roast and delivered to the potential customer. He liked it, and over the years bought thousands of them. A large restaurant wanted a cooked dark and white meat turkey roll. Bob went back to the farm, made one and took it to the restaurant. The restaurant liked it and continued to buy them. Soon, these two boneless products were sold to many other customers. Responding to customers' needs and continuing to make a profit were important business goals.

On June 15, 1959 a little brother for Cynthia by the name of Mark Ward arrived. He, like his sister, was healthy. The farm's finances were healthy too.

In 1960, annual production had increased to 15,000 and the turkeys continued to sell well enough that Bob moved into year-round sales. Bob was a bit shocked when he received word that the City of Syracuse Department of Health ruled that all facilities, where meat or poultry was processed, had to pass inspection if they were to sell their products in the city. Since most of the farm's products were sold in Syracuse, compliance with the rules was critical. An inspector visited the farm and filled out a sheet with some things needed to changed. Bob got those done. When the inspector visited again, the farm was in compliance and could continue to sell in Syracuse.

It is said that for every problem there is a solution. By selling boneless and roast turkey breasts, the problem of surplus large tom turkeys had been solved, but another was created. It took many years to figure out what to do with the surplus of drumsticks, thighs, necks, giblets and of course the remaining turkey carcasses that no one wanted. Over the years, the farm produced a multitude of products to try to utilize these parts. All of them were liked by a few people but not enough to make them marketable. Several of the products made, including ground turkey, turkey bologna and turkey hot dogs, were years ahead of their time. Almost everyone wanted the turkey's breast. Fortunately, the farm received more for the white meat than for the whole turkey.

One of the more interesting products that was packaged and sold was turkey fries. The testicles of a large tom turkey are about the size of a pecan in its shell. Some people enjoy them battered and deep fried or sautéed. Not very many were sold, but it was a lot of fun serving them to unsuspecting friends. Most liked the delectable morsels that were ahead-of-their time, until they asked what they were and heard the answer.

Another product was organic turkey fertilizer. One winter Bob visited some lawn and garden stores and gave each one a few bags to try. It was a good fertilizer but hadn't been through a composting cycle so was dusty, smelled bad when it got wet and did not sell well.

As the business grew, so too did its workforce of high-quality employees. A small retail store was also opened in the plant, managed by an employee who also handled calls to the wholesale customers. Metta and Bob had always done all the bookkeeping, but now an office was set up in the processing plant. Janice had been doing much of this but with two little children it became too much.

By now the traditional small farm diversification was coming to a close. The potatoes, cabbage and red kidney beans were gone and the cows were about to go. These products would have left the farm when Bob returned from college, but he knew Harry enjoyed them. Bob believed it wouldn't be wise to change things too rapidly until he had proven the wisdom of his decisions.

One of his decisions that worked out extremely well, and added substantially to the farm's bottom line, was the manufacture of turkey feed. At first the farm purchased a concentrate and mixed its own home grown grain with it. Later, all ingredients were bought and manufactured on the farm. This enabled the farm to formulate its own mixes, control the quality of the ingredients and produce a better turkey at a lower cost.

The turkey industry was suffering across the entire country in the 1960s. Almost everyone was losing money and both large and small turkey farms were going out of business. Many in the industry wanted to have the U.S. government establish a marketing order to limit turkey production. Bob testified against it and fortunately one was not enacted. If it had passed, consumers would have paid more for their turkey in order to keep inefficient producers in business. It also would have put limits on Plainville farm's ability to expand.

As the business grew, the farm had to periodically purchase land and build additions to the processing plant every few years to continue an efficient operation. The goal was to grow as much of their feed as possible. But, as the business grew, more and more feed was purchased from other farmers each year.

On June 22, 1964, Janice and Bob had their third and last child, Bruce Wayne. He was a real bundle of a boy weighing in at ten and three-quarters pounds. Janice said that she had had enough children. She wasn't going to take any chances on the possibility of having a larger one.

When Bruce was a year old, she put her teaching skills back in use and started giving tours to schoolchildren. She gave each of the children an apple, a turkey feather and a Plainville Turkey Farm pencil. The tours were free but it didn't do any harm to make sure each child's parents knew about the farm. Many of the children had never been on a farm so it was a special learning experience for them. A neighbor came to take care of Bruce and since the tours were very popular, Janice was busy every day from September until early November.

By the middle 1960s Harry had gradually turned over the farm decision-making to Bob. Sometimes he delivered small orders of turkeys or turkey rolls that would fit in the station wagon to customers 50 to 150 miles away. He kept a team of horses and used them to do some mowing around the buildings. He also had a large vegetable garden and used one of the horses to cultivate. Mark enjoyed spending time with him helping with the horses. Cynthia and her grandmother spent a great deal of time with each other and became very close.

Although Ruth Charlotte lived near Boston, her family, consisting of husband Al and three children, Albert, Robert and Susan, came to visit their parents and the farm several times a year. Whenever they did, Bob's and her children had good times together. There was always a big dinner for the entire family at home or in a restaurant. Although Ruth lived 300 miles away, family and farm stayed close to her heart. Ironically, she and Al had moved back to the area where William Ward had settled when he came from England with his family 300 years earlier.

About 1970, Bob was having a health issue and decided it was time he shared some of the responsibilities of operating the farm, which now grew 45,000 turkeys and had 20 employees. He hired a young man who grew up on a small turkey farm to take over the daily management of the field crops and the live turkeys. He was very conscientious and helped out a great deal.

It was a wise move as Bob had not only been busy on the farm, but was also involved with a great variety of volunteer activities on both a local and state level. Bob and Janice were able to spend a week vacationing in a warm spot each winter and to take the whole family on a one week vacation in the summer. Soon Bob's excellent health returned.

Another challenge arrived in 1970 when New York State required individual bird inspection. An inspector was assigned to the farm who examined each bird processed and monitored the cleanliness of the plant. In retrospect, it didn't prove to be too difficult and actually benefited the business. It required a change to a moving line rather than work on stainless steel tables. It increased production and efficiency. Five years later the farm changed to USDA inspection and was able to sell its turkey products outside of the state.

STATE OF NEW YORK
DEPARTMENT OF AGRICULTURE AND MARKETS
C. CHESTER DU MOND, COMMISSIONER
ALBANY 1

BUREAU OF FOOD CONTROL
C. R. PLUMB, DIRECTOR
CHARLES H. FOGG, ASST. DIRECTOR

November 23, 1949

Mr. Harry C. Bitz
Plainville Road
Plainville, New York

Dear Sir:

We are in receipt of a report of inspection and investigation of your activities in slaughtering and dressing turkeys both for retail and wholesale purposes.

The building equipment and methods used in this operation are very unsatisfactory to say the least. As a bona fide farmer raising your own domestic turkeys on your own farm you are not subject to the licensing provisions of Article 5 A. However, you are required under Article 5 A and Article 17 to maintain your place of operation in a sanitary condition and perform such operation in a sanitary manner.

We are taking this opportunity to inform you that the slaughtering and dressing of turkeys for resale must be discontinued at once, and we are notifying our representative to make a reinspection and if you are still operating under these unsatisfactory conditions you will be referred to our Legal Bureau for penalty action.

Very truly yours,

C R Plumb

CWN/ms   Director   n.

A 1949 letter received from the New York State Department of Agriculture and Markets stating that the farm's turkey dressing facilities were inadequate. This was a wakeup call to build a new dressing facility or stop processing turkeys. The family temporarily made improvements to the old facility. When Robert decided he wanted to come back to the farm after college they built a new processing plant in 1950.

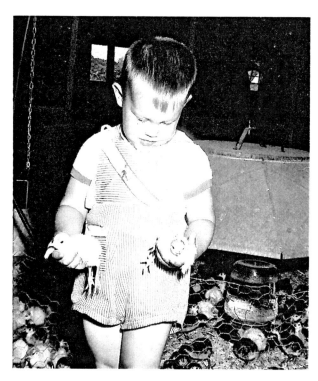

A 1961 photograph of Mark Ward Bitz with a day-old turkey poult in each hand.

A 1963 photograph of Harry Bitz with a birthday cake for his grandson, Mark Ward Bitz. Mark's father, Robert, is also enjoying the occasion.

A 1963 photograph of the family celebrating Harry and Metta's 40th wedding anniversary. From left to right. Albert Dettbarn, Susan Dettbarn, Al Dettbarn, Robert Dettbarn, Ruth Dettbarn, Harry Bitz, Metta Ward Bitz, Janice Bitz, Cynthia Bitz, Robert Bitz, Mark Bitz.

A circa 1976 photograph of the Robert and Janice Bitz family. Left to right are Mark, Janice, Robert, Bruce and Cynthia.

By 1975, three-quarters of the 75,000 turkeys grown were large toms. It was now possible to purchase sex-separated poults. The boneless products produced were selling well and it was more efficient to bone the larger toms rather than the smaller hens. Rather than grow all the turkeys on one farm, a nearby neighbor farmer was hired to start 8,000 turkeys every 10 weeks. It worked well; Bob decided to buy a farm two miles away to grow additional turkeys.

When Mark was about to turn 16, Bob and Janice inquired what he might like for his birthday. He had an unusual request. He said he would like a tree! Bob replied that he would be happy to oblige him. Mark had been taking wood shop as a course in high school and Bob had seen that he was talented. One Saturday Mark, Bruce and Bob headed to the family wood lot with tractor, wagon, chainsaw and other necessary equipment. They notched the tree on the side of the direction it should fall and then went to work cutting a beautiful wild cherry tree. When the tree was almost completely cut the saw blade caught so they drove in a wedge and finished sawing the tree. Although it was totally cut the tree would not fall. They drove another wedge into the cut and the tree still stood perfectly straight. What should they do? While they were talking, Bruce pushed on the tree and to everyone's amazement it fell to the ground. Bruce was kidded about his immense strength! Mark now had plenty of wood to make things, but while there, a second tree was cut for him, which fell without Bruce having to push it over. He had enough lumber to last him a lifetime!

Bruce enjoyed being in the Boy Scouts. He earned many merit badges and enjoyed camping and the outdoor activities associated with scouting. He completed a required project successfully to become an Eagle Scout. It was a wonderful experience for him.

It had always been Bob's goal to produce a product which added as much value as possible. In 1973, he contacted a friend who owned a restaurant to see if he would be interested in becoming his partner in building a new restaurant that specialized in Plainville turkey. They joined together and by late summer opened Plainville Farms Restaurant and Store. There were two challenging years, especially since it was

absentee ownership. Eventually the restaurant became profitable
and prospered for over 30 years. Because of its success, two fast food
turkey restaurants were opened in local shopping malls. But profits
were marginal, so the two were closed. Bob opened another sit-down
restaurant, but after a few years also discontinued it. Knowing when to
quit is far better than persisting and failing.

Janice and Bob's children seemed to grow up rapidly. In 1974 they
packed Cynthia's things in the car and took her to college at Putney,
Vermont. It was only a few miles from where her ancestor William
Ward, who had settled the farm at Plainville, was born. The family nest
was already beginning to empty. Since her room was on the second floor,
Bob, who had heard of fires where the people inside were trapped, went
to the local hardware store, bought her a rope and instructed her on
how to use it in case of an emergency. Fortunately it came home from
college with her totally unused!

Three years later it was time for Mark to head off to college. Bob wanted
him to apply to Cornell where he had gone, but Mark wanted to save
Cornell for graduate school. Bob took satisfaction in that he chose the
College of Agriculture at Purdue University in Indiana. He was going to
study agriculture and planned to come back to the farm!

From the time he was just a toddler, Mark was independent like so many
in the family. He could see things that most adults overlooked and always
wanted to do everything. Bob called him "Doey" sometimes because when
something needed to be done he would blurt out, "I do, I do!"

Mark majored in agricultural economics and economic development
and earned his Bachelor of Science degree in only three years. He
traveled extensively during two summer vacations. At Purdue he saw an
opportunity to live in another country for a year, and was interested in
Poland and Israel. The exchange decided he would go to Poland, behind
the 'Iron Curtain'. While there he worked on a collective farm and
taught scientists English. It was the year the Poles started standing up
to the Soviet Union to throw off the yoke of communism. It was a great
learning experience and taught Mark that conventional wisdom is often

wrong and the seemingly impossible can be possible with excellent
leadership, teamwork and determination. It made him appreciate life in
the United States much more.

Cynthia found the right man, got married and moved away from home.
Although she lived 300 miles away she, like her Aunt Ruth and her
great aunts of a generation earlier, kept close ties with her family and
the farm, often coming back home to visit. She and her husband, Sean,
presented Robert and Janice with two precious granddaughters, Rebecca
and Elizabeth.

In 1982, Bob and Janice packed the car with Bruce's things and took
him to college. He had decided to go to his father's alma mater, the
College of Agriculture at Cornell University. Would it be possible that
both of the boys might be coming back to the farm?

Bob and Janice were now all alone in the family homestead. The house
seemed so empty! Harry had passed on but Metta still lived in the house
next door so Bob stopped daily to see her.

It is traditional, on a small farm, for the occupants to be able to handle
almost all of the challenges that are bound to present themselves.
Plainville Turkey Farm was no exception. As their employee numbers
increased they began to employ people with specialized skills. Gradually
they were able to employ a mechanic, a plumber, an electrician and an
accountant. These people were of great help to the enterprise.

Treating employees as you would like to be treated is critical for the
success of any business. Plainville Turkey Farm provided generous
amounts of time off, especially for a farm, as well as numerous fringe
benefits. Although it was beginning to be a large farm operation,
it was always considered to be a family farm where employees were
treated like family. As Mark and Bruce matured, they were given more
responsibilities and taught the values that their family had possessed for
several generations.

As a young boy, Bob's dad had him take care of several pigs which Bob
enjoyed. He decided that it would be a good project for both Mark and

Bruce. Cynthia had gained both knowledge and responsibility learning to cook and sew through 4H projects. Mark bought ten pigs when he was 11 years old and was totally responsible for caring for them. He had to weigh the feed he used and care for them morning and night until they were about six months old and ready for market. It was a real challenge and an experience for both he and his father to load ten 200 pound pigs on the back of one of their trucks and haul them 14 miles where they were sold to a processing plant. The pigs did not cooperate! Six years later, after Bruce had grown his pigs, Bob learned that it was smarter to sell them to a livestock dealer and let him load the pigs!

In 1981, Harry's life came to an end. He had started his career with nothing other than the clothes on his back and plenty of ambition. He had been a good honest community member, and worked hard to obtain what he had. He set a fine example for Ruth Charlotte and Bob to follow.

In 1985, the farm celebrated its 150th anniversary. Larger customers, friends, neighbors and employees were invited to help celebrate the occasion. At that time the farm had 60 employees, grew 225,000 turkeys and had over 700 acres of corn. Plainville Turkey Farm was growing almost all of the turkeys produced in New York. When Bob had come home from college 33 years earlier, the farm was one of over 100 turkey farms in New York that were growing from one to five thousand turkeys a year.

CHAPTER 12
Ward-Bitz Family After 1985

The farm was becoming a large business. Throughout Bob's life he had benefited from the wisdom of others. He wasn't hesitant to ask questions and exhibit his ignorance. Since there was no Board of Directors to provide advice, he decided to form a farm advisory board. He asked a banker, a businessman and a college professor, with all of whom he was slightly acquainted. Each agreed to serve and the four of them met quarterly. It was like having an extended family to go to when help was needed to make business decisions.

While Mark was in Poland he became well-acquainted with a Polish girl who had lived six months with Janice and Bob in a 4-H exchange program. She was a farm girl who had studied poultry husbandry while in college and there seemed to be perfect chemistry between them. They fell in love and married. She was a lovely girl who had become close to Bob and Janice while here during the exchange program.

Bob, Janice and Bruce had made arrangements to meet Mark and Lou at the customs office at the airport in Geneva, Switzerland. Unknown to Bob, the customs office was refusing to give Lou entrance to Switzerland because she didn't have a return ticket to Poland. Mark and Lou had arrived but there was no Bob and Janice to meet them. Bob and Janice had arrived and there was no Mark and Lou to meet them. There was a bank of telephones on each side of a glass divider separating the customs side from freedom. Mark went to the phones to call the farm back in Plainville at exactly the same time that Bob went to the bank of phones on the other side of the divider to call the farm. Bob rapped loudly on the glass divider. Mark saw him, smiled widely and motioned to Bob to go to the customs office. The customs officer saw that Bob was obviously irritated with him and once Bob explained the situation they allowed Lou to come into Switzerland. It was a miracle!

Poland was still behind the iron curtain so there was a great deal of corruption. Although Lou had all the necessary papers, Mark had to bribe the officials at the airport to allow her to get on the plane in Poland.

When Mark and Lou arrived back home in 1981 they lived with Metta a few months while Mark waited for classes to start for his advanced college degrees.

Mark received a fellowship for a graduate degree, during the years 1982-85, at the College of Agriculture at Cornell and he and Lou lived in the married students' housing complex. Since it was only 60 miles from the farm, they occasionally returned home for a few days. Bob was elated that Mark was going to his old alma mater. In fact, Bruce was also there at the same time working toward his bachelor degree.

Gradually the turkeys were consuming more and more feed making the farm's storage facilities inadequate. At times sufficient corn was not available from local farmers. They would have railroad cars full of corn shipped in from the Midwest, but didn't have a convenient place to unload the cars.

There was a large grain storage facility scheduled to be sold at a bankruptcy sale. It was only eight miles from the farm and was located on the main railroad line. Mark and Lou were back home on a break from classes at the time. He and Bob talked it over and agreed to have Mark go to the auction and purchase the facility if the price was right. Mark was able to buy it for the farm at a reasonable price. It provided both a large grain storage and a good railroad siding.

In the fall of 1987 Metta passed away at 91-years-of-age. She had remained quite healthy until the last few months of her life. She had seen many changes to the farm and was very proud of the family's accomplishments. The house was filled with many memories and artifacts depicting multiple aspects of the family's history. It was difficult for Bob when he went into the house. It reminded him of family members that he had loved and were now deceased, and it was filled with childhood memories.

Disposing of everything was also difficult. Ruth Charlotte and her family took whatever they could use and Bob and his children took a number of other things. Bruce had graduated from college and had decided to go into teaching so was able to use quite a few items for his apartment. Mark and Lou were also able to take some of the things. The dining room table that Will and Lilly had purchased when first married, on which Will had his appendix removed, went to Ruth's daughter, Susan, who lives in Massachusetts. The entire family, in later years, enjoyed several family meals around the old table.

On June 26, 1987 another member of the next generation arrived to continue the family line. Karl Ward Bitz came into the world. Karl joined the family while Metta was still living so she had the joy of holding her first great-grandson. Six years later, on April 15, 1993, Karl was joined by a brother named Asher Ward Bitz. Now Bob and Janice were blessed with four grandchildren, two girls and two boys.

A decision was made to hire someone to supervise the corn and soybean production. A man from Kentucky was employed and moved into Metta's old house with his family. After a year he decided to purchase his own house leaving Metta's house empty again. Mark, wisely, didn't want to live so close to the center of all the farm's activities. There were trucks and cars coming and going all the time. It was now much different than when Bob had moved there 35 years earlier. The family considered moving the house to a quieter spot on the farm but the cost of moving it and bringing the house up to current standards was greater than building a new home. It was too close for Bob and Janice to have non-family neighbors so the decision was made to tear it down. The old family homestead said goodbye to its younger sister that had stood next to it for the past one hundred years.

That same year the farm started publishing a monthly newsletter for all of its team members. With about 100 employees working in the farm's various activities, it was important to keep them informed about each other and what was happening all over the farm. Bob regularly wrote an article entitled, 'A Page in History' that shared with them what life was like on the farm for previous generations. There was also a section devoted to team member achievements and recognitions.

For many years, once the turkeys reached eight weeks of age they were moved to fenced pastures to be finished for marketing. This was fine when the weather was good but when it turned cold in the fall and snow came, it was very hard on the turkeys. Moving to year-round production made growing them inside a necessity. Gradually, more growing buildings were constructed where the turkeys could run freely in large areas inside a building. The farm's intent was to indefinitely continue to have turkeys on pasture during the summer and early fall. Trees were even planted on portions of the fields to provide the turkeys with natural shade during hot weather. One fall wild birds brought avian influenza to turkeys in the fields. Fortunately it didn't spread to the turkeys in the buildings. When avian influenza hit the flocks on pasture, the decision was made that the turkeys could no longer be sent to the fields where contact with wild birds could occur.

The family had always had a serious concern for its livestock and had the same feeling for its turkeys. The Wards and Bitzs knew that animals were no different than people in that the better you treated them, the better they did for you. More space was provided for the turkeys than was required or standard by the industry, but was the norm at the Plainville Turkey Farm. For many years workers had caught the turkeys and put them into crates before processing. Later many of the turkeys were herded, like cattle, into the processing plant. Mark devised large trailers with a platform that could be moved up or down so that the turkeys could walk directly onto the trailer and have a quick comfortable ride to the processing plant where the trailer was raised up to dock height for easy unloading.

As satellite farms were developed a few miles away, this method of moving turkeys to the processing plant was ideal. The normal practices in the turkey industry were to load the turkeys into small cages, stacked six tiers high and haul them many miles to the processing plant. Often they are in these cages for over 12 hours and it puts a great deal of stress on the birds.

Because of the farm's excellent care and concern for the turkeys, Plainville Turkey Farm was recognized by the federal government and the American Humane Association for its animal friendly practices. It was a sad Sunday morning, shortly afterwards, when Bob received a call from the restaurant manager telling him that the restaurant had been vandalized during the night by animal rights activists. They had spray painted activist slogans on all sides of the building, put glue in the door locks and broken windows. As a local turkey producer easy to reach, they chose Plainville's facilities to protest the inhumane practices of others. It was especially sad because the Plainville operation was far friendlier to our turkeys than the rest of the industry.

An increasing number of customers were coming to the little sales area in one corner of the processing plant. It was located close to Plainville Road and when customers drove in and out the sight distance was limited. As a result there had been a couple of minor accidents and some close calls. What was needed was a new sales facility. The decision was made to build one on the farm which provided good visibility to the highway and allowed for expanding of the sales facility. Thousands of schoolchildren were visiting the farm each year, but the tours were outside and the weather was not always desirable. A visitor center was built that connected to the new sales store.

A great deal of thought was put into the buildings and the results were rewarding. An ice cream machine was installed for the sale of fifty cent cones. There was also a sampler plate to give visitors a taste of several of the turkey products. In the visitor's center, in addition to a variety of farm animals, there was an animated farmer sitting on an old tractor that carried on a conversation with an animated turkey named Professor Plainville. The visitor center provided educational entertainment for adults as well as children. On the wall in one end of the building was a picture of William Ward, who originally settled on the farm.

A circa 1996 photograph of Mark, Asher, Karl, Robert and Lou Bitz enjoying a watermelon in the front yard of the 1840 Ward home.

A circa 1998 photograph of the farm's retail store, visitor center and the Pioneer Experience.

A view of one area of the Pioneer Experience building showing some of the farm equipment similar to that used by the Ward families in previous generations.

A view of the log cabin in the Pioneer experience building similar to the original home on the farm when it was purchased by William Ward in 1835. In the foreground is the top of a cast iron stove similar to what William Ward used to heat his new home constructed in 1840.

Robert and Janice Bitz riding in a surrey next to the 1840 Ward home where they lived. This is how the old home looked, after remodeling several times, when this photo was taken on 1998.

Karl Ward Bitz and Robert Ward Bitz at Karl's graduation from Cornell University in 2009.

Robert, Karl and Asher Bitz on their way out to a farm field so Bob can pose with a horse and plow in the development of a new farm logo.

A circa 2000 photograph of most of the farm's team members taken in front of the retail store and visitor center. At the time the turkey business was sold in 2007 the farm employed over 200 people.

In the visitor center were baby turkeys, full grown turkeys, pigs, goats, sheep, rabbits, a pony and a cow. Schoolchildren from a wide area enjoyed seeing farm animals that many had never before seen. A neighbor, who was a retired farmer, took care of the animals morning and night.

One time when Bob's small granddaughters were visiting, he put one at a time on the back of the pony and led the pony in a field near the visitor center. All of a sudden the pony must have thought it was in a rodeo because Elizabeth went flying over the pony's head. Bob was frightened for fear Elizabeth might have been seriously hurt, but was greatly relieved when Elizabeth arose with a big grin on her face saying that she was fine.

Bob didn't want to have the possibility of something like that happening again, so he sold the pony. He then found a farm where they sold miniature horses. He bought a colt and brought it to the farm in the back of his station wagon. Jeff, the small grandson of the gentleman caring for the animals, trained the little horse, as it grew, to lead and then to drive. Bob bought a small sulky and Jeff drove the little horse, advertising Plainville Turkey Farm in parades.

Bob had more spare time now as Mark was gradually assuming more responsibility. Bob had never been as much of a horse lover as his father but decided to purchase a horse for both riding and driving. He also decided to buy an old riding horse that would be safe for his grandchildren to ride and keep the other horse company. The younger horse was quite high strung but worked well attached to the buggy for driving. One day Bob put the saddle on the younger horse and went for a ride. The horse did a little bucking and the next thing Bob remembered was getting up off the ground with no horse around. After that experience he decided to give up riding horses!

When Bob's granddaughters didn't care about riding the old horse any longer he purchased a matched team of Haflingers. They were both mares and although Bob didn't realize it, they were both carrying foals. A few months later they both foaled in the middle of the night and amazingly, both at the same time. A young man who was helping Bob had checked on the mares an hour earlier in time to see them give birth. Both of the foals were mares and looked almost exactly alike.

Bob had a great deal of enjoyment the next two years training the foals. When he harnessed the mares to drive, he tied each colt to its mother to give the colts exercise and to start teaching them to drive. In a little over a year the horses were hitched one at a time, by the side the mother, to learn to be driven. Later, the colts were hitched together as a team and had no problem driving them. Bob had reverted back to training horses similar to how his grandfathers had done generations earlier.

The horses soon had company in the building where they were housed. Sixteen pens were constructed to compare various turkey feed ingredients against each other. Four different rations or ingredients were compared with four replications of each one. Through these feed trials valuable information was acquired that led to the feeding of a vegetarian diet to the turkeys and helped keep them superior to those of the competition. Three completely different tests were made each year for over fifteen years. Often appreciable differences in the ingredients used wasn't seen but occasionally it paid off very well.

The processing plant was busy every week of the year but the weeks before Thanksgiving were especially busy. To get all the necessary turkeys dressed extra people were employed. In earlier years the extra employees came from within a few miles of the farm. By the year 2000 there were not a sufficient number of area residents who were interested in working part-time, so some Hispanics were hired that had harvested fruits and vegetables for another farmer earlier in the year.

Everyone was busy prior to Thanksgiving when, to our surprise, immigration officers arrived to see if all of our employees were legal. We had checked all of their papers to be sure they were legal before employing them, but were shocked to learn about a dozen provided us with falsified documents. Mark requested that immigration allow them to work a few days longer but they refused. Understaffed, the work got done by everyone working longer hours. The lesson learned: always verify papers with immigration authorities before employing a new person.

Mark was a strong leader for the farm bringing several fine people to make up the farm's leadership team. They were knowledgeable, honest and hard working. He seemed to have the talent to select the right people for each area of responsibility. In 1990 the farm constructed a new feed mill at its Jordan property. Now railroad carloads of ingredients could be unloaded, stored and transferred directly into the various turkey feeds as needed. A tractor trailer with a self unloading body, that could haul 25 tons of feed to the farm at a time, was purchased. The new mill was a major cost considering the initial feed tonnage but became more valuable each year after construction. By this time production was up over a half million turkeys per year.

One year during the middle of the night Mark received a call that there was a big fire at one of the farm's buildings. By the time he arrived someone had called the local fire department and their trucks soon arrived. Several other fire departments were called and many gallons of water were pumped to extinguish the fire. Both ends of the building were saved but 124 feet in the middle were destroyed. The worst part was that 9,000 young turkeys were lost due to smoke inhalation. Prior to the fire starting, 16,000 just hatched poults had been placed in a special truck in North Carolina and were on their way to arrive the next morning in the part of the barn that had burned. With only a few hours to prepare, a barn had to be made ready for those poults. They couldn't be sent back to the hatchery!

All the farm crew and some neighbors went to work preparing another building from which the turkeys had just been removed. Stoves had to be set up, feeders and waters filled and litter put down on the floor. The local hardware store even opened early to supply us some parts to run propane gas to the stoves. The crew worked all night and shortly after the truck with the babies arrived they had the building ready for the poults!

At 6:00 in the morning Mark contacted the farm's insurance company who had a representative at the fire in two hours assessing the damage.

The fire was still smoldering and a fire truck was standing by. Even before the insurance agent was there, Mark had a general contractor on the site measuring the building and making preparations for a crew to be on the job the next day. More poults were coming for that building in five weeks so it had to be ready to use by then. It was completed in time. Bob was amazed and pleased at the way Mark and his team handled the entire disaster.

Bob had always enjoyed history and started collecting farm and home antiques in his semi-retirement. By 1997, he had quite an accumulation of antiques stored in the old gambrel roof barn which his grandfather had constructed 90 years earlier. Turkeys were now the only livestock on the farm; there were no more potatoes grown and grain was combined in the fields so the barn was no longer in use. The old barn was not a good place to display the antiques for people to enjoy so he decided to construct a large new building adjacent to the retail store. He named it the Pioneer Experience. Inside he constructed an authentic log cabin like his Ward ancestors had used several generations earlier and equipped it with artifacts of the time. He displayed his collection of farm antiques that his ancestors would have used in the 1700s and the 1800s.

Tours of the building were given to both scheduled groups and to individuals at specific times during the week. Bob found that very few people had any idea of the way people lived in earlier times. It was also interesting for him to learn of the lack of interest most people had of the way their ancestors lived. When the sales store was closed some years later and turned into offices, he closed the Pioneer Experience and sold most of his antiques at auction. Having the Pioneer Experience had been a joy for Bob to set up and share with many people.

In 1996, a disease came to the farm on some of the poults that was difficult to overcome but actually ended well. To get rid of the disease, one farm at a time was depopulated and thoroughly cleaned. Having turkeys scattered on several farms made it possible to continue almost normal production for customers during this period of time. After each farm was depopulated, each team member caring for the farm showered and put on clean clothes prior to entering any turkey buildings and showered again before leaving. All of the turkeys were provided with additional space and no more antibiotics were used. After this was done, the livability of our turkeys increased so it even exceeded that of the rest of the industry, which was still using antibiotics.

Mark was invited to speak about the program Plainville Turkey Farm was using at a National Turkey Federation, but the rest of the industry ignored the success that could result with the removal of antibiotics. About ten years later customers began to be concerned about the regular use of antibiotics by the livestock and poultry industry because of resistance of bacteria when antibiotics were used for humans. The Food and Drug Administration, 20 years after Plainville's success, is phasing out the therapeutic use of drugs in animal feed.

Another huge benefit came to Plainville by removing the use of antibiotics from their turkeys. The leading retail supermarkets now wanted to offer their customers Plainville's drug-free products as almost none other than Plainville had any available.

Almost every family has its traditions that are passed on from one generation to the next. In the Ward-Bitz family celebrating Christmas similarly each year was a family tradition. Everyone came back to the farm from wherever they lived. The children hung up their stockings on Christmas Eve and the next morning it was evident that Santa had visited during the night. The children were taught delayed gratification because they could not open their stockings until dad had completed his morning chores and come back to the house. After the stockings were opened everyone enjoyed a big breakfast together. The presents then to be exchanged were placed under the tree in the bay window of the house. The family then opened the presents, each person taking a turn, one at a time. Following the opening of presents around the Christmas tree, the women prepared a big Christmas dinner while the children played.

Way back in the 1930s, when Ruth Charlotte and Bob were children, they played with the same wooden blocks that their mother and grandfather had played with when they were little children. Next

Ruth Charlotte's and Bob's children played with them when visiting at Christmas. Bob moved the blocks to his home after Harry and Metta had passed on. Then Ruth's grandchildren and Bob's grandchildren played with them at Christmas time when they were all together at Bob and Janice's home. Even Ruth's oldest great grandson played with the blocks. One Christmas we took a picture of each of the three living generations playing with those blocks. The blocks have no monetary value because they are all well used but have tremendous sentimental value.

The farm continued to grow and prosper under Mark's guidance. In 2007, Mark sold the turkey business and some of the land to a large corporation that was better equipped to handle the risks associated with the production, processing and sale of animal products over the entire country. He retained much of the land so that part of the original 1835 purchase remains in the family.

In this book Bob has only told the story of his Ward ancestral heritage. In each generation William Ward's progeny have scattered to almost all corners of the world. Now the same thing is happening to Bob's family. Perhaps in 375 years, or more likely sooner, one of Bob's progeny will trace his or her ancestral heritage back to Bob or some other family member.

Ruth Charlotte and two of her children's families have moved back to their original roots in New England. Her oldest son and family live in Florida. Cynthia and family also returned to live in New England. Mark has moved to Florida and Bruce remains in New York. Bob and Janice moved only seven miles from the farm and live in Baldwinsville.

One thing Bob has seen that continues to be passed down from one generation to the next are the precious family values. A handshake by one of the family's members is as strong as a written contract. Each family member respects America and believes in performing our individual responsibilities in the best way possible. Bob jokingly tells friends, "I chose my parents well!" He often wishes that everyone had the opportunity to have the ancestral heritage that he has enjoyed.

A 2011 photograph of the Bitz family. From left to right are Mark, Lou, Karl Kristi, Asher, Robert, Janice, Rebecca, Cynthia, Sean and Elizabeth.

A 2011 photograph of the Dettbarn family. From left to right are Albert, Ruth, Almudena, James, Jason, Annie, Susan Bonaiuto, Andrea Bonaiuto, David Bonaiuto and Seb Bonaiuto.

A 2014 celebration of Ruth Bitz Dettbarn's 90th birthday. From left to right. Back row: Seb Bonaiuto, Annie Dettbarn, Karl Bitz, Lou Bitz, Elizabeth Bowen, David Bonaiuto, Rebecca Bowen, Sean Bowen, Bruce Bitz, Nicholas Dettbarn, Gisella Dettbarn, Jason Dettbarn. Middle row: Robert Dettbarn, Albert Dettbarn, Susan Bonaiuto, Ruth Dettbarn, Robert Bitz, Cynthia Bowen, Mark Bitz. Front row: James Dettbarn, Kevin Dettbarn, Andrea Bonaiuto, Kristi Bitz

APPENDIX 1
Notes

CHAPTER 1 – William Ward, Elizabeth and the five older children were all born in England, probably in East Anglia, on the approximate dates given. We know they sailed to Boston in 1638 but the name of the ship and what happened on it is fiction. William married Elizabeth after his first wife Rebecca died.

CHAPTER 2 – We have no record of where the Wards spent their first year. They could have gone to Sudbury in either 1638 or 1639. The settlement of Sudbury is well documented from 1639 through the following years. The Belchers are fictional but the other names are factual. The experiences encountered while settling in Sudbury are all fictional.

CHAPTER 3 – Cato was the leader of the Indians who was peaceful and helpful to the settlers. The Johnson and the Freeman families are fictitious. The daily activities of Sudbury are also fictitious but are written to closely resemble what may have occurred.

CHAPTER 4 – The reasons given for moving to Marlborough, the years given, the land distributed and the family members that moved are all factual. The fortified houses, the blockhouse and the soldiers stationed there are also factual. The dates of the Indian attacks, the size of the Indian Reservation the people killed or injured and the results of the attacks are factual. The dates of death and burial locations are factual as is the move to Ashford, Connecticut. The teaching by Elizabeth and the interactions between William Ward of the third generation and Will Ward of the first generation are fictitious. The Hiles and the dog

Nosey are fictitious as also is the reason the family moved to Union, Connecticut.

CHAPTER 5 – We do not know why the family moved to Somers, CT or if Jacob was ill. Nothing is known of Peter's youth. He did marry Lucretia Jones who married a man with the last name of Pinney after Peter died. All able-bodied men were required to serve in the militia. Connecticut was required by the British to furnish several thousand men during the French and Indian Wars. Peter served for several years. Peter served in the British Colonial Army under Major General Lyman. Both he and his brother Giles died in Havana from Yellow Fever, along with several thousand others. The author owns Peter's commission to Sergeant, which is dated October 16, 1762. He died a little over a month later. We do not know why he was promoted but it was likely because of extraordinary service in Cuba. The name Nate Pinney is fictitious.

CHAPTER 6 – Abner was bound out but we don't know to whom or why. Perhaps his mother's second husband didn't want him or it could have been to teach him a trade. Abner's service in the Revolutionary War is documented in the Massachusetts records of those serving in the war. He is listed at Concord and Lexington and enlisted almost continually during the Revolutionary War. His service is also shown in numerous regiments during the war. We have no idea of the experiences he encountered. Edna was a fabrication. He did marry Hannah Garfield, who was his brother's sister-in-law, on July 24, 1784. They had twelve children whose dates and places of birth are listed in the William Ward genealogy, which gives information as to the approximate times they moved. Why they moved and whether they purchased property is unknown. Abner is said to be buried in an unknown family cemetery on an adjoining Ward farm. Hannah is buried in her daughter Harriet Beardsley family's lot in the North Lansing, NY cemetery. There is a memorial monument to Abner Ward next to her grave.

CHAPTER 7 – The Ward Genealogy and family lore tell us that William served in the War of 1812. There are at least two William Wards from New York listed in the US archives but we do not know if one of them was our William Ward. William Ward did purchase a 43 acre farm along Owasco Lake on November 3, 1814 for $215 and then sold it to his younger brother Hiram on April 20, 1825 for $1,000. The Finch family is real as well as the fact that they were financially comfortable. Mr. Finch did loan William $1,000 and we have records showing that William paid it back. We do not know where William and Hannah or where the Finchs lived in Schuylerville. The Ward Genealogy reports that William, Hannah and children made the trip from Schuylerville to Scipio by ox pulled sled. The author has a copy of William Ward's deed to the property near Owasco Lake. Both the purchase price and the selling price of that land is factual. All conversations are imaginary.

CHAPTER 8 – The Ward Genealogy states that William Ward purchased 50 acres of forested land in Lysander around 1825 but the author has not located the property. He did purchase the farm at Plainville on a land contract and did make the approximate payments indicated before receiving the deed. Jeb Smith is fictional. The description of the well is based upon the actual well used by the family for several generations. Census data tells us that Ida was born in Ohio and is listed in the census as Hiram's daughter. The family has always considered her to have been Hiram's daughter. Celestia did not die in childbirth but did live until 1896 and had a son in 1862. Billy Wilson and the information about tobacco are fact. The Plainville church burned in 1852 and was replaced in 1854. The author has the deeds to two of the pews.

CHAPTER 9 – This chapter is almost entirely fact. Liz is a fictional person.

CHAPTERs 10,11 and 12 – All are factual.

Appendix 2

EARLY SUDBURY SETTLERS: LAND AND TOWN OFFICES

From *Puritan Village* copyright 1963 by Sumner Chilton Powell.
Reprinted by permission of Wesleyan University Press.

Early Sudbury Settlers: Land and Town Offices
1638-1655

NAME (*MARRIED IN 1640)	ACREAGE IN ENGLAND	ACREAGE IN WATERTOWN	SUDBURY: MEADOW	SUDBURY: UPLAND	SELECTMAN	DEPUTY TO GEN. COURT	CONSTABLE	FENCE VIEWER	JUDGE OF SMALL CAUSES	SURVEYOR OF HIGHWAY	INVOICE TAKER	TIMBER KEEPER	SWINE WARDEN	MILITARY POST	NEW LOT GRANTED 1655	TOTAL POSTS
Edmund Brown*	?	0	74	38			Minister									
B. Pendleton	?	92	57	76	6	0	0	0	0	0	0	0	0	0	Yes	6
T. Cakebread*	?	66	50	124			Miller							Ens	Yes	1
W. Pelham	?	0	50	0	2	0	0	0	1	0	0	0	0	Capt	Yes	4
P. Noyes*	116	111	48	73	14	2	1	3	4	2	0	0	0	S. Arm	Yes	26
E. Goodnow*	?	0	43½	30	13	3	0	1	3	2	2	3	3	Ens	Yes	30
J. Knight	?	394	38½	61	0	0	0	0	0	0	0	0	0	–	No	0
E. Rice*	15	0	33½	54	11	5	0	1	3	1	1	0	0	–	Yes	22
G. Munnings*	?	109	28	10	1	0	0	0	0	0	0	0	0	–	No	1
W. Ward	?	0	25	20	11	1	0	3	2	0	2	1	1	–	Yes	21
W. Haines*	?	0	23½	57	14	5	0	1	3	1	2	0		–	Yes	28
T. Brown	?	0	23	25	0	0	0	0	0	0	0	0	0	–	No	0
T. Noyes	0	0	22	0	2	0	1	1	0	2	1	0	0	–	Yes	7
R. Darvell	22	68	20½	27	1	0	0	4	0	2	1	0	0	–	Yes	8
R. Be(a)st	?	0	19	0	0	0	0	0	0	0	0	0	0	–	Yes	0
A. Belcher*	?	–	18½	19	0	0	0	0	0	0	0	0	0	–	No	0
J. Goodnow*	?	0	14	17	3	0	2	3	0	1	0	0	0	Drum	Yes	10
J. Bent	45	0	11½	29	2	0	0	0	1	2	0	1	0	–	Yes	6
J. Wood	?	0	10½	4	1	0	0	1	0	0	0	0	0	–	Yes	2
S. Johnson*	?	0	10	11	0	0	0	0	0	0	0	0	0	–	Yes	0
A. Buckmaster	?	0	10	0	0	0	0	0	0	0	0	0	0	–	No	0
"Wid" Hunt	?	0	10	14½	0	0	0	0	0	0	0	0	0	–	No	0

Appendix 3

MARLBOROUGH, MASSACHUSETTS

From Puritan Village copyright 1963 by Sumner Chilton Powell.
Reprinted by permission of Wesleyan University Press.

Marlborough, Massachusetts

Land Grants and Town Offices (1660-1665)

(Total: 6 elections)

	VOTE IN SUDBURY	SUDBURY MEADOW (ACRES)	SUDBURY UPLAND (ACRES)	GRANTED FARM IN SUDBURY?	MARLBOROUGH — UPLAND	MARLBOROUGH — MEADOW	SELECTMAN	CONSTABLE	CLERK	TIMBER KEEPER	HIGHWAY SUPERVISOR	TOTAL POSTS
E. Rice*	No	47	164	Yes	50	25	5	0	0	0	0	5
W. Ward*	No	25	65	Yes	50	25	6	0	0	1	0	7
J. Ruddock*	No	17	35	Yes	50	25	6	0	5	2	1	14
T. King*	No	3	6	Yes	39½	20	6	2	0	1	1	10
T. Rice	No	0	0	Yes	35	17	0	0	0	0	0	0
Edw. Rice*	No	0	0	Yes	35	17	0	0	0	0	0	0
T. Goodnow*	No	10	28	Yes	32	16	2	0	0	0	2	4
"Minister"	–	–	–	–	30	15	–	--	–	–	–	–
W. Kerley*	–	2	18	Yes	30	15	1	0	0	0	3	4
J. Johnson*	–	0	0	No	30	15	1	0	0	0	0	1
R. Newton*	No	9	15	Yes	30	15	0	0	0	0	0	0
J. How, Sr.*	No	11	19	Yes	30	15	4	0	0	0	0	4
J. Woods, Jr.*	No	28	49	Yes	30	15	3	0	0	0	0	3
P. Bent*	No	0	0	No	30	15	0	0	0	0	0	0
J. Rutter	No	0	9	Yes	30	15	0	0	0	0	0	0
"Blacksmith"	–	–	–	–	30	15	–	–	–	–	–	–
Ab. How	–	0	0	No	25	12	0	0	0	0	0	0
B. Rice	–	0	0	No	24	12	0	0	0	0	0	0
S. Johnson*	–	16	37	Yes	23	11	4	3	0	0	0	7
J. Maynard, Jr.*	–	0	0	No	23	11	0	0	0	0	0	0
Jos. Rice	–	0	0	No	22	11	0	0	0	0	0	0

Appendix 3

MARLBOROUGH, MASSACHUSETTS

From *Puritan Village* copyright 1963 by Sumner Chilton Powell.
Reprinted by permission of Wesleyan University Press.

APPENDIX VIII *(cont.)*

	VOTE IN SUDBURY	SUDBURY MEADOW (ACRES)	SUDBURY UPLAND (ACRES)	GRANTED FARM IN SUDBURY?	MARLBOROUGH — UPLAND	MARLBOROUGH — MEADOW	SELECTMAN	CONSTABLE	CLERK	TIMBER KEEPER	HIGHWAY SUPERVISOR	TOTAL POSTS
P. King	No	0	0	No	22	11	0	0	0	0	0	0
J. Rediat*	No	0	12	Yes	22	11	0	0	0	0	0	0
Ob. Ward	—	0	0	No	21	10	0	0	0	0	0	0
Sam. Rice	—	0	0	No	21	10	0	0	0	0	0	0
A. Belcher	—	18½	36	No	20	10	0	0	0	0	0	0
J. Bellows	—	0	0	No	20	10	0	0	0	0	0	0
T. Goodnow, Jr.*	—	0	0	No	20	10	0	0	0	0	0	0
H. Kerley	—	0	0	No	19½	10	0	0	0	0	0	0
Rich. Ward	—	0	0	No	18	9	0	0	0	0	0	0
J. Barrett	—	0	0	No	18	9	0	0	0	0	0	0
Jos. Holmes	—	0	0	No	18	9	0	0	0	0	0	0
C. Baynster*	—	0	0	No	16	8	0	0	0	0	0	0
J. How, Jr.	—	0	0	No	16	8	0	0	0	0	0	0
Rich. Barnes	—	0	0	No	16	8	0	0	0	0	0	0
Sam. How	—	0	0	No	16	8	0	0	0	0	0	0
J. Newton	—	0	0	No	16	8	0	0	0	0	0	0
H. Axtell	—	0	0	No	16	8	0	0	0	0	0	0

(*) Signed First Petition for Marlborough Settlement.
(Yes) Received 130-acre farm in W. Sudbury, 1658. (No) — did not.
"No" those recorded as voting against the limitation of Sudbury commons.

Appendix 4a

An 1830 receipt for a pew in the first Plainville church which was
constructed of wood and burned in 1853

This Indenture, made the *Twenty fifth*
day of *February A.D. 1830* ———————— Between the Trustees
of the first *R*eligious Society in Lysander and Cato, who are also a building committee of the first free church, which is to be free for all religious denominations
when not occupied by regular or stated appointments for preaching in the town
of Lysander, in the county of Onondaga and state of New-York, and their successors in office, of the first part, and *Elijah Osborn of the town
of Ira county of Cayuga* ————————————
———————————————— of the second part witnesseth, that the said committee
for and in consideration of the sum of *thirty* ————————— dollars and
————— cents to them in hand paid, the receipt whereof is hereby acknowledged, have granted bargained and sold, and by these presents, do grant, bargain,
and sell unto the said *Elijah Osborn* ——— to *his* heirs,
executors, administrators or assigns forever, the pew or seat No. *42* — with the
appurtenances thereunto belonging to have and to hold the said pew or seat No.
42 to the said *Elijah Osborn* and *his* heirs, executors,
administrators or assigns forever.

In witness whereof we have hereunto set our hands and seals the day and year
past above written.

SEALED AND DELIVERED ⎰
IN THE PRESENCE OF ⎱

Francis Brott
Gilman ...

James L. Voorhees

M.B. Scofield

⎰ BUILDING
⎱ COMMITTEE.

John Paul

Alfred Wilson

Thomas Sandborn

... Simmons

Appendix 4b

An 1854 receipt for a pew in the second Plainville church which was
constructed of brick and still serves the Plainville area in 2015

This Indenture, Made the *Eighth* day of *April* A. D. 1854, between the Trustees of the CHRISTIAN CHURCH AND SOCIETY, of Plainville, in the county of Onondaga, and State of New York, and their successors in office, of the first part, and *William Ward* of the second part—

WITNESSETH, That the said Trustees, for and in consideration of the sum of *forty five* dollars and — — — — cents to them in hand paid, the receipt whereof is hereby acknowledged, have granted, bargained and sold, and by these presents do grant, bargain and sell unto the said *William Ward* of the second part, and to *his* heirs, executors, administrators or assigns, forever, the Pew or Seat No. *32* situated in the Christian Meeting House in Plainville, belonging to said CHRISTIAN CHURCH AND SOCIETY, with the appurtenances thereunto belonging, to have and to hold the said Pew or Seat No. *32* to the said *William Ward* part*y* of the second part, and *his* heirs, executors, administrators or assigns, forever.

In witness whereof, We have hereto set our hands and seals, the day and year above written.

IN PRESENCE OF

D G Smith

George Hopkins
Chester Barns
Wm Dick

Deed of Pew.

THE TRUSTEES OF THE

Christian Church & Society,

OF PLAINVILLE,

TO

Wm Ward

ONE $3 D

Gazette Print, Baldwinsville.

Appendix 5a

Deed for land in Cayuga County purchased by William Ward in 1815

Appendix 5b
Deed for land in Cayuga County purchased by William Ward in 1815

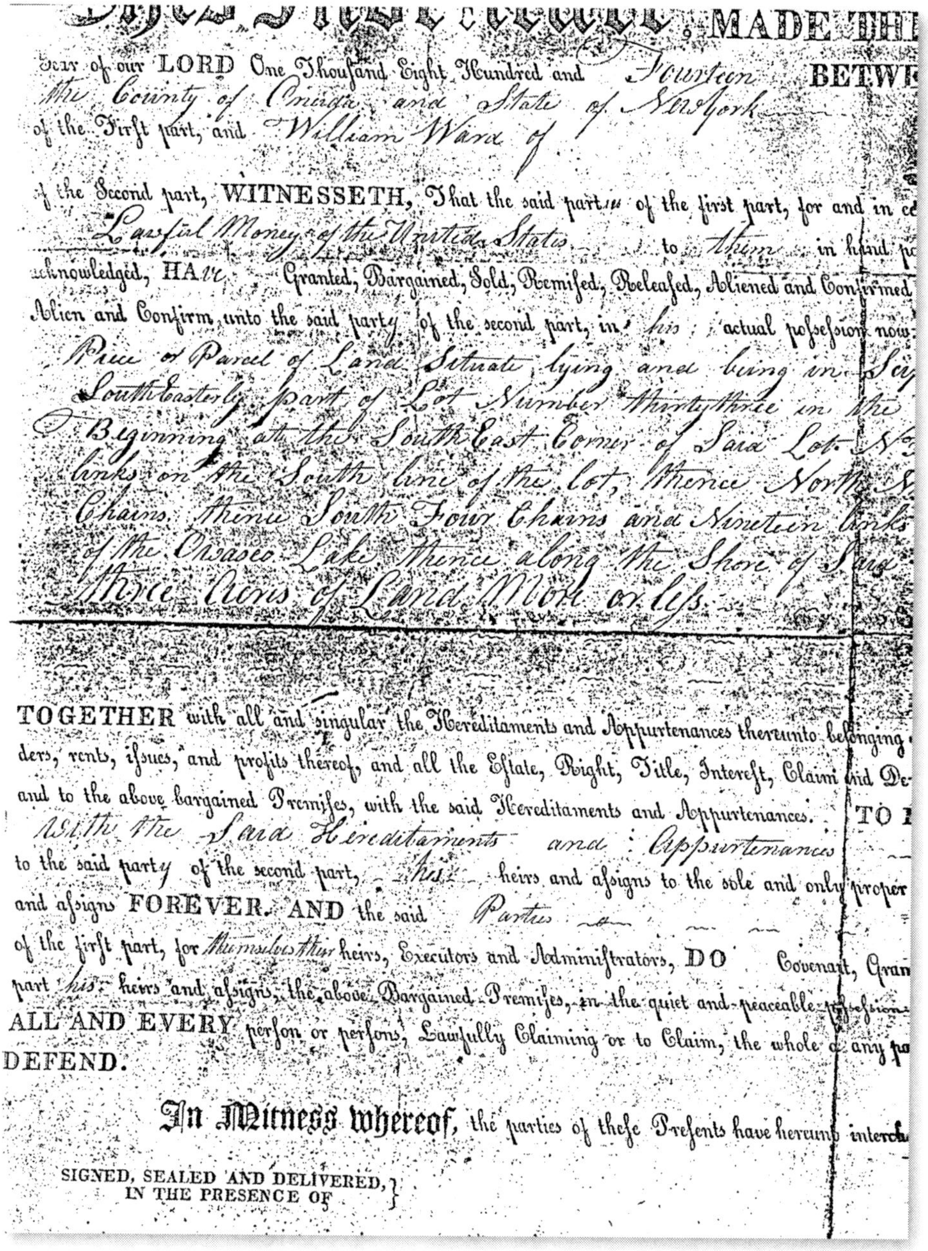

[Handwritten and printed deed text, partially legible:]

... year of our LORD One Thousand Eight Hundred and *Fourteen* BETWE...
... the *County of Oneida* and *State of New York* ...
of the First part, and *William Ward* of ...

... the Second part, WITNESSETH, That the said part... of the first part, for and in co...
Lawful Money of the United States ... to *them* in hand ...
acknowledged, HAVE ... Granted, Bargained, Sold, Remised, Released, Aliened and Confirmed
Alien and Confirm, unto the said party of the second part, in *his* actual possession now ...
Piece or Parcel of Land Situate lying and being in *Si...*
Southeasterly part of *Lot Number Thirtythree* in the
Beginning at the South East Corner of Said Lot N...
links on the South line of the lot, thence North ...
Chains, thence South Four Chains and Nineteen links ...
of the Oasco Lake, thence along the Shore of Said ...
Three Acres of Land More or less.

TOGETHER with all and singular the Hereditaments and Appurtenances thereunto belonging ...
ders, rents, issues, and profits thereof, and all the Estate, Right, Title, Interest, Claim and De...
and to the above bargained Premises, with the said Hereditaments and Appurtenances. TO ...
With the Said Hereditaments and Appurtenances
to the said party of the second part, *his* heirs and assigns to the sole and only proper ...
and assigns FOREVER. AND the said *Parties* ...
of the first part, for *themselves, their* heirs, Executors and Administrators, DO Covenant, Gran...
part *his* heirs and assigns, the above Bargained Premises, in the quiet and peaceable ...
ALL AND EVERY person or persons, Lawfully Claiming or to Claim, the whole or any pa...
DEFEND.

In Witness whereof, the parties of these Presents have hereunto interc...

SIGNED, SEALED AND DELIVERED, }
IN THE PRESENCE OF }

Appendix 5c

Deed for land in Cayuga County purchased by William Ward in 1815

Appendix 6a

Envelope to William Ward at Cato in 1824 from his brother-in-law
Joseph Finch who lived near where William had recently lived in
Schuylerville, New York

Appendix 6b

Letter written to William Ward at Cato in 1824 from his brother-in-law Joseph Finch who lived near where William had recently lived in Schuylerville, New York

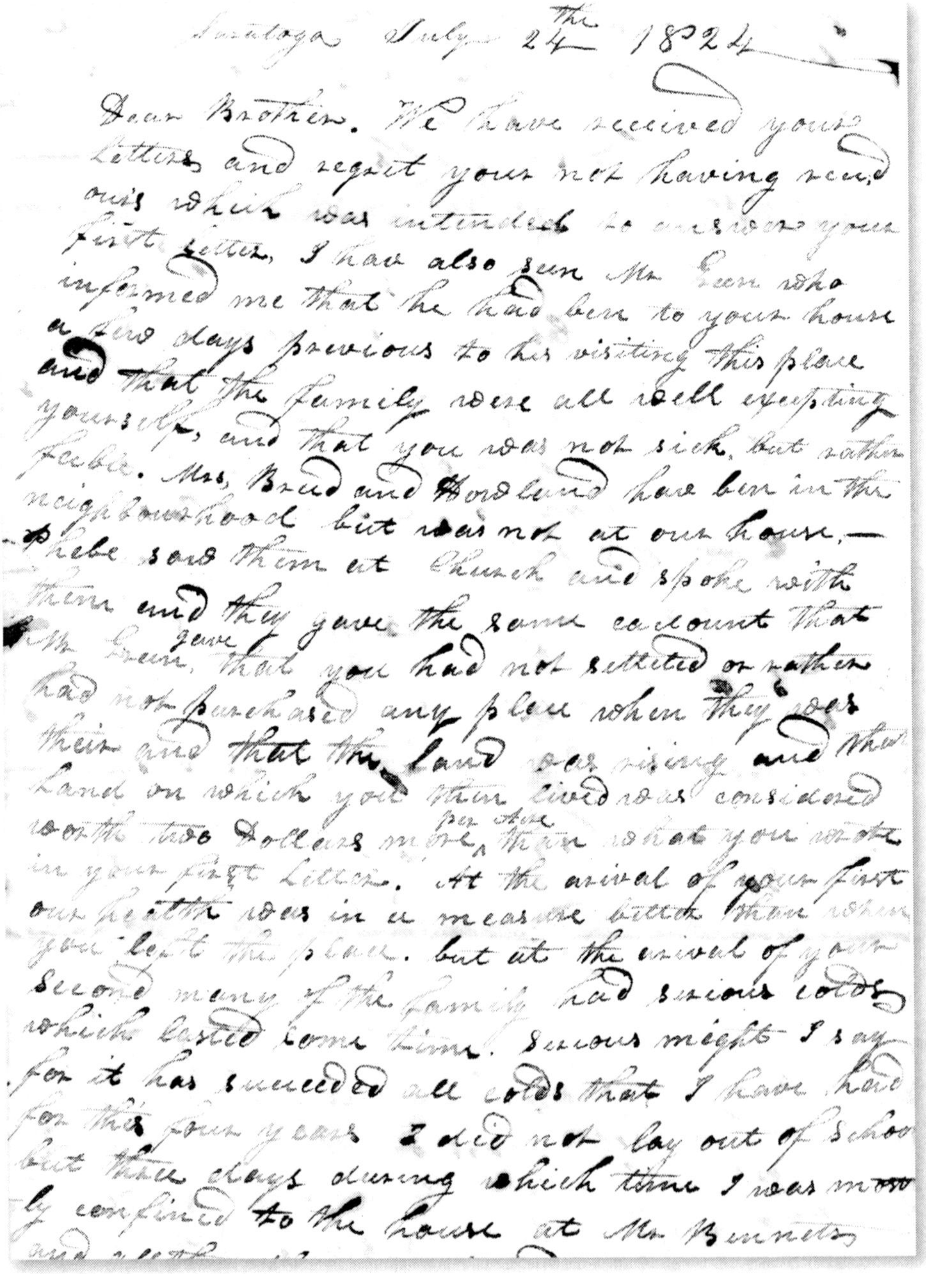

Saratoga July 24th 1824

Dear Brother. We have received your letters and regret your not having rec'd ours which was intended to answer your first letter, I have also seen Mr Green who informed me that he had ben to your house a few days previous to his visiting this place and that the family were all well excepting yourself, and that you was not sick, but rather feeble. Mrs. Breed and Howland have ben in the neighbourhood but was not at our house,— Phebe saw them at Church and spoke with them and they gave the same account that Mr Green gave that you had not settled or rather had not purchased any place when they was their and that the land was rising and the land on which you then lived was considered worth two Dollars more per Acre than what you wrote in your first Letter. At the arival of your first our health was in a measure better than when you left this place. but at the arival of your second many of the family had serious colds which lasted some time. Serious might I say for it has succeeded all colds that I have had for this four years I did not lay out of School but three days during which time I was mostly confined to the house at Mr Bennets and [illegible]

Appendix 6c

Letter written to William Ward at Cato in 1824 from his
brother-in-law Joseph Finch who lived near where William had
recently lived in Schuylerville, New York

I have commenced my third quarter in the
same place, after the expiration of which
I shall leave the place if providence permit
We have had some talks of selling
Mr Asa Clements said that if we would
make out a Deed for twenty Dollars per
Acre the man Money should be counted
Down! Mr Esmond will call probaly to
morow and see the premeses Uncle ___ says
you cannot sell and if you could what the
Devel would you do! But if any man
will give me my price, I will show ____
Mr ___ that I would take the money
$27 Dollars the price, $25 the lowest cent

N.B. Phebe says she is going to call and
see the old Bachelor you was to procure
in that Cuntry! when I dont know
give our respects to all enquiring friends
So I remain your ___ Brother
Mr
William Ward

___ Finch

N.B. all live at home and are generally
speaking well Crops small wheat worth
most nothing attall ___ friends all well
and Grandmother has got another
Daughter

Appendix 7a

Envelope to William Ward, now living in Plainville, in 1841 from his
son William Finch Ward who was visiting his mother's family near
Schuylerville, New York

Appendix 7b

Letter written to William Ward, now living in Plainville, in 1841 from his son William Finch Ward who was visiting his mother's family near Schuylerville, New York

Warrensburgh March th 2 1841
Dear Parents
                    I take the present
to inform you where i am and
where i am a going i left syracuse
at 8 oclock in the evening and arived
in troy about 8 in the morning and to
schuylerville at about one in safty i found
uncle roswell folks well also uncle daniels
i started this morning for indian river and have
put up at the above named place i should
have wrote to you before i left saratoga
but i hope to find uncle james to the falls
but finding him gone and would not be
back in some two or three weeks i went ahead
and shall see him to morrow when i return
i will weight again Nathan wished me
to weight as soon as possible and send him
his note which i shall enclose in this letter
i took it up the next day after i got to
roswells acording to directions
                    Yours in haste
                        Wm F Ward
i shall put this into the office to morrow
morning providing all is safe

Appendix 8a

Envelope of letter that was written to and delivered to William Ward in
Lysander, New York in 1825

Appendix 9

1901 letter written to William and Lilly Ward
by their uncle Nathan Ward

Gilberts Mills Oswego Co. N. Y.
Oct. 4- 1901
To William E. and Lilly M. Ward.
Dear Nephew and Niece,
Lillys letter was duly received, and
I thank her for her rememberence of me
in my old age, and for the kind words
she has written. Will, if you cannot, or
do not write much, you are fortunate
in haveing a good wife who can,
John brought me the letter from the
Office in the evening after I had
retired for the night, I sat up in bed
drew up the table close, turned up
the lamp, put on my speckes and
read it, and then lay down to
sleep, I was pleased to hear you were
all well, and enjoyed your trip to the
Pan American,
Thinking you would like to
know something of our ancestral
history, I drew off a copy of my family record and sent

Appendix 9

1901 letter written to William and Lilly Ward
by their uncle Nathan Ward

you, and as you all appear to be
pleased with it, I am glad I done it. I
am the only man liveing that could
do the most of it, and it cost me no
great loss of time for I done the most of
it when I could do nothing else.
I have seen my Great Grand Mother Finch
many times, and all of Grand Father
Joseph Finches brothers and Sisters except
one, and probably have seen her but do
not now remember it. I think Jeremiah
was the oldest, and am sure that
Samuel was the youngest; but the
order in which the others were born
one after another as I have set them
down may not be quite correct.
And I have seen Grandfather and
Grandmother Ward, and all of their
children, except Aunt Polly Wilson
who died before we mooved from Saratoga
to this country. I think Josiah was
the oldest, and I am sure that Betsy
was the youngest, and Sidney was
the next older than Betsy. But except

Appendix 9

1901 letter written to William and Lilly Ward
by their uncle Nathan Ward

Father, I have no figures to tell when the others were born, and the order in which I have set them down may not be quite correct.

Grand Father, Grand Mother, Aunt Sally and Aunt Caroline Finch, were all members of the Baptist Church. Aunt Phebe, was a Methodist.

It is not known to me whether Grand Mother Ward ever united with a church or not, but she was a Christian; and in her latter years would often say, "We must keep our Lamps trimed and Burning."

William Ward who once resided on the first place North, and adjoining David Tillotsons, has twice told me that his Great Grand Father Ward was sold to pay his fare for crossing the Ocean, and a Widow Woman bought, and afterwards married him. Of course he must have been one of those three Brothers that came over.

Father knew there was a family by the name of Ward residing in Skaneateles who claimed to be decendants from those

Appendix 9

1901 letter written to William and Lilly Ward
by their uncle Nathan Ward

three Brothers. After Oscar went to Phoenix and before he was married, there came a lady from Ikancatles to the house where he borded (whos name was Ward) who said she was a descendant from those three Brothers. So, so far as I can see the tradition about the three Brothers comeing over must be correct. When the Lady went away from Phoenix she sent her complimentes up to her cousins as she called us.

I have understood you both were members of the Christian Church, and I congratulate you on that account. To be true and worthy members of Christs Family, is an assurence that we shall receive an immortal life beyond the grave, and that is the greatest gift our Heavenly Father can give us.

see 1 John 2-25 "And this is the promise that He hath promised us, even eternal life."

Marke 16-16 "He that believeth and is baptized shall be saved."

Appendix 9

1901 letter written to William and Lilly Ward
by their uncle Nathan Ward

first of August, my strength, and
my endurance which never was the
very best, has wonderfully fallen
off and I find myself a feble old
man, I can walk about the house
a little but am obliged to keep my
bed much of the time, and at most,
it cannot be long before the boys
will carry and deposit me at
Plainville where I have a good
wife, two small children, Father,
Mother, Brother, Sister, Nepew,
Niece, Fatherinlaw, Motherinlaw,
two Brotherinlaws, and two or
three Sisterinlaws; and there
shall we all sleep till the bright
resurrection morn.
    I will be pleased to receive
a letter from you at any time, and
if I can I will answer.

Appendix 9

1901 letter written to William and Lilly Ward
by their uncle Nathan Ward

Your Uncle
Nathan Ward

Appendix 10

An 1830 paper describing a loan of $1,000 to William Ward
from Roswell Finch

Know all men by these Presents that We Roswell
Finch James C. Finch of the Town of Senetoga
County of Senetoga and State of New York one held
and Firmly Bound unto William Ward of the Town
of Lysander County of Onandaga and State aforesaid
in the Penal Sum of one Thousand Dollars to be Paid
to the said William on his Certain attorney his heirs
Executors or administrators and assigns Which Payment Well and Truely to be made We bind our selves our
heirs Executors and Administrators Jointly and Securely
firmly by these Presents Sealed With our Seals and Datte
this Twentieth Day of February in the year of our Lord
one Thousand Eight hundred and thirty

The Condition of the above obligation is Such that Where
the above Bismched William Ward Was Indebted to Joseph
Finch Late of the said Town of Senetoga Decea[s]t on to the
Executors of the said Joseph as Executors of the Last Will
and Testment of the said Joseph Finch Decea[s]t on to the
h___ s of the said Joseph as a Part of the Portion of
his Estate that the said Joseph Deced Seised of in the ___
be yeelded unto the Daughter Hannah of the said
Joseph Finch Decea[s]t who is the Wife of the said
William Ward
Now in Case the above Bound Roswell Finch and
James C Finch their heirs Executors and Adminis
trators Shall from Time to Time and at all Times
Save and Keep harmless the said William and
Hannah their heirs Executors Administrators Charges
from all Claims and Demands Costs and Charges
that the said Joseph Finch their Father had against
them at the Time of his Deceas and all Claims of
the Executors of the Last Will and Testment of
the said Joseph and all Claims of the Heirs of the
said Joseph Then this obligation is to be Void
otherwise to be and Remain in full force
and Virtue
In Witness Whereof We have hereunto set our hands
and Seats in Presents of

Charles Ray   Roswell Finch

Chauncy Betts   J. C. Finch

Appendix 11a

Papers regarding the 1835 purchase of William Ward's
72 acre farm in Plainville

Appendix 11b
Papers regarding the 1835 purchase of William Ward's
72 acre farm in Plainville

Appendix 11c

Papers regarding the 1835 purchase of William Ward's
72 acre farm in Plainville

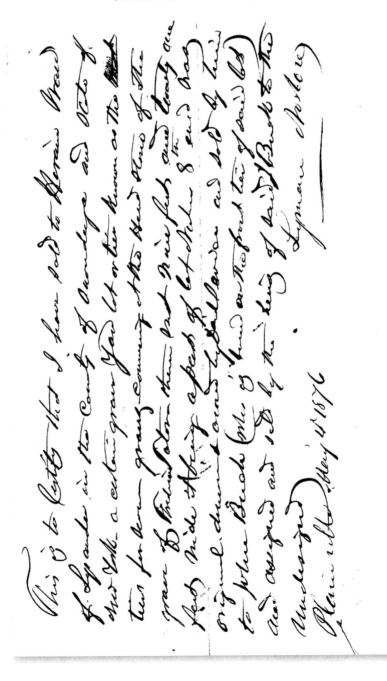

Appendix 11d

Papers regarding the 1835 purchase of William Ward's
72 acre farm in Plainville

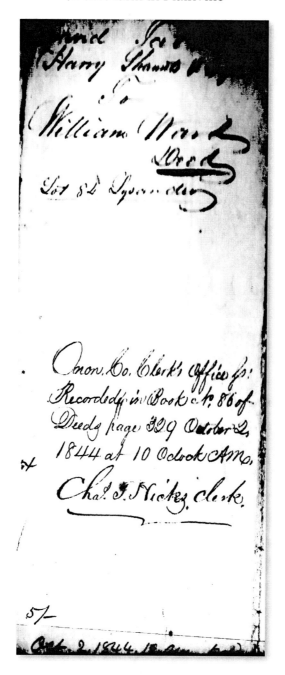

Appendix 11e

Papers regarding the 1835 purchase of William Ward's
72 acre farm in Plainville

Know All Men by these presents, that I William Ward
of late in the County of Cayuga and State of New York
am held and firmly Bound unto Hiram Ward
of Scipio in the County aforesaid in the just Sum of
One Thousand Dollars for the payment there of
I do by these presents bind my Self and Legal
representatives heavenly to pay the same to the said
Hiram or his Assigns or legal representatives

Witness My hand and Seal this 23d April 1824.

The Condition of this Obligation is Such that
whereas the said Hiram have this day given
me his several Notes of hand amounting to the
Same of five hundred dollars to be payed as follows
Fifty Dollars on the first day of July Next
Fifty Dollars on the first day of January Next
One hundred Dollars on the first day of Jany 1826
One hundred Dollars on the first day of Jany 1827
One hundred Dollars on the first day of Jany 1828
One hundred Dollars on the first day of Jany 1829
And It is Agreed that when the said Hiram
has paid the aforsaid Notes, then I the said William
am to make an Execute a Deed of Warrantee to
the said Hiram of the fowling premises to Wit
Forty three Acres of Land in the Town of
Scipio afore said it being the same Land that my
Honored Father Abner Ward now lives on and has
lived on for twelve years last past Bounded on
following Northerly by Joshua Banker Land
Southerly by Wells ....

....
....

....

....

Appendix 12a
Papers regarding Abner Ward estate

We, the undersigned, appraisers, appointed by the Surrogate of the county of Cayuga, having first taken and subscribed the oath herein inserted, certify that we have estimated and appraised the property of _Abner Ward_ deceased, exhibited to us, according to the best of our knowledge and ability, and that we have signed duplicate Inventories thereof. *Whipple Cloth*

Elisha Barnes

Cayuga County, ss. I,

do swear that the foregoing inventory is in all respects just and true; that it contains a true statement of all the personal property of the said deceased, which has come to my knowledge; and particularly of all money, bank bills and other circulating medium, belonging to the said deceased; and of all just claims of the deceased against me, according to the best of my knowledge.

Sworn and subscribed, this

day of   before me,

Note

One against Norman Sharp of One Hundred Dollars Spurious Dated March 15th 1834

One other note against Norman Sharp of ninety three Dollars Spurious Dated April 1st 1835

One other note against Norman Sharp of ninteen dollars Dated January 5th 1838

One other note against Elisha Byrnes of forty dollars fourteen Cents Dated april 30th 1835

One other note against Oben Griswold of One Hundred forty five dollars ninety Cents Dated Oct 31st 1857

One other note against Abner Ward Jun of twenty seven dollars ninety seven Cents Spurious Dated april 1st 1857

One other note against Abner Ward Jun of five dollars fifty six Cents Spurious Dated December 9th 1842

One other note against Hiram Ward of forty three Dollars eighty three Cents Dated Dec 9th 1842

Appendix 12b

Papers regarding Abner Ward estate

November the 2 1843

Names of articles sold at Publick sale this day

To Amos Ward one coat	4-5-0
To Pantaloons and vest	3-0-0
To one hat	1-25
To Hannah Ward one cloak	2-0-0
To Hiram Ward one chest	2-0-0
To Whipple Clark one lather box	0-08
To Hiram Ward one Raisor	0-0 9
To Hiram Ward one box	0-13½
To Hiram Ward one book	0-13½
To Hiram Ward one tobacco box	0-04
To Hiram Ward one cap	0-13½
To Hiram Ward one pair of mits	0-10
To Hiram Ward one bottle	0-04
To Jehial Ward one pair of socks	0-06
To Hiram Ward one comefited	0-04
To Sally Ward one pair of specks	0-12½
To Hiram Ward one pair of drawers	0-12½
To Hiram Ward one bottle	0-08
To Rehesa Banks one raisor strap	0-08
To Smith Banks one raisor strap	0-06
To Hiram Ward one vest	0-12
To Hiram Ward one vest	0-04
To Hiram Ward one roundabout	0-13
To Hiram Ward one pantaloons	0-10
To Hiram Ward do do	0-09
To Hiram Ward one pocket book	0-04
To Jehial Ward two shirts	0-12½
To Wm Ward one buffalo robe	2-50
To Hiram Ward one pair of boots	0-25
To Abner Ward one pair of stillards	0 25

Appendix 12c

Papers regarding Abner Ward estate

			$
to	one	Coat	4. 50
to	one	hare Cap	0. 50
to	one	Cloak	2. 00
to	one	trousers	0. 12½
to	one	Coat	0. 25
to	one	round about	0. 12½
to	one	prantaloons and vest	3. 00
to	one	drawer	0. 62
to	one	vest	0. 25
to	one	vest	0. 37½
to	two	shirts	0. 25
to	one	pantaloons	0. 06
to	one	drawers	0. 03
to	one	pair of socks	0. 18
to	one	hat	1. 25
to	one	pair of mits	0. 18
to	one	Comforter	0. 12½
to	raisor strap		0. 25
to	Cash		13. 10
to	one	leather Case	0. 12½
to	one	raisor	0. 25
to	one	cliner box	0. 12½
to	one	pocket book	0. 06
to	one	Book	0. 25
to	one	pair of spoeks	0. 12½
to	one	tobaco box	0. 12½
to	one	Chest	2. 00
to	one	Buffaloe Skin	2. 50
to	one	pair Boots	0. 25
to	one	Stillyards	0. 25
to	two	bottles	0. 25

Appendix 12d
Papers regarding Abner Ward estate

Received of Wm Ward Administrator of the Estate of Abner Ward deceasd late of sipio Cayuga County the sume of fore teen Dollars And twelve cents in full of all claims and demands Whatsoever Which I have or may have against the said Estate as an heir at law or otherwise Witness my hand and seal this 31 Day of August 1844 At Venice

Abner X Ward
Mark

Received of Wm Ward Administrator of the Estate of Abner Ward deceasd late of sipio Cayuga County the sume of Seventy seven Dollars and 66 cents, in full of all claims and demands Whatsoever Which I have or may have against the said Estate as an heir at law or otherwise Witness my hand and seal this 2 Day of september 1844 At Lansing

her
Hannah X Ward
Mark

Received of Wm Ward Admenishator of the Estate of Abner Ward deceasd late of sipio Cayuga County the sum of Fore teen Dollars Dollars And twelve cents in full of aall claims and demands Which I have or may have against the said Estate as an heir at law or other wise Witness My hand and seal this 2 Day of September 1844 At Lansing

Appendix 13a
William Ward Will

This is the last will and testament of William Ward of the town of Lysander in the County of Onondaga and State of New York Know all men by these presents that I William Ward aforesaid do make and publish this Instrument as follows to wit;

1st I do hereby order and direct that all my liabilities, funeral expenses and testamentary charges whatsoever be paid from my personal property

2° I do give and bequeathe all of the Remainder of my personal property after paying the charges (liabilities) and expenses aforesaid to My sons Nathan Ward William Ward & Hiram Ward to be equally divided among and between them (except that the said Hiram Ward is to have all of the crop of Tobacco now on hand) that is to say in proportion to what they shall respectively have done for me, my said sons to be satisfied from the personal property for and for their care and attention to me while living and the same to be divided between them so as to make their respective shares equal after satisfying each for what he may have done for me while living

3. My Real Estate I give divise and bequeathe to My Sons Nathan Ward, William Ward & Hiram Ward and to the children of my deceased daughter Nancy Jane Pattisson (late wife of Sandford Pattisson) to be equally divided into four parts so that the said Nathan Ward or his heirs shall receive one part, Wm Ward or his heirs one part, Hiram Ward or his heirs one part, and the children of my said Deceased daughter the other part making four equal parts,

4ª I do hereby constitute and appoint Nathan Ward

Appendix 13b
William Ward Will

true & lawful Executors of this my last Will and
testament with full power to do all that may be
necessary to close up and divide my estate accor
ding to the provisions of this my last Will and testment
and to sell my real estate & execute deeds of conveyance
for the same as may be necessary

9th I do also order and direct that in case I
should depart this life before the ensuing Autumn
that is before the 1st of Decr 1865, that in that event
my said son Hiram Ware who is now residing
on my farm — & within whom I am living
shale have the rights to remain on the farm
up to that time with the same rights & privileges
that he now enjoys ...

In witness my hand and seal this 9th day of Decr 1864   Wm Ward

Subscribed and acknowledged & seal by the
testator William Ware in the presence of
Each of us who have subscribe our names
as attesting witnesses thereto, at the Request
of the said testator and the said testator
... at the time of making such ...
... and acknowledgement ...
... this instrument to subscribed
... to be his last Will & Testament
... ... Plainville N.Y

Eliza Cripps   Plainville N.Y.

Appendix 13c
William Ward Will

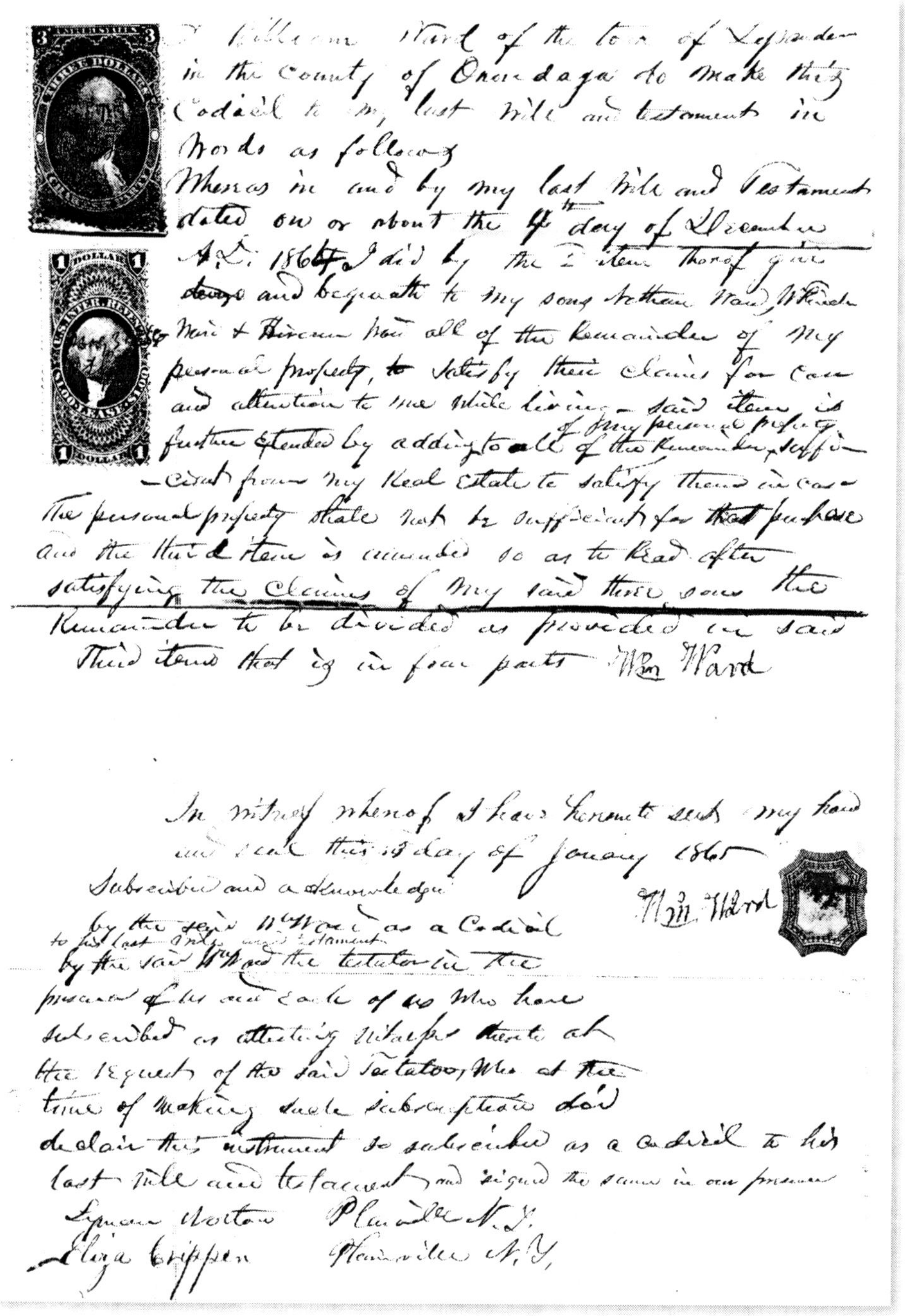

Appendix 14a

Inventory of William Ward Estate

Onondaga County, ss. I *Lyman Norton* an Appraiser, duly appointed by the Surrogate of said county, do *solemnly swear* and declare, that I will truly, honestly and impartially appraise the personal property of *William Ward* late of the town of *Lysander* in the county aforesaid, deceased, which shall be for that purpose exhibited to me, to the best of my knowledge and ability.

Sworn this *15* day of *May* 1865, before me.   *Lyman Norton*

John Schenck Justice of the Peace

Onondaga County, ss. I *Benjamin B. Schenck* an Appraiser, duly appointed by the Surrogate of said county, do *solemnly swear* and declare, that I will truly honestly and impartially appraise the personal property of *William Ward* late of the town of *Lysander* in the county aforesaid, deceased, which shall be for that purpose exhibited to me, to the best of my knowledge and ability.

Sworn this *15* day of *May* 1865, before me.   *Benj. B. Schenck*

John Schenck Justice of the Peace

INVENTORY.

A true and perfect inventory of the goods, chattels and credits, which were of *William Ward* late of the town of *Lysander* in the county of Onondaga, deceased, made by *Hiram Ward and Nathan Ward Executors* of the estate of the said deceased, with the aid and in the presence of *Lyman Norton and Benjamin B. Schenck* they having been duly appointed and sworn or affirmed as Appraisers; containing a full, just and true statement of all the personal property of the said deceased, which has come to the knowledge of the said

Hiram Ward and Nathan Ward Executors

of said estate, and particularly of all money, bank bills and other circulating medium, belonging to the said deceased, and all just claims of the said deceased against said *Hiram Ward & Nathan Ward* and all bonds, mortgages, notes and other securities for the payment of money belonging to said deceased, specifying the name of the debtor in each security, the date, the sum originally payable, the endorsements thereon, with their dates, and the sum which, in the judgment of the appraisers, may be collectable on each security.

Upon the completion of this inventory, duplicates thereof have been made, and signed at the end thereof, by the appraisers.

ARTICLES INVENTORIED.

	Dolls.	Cts.		Dolls.	Cts.
Silver Coin		36	Amt Brot Up	526	80
Bank Bills on hand at the death of Testator	434	86	1 Alapaca Coat	1	50
Bank Bills Rec for Property Sold by Hiram Ward	81	48	2 Vests	2	00
			2 old Vest	1	00
			2 old Coat		
4 pair old Pants		10	3 pairs wool Drawers	2	00
2 " Pants good	5	00	4 " old Shirts		50
1 Over Coat	3	50	2 Red wool Shirts	2	00
1 Drap coat	1	50	4 pair Socks	1	00
			4 " old Do		10
			4 " Cotton Do		15
	526	80	Amt Cond forwd	534	05

Appendix 14b
Inventory of William Ward Estate

Am of Inv'd Br'd flannel	$534.05
2 Silk Pocket Hkfs 3/each	75
1 Cotton Clo 15 1 Necktie 25	40
One Umbrella	50
2 Hts 15 2 Caps 50	75
3 pair ... 1 pair ...	1.50
1 pair Gloves	15
1 Hants Patent Truss	50
4 Small Baskets 10/Each	40
2 Old Mops 10 & 5 Snaps 5	15
1 Butcher Knife	50
1 Family Bible & Bible Dictionary	1.25
16 Vol. Books	3.25
8 " Books	.50
1 money purse	.15
1 Craigs Microscope	1.00
1 Hourly Glass	50
1 Hand Glass	1.25
3 Lead Pencils 5 Powder & Shot 30	35
1 pair silver Bowed Spectacles and Case	1.50
2 Jack Knives	40
1 Lot of Old Razors, Strops and 1 Cork Screw	.75
1 Picture frames & Picture	30
1 Old Satchel	15
1 Silver Watch	5.00
15 Grain Bags	2.35
1 Bed Quilt (Star Pattern)	2.50
1 Linsey Walsey Blankets	75
1 Comforter	75
1 Plaid Woollen Blanket	1.50
4 Woollen Sheets	4.50
Am't Carried Up	$

Am't Bro't up	$570.35
1 Remnant Flannel	50
2 Yds factory	50
4 pair Cotton sheets	8.00
1 Pillow Case	.85
1 pocket Book 2/	25
1 Stand & Stand Clothe 8/	1.00
1 Chest	.50
1 Feather Bed & Straw Tick	19.50
2 Old Bedsteads & Cords	1.50
50 feet pine (dry fir) Lumber	1.00
1 Parlour stove & pipe	2.50
4 Jugs mixe (damaged)	2.75
1 Parlour stove Furniture	4.00
1 Tether Jar	25
1 pair Stilyards	25
2 Steel traps 2/	50
1 Wrench	.05
2 Small Linnen Wheels	50
1 Fill Wheel 2/	25
1 Real 2/ 1 pr Swifts 10d	35
1 Hetchel	10
1 Dye tub 10 1 Kanaup 10	20
1 Reed 5 1 Copper Tea Kettle	.45
2 Sheep Skins	.40
1 Shoe Makers Bench & kit	1.00
1 Auger 10 1 Steel fool 10	20
1 St measure & Funnel	20
1 Stove Brush	10
1 Apple Rack	10
1 Maves cover	25
1 Lot of Old Iron	1.00
Am't Over	621.33

Appendix 14c
Inventory of William Ward Estate

Appendix 15a
Expenses and receipts for expenses of the William Ward Estate

	dolars	cents
Account of the money [...] out for the estate		
for the [...]	32	00
to vanhorn for services at the funeral	5	00
to Murphey to dig and cover grave	2	50
to Simpson for preaching at funeral	2	00
to Scott for toling the bell and tinding [...]		50
to B B French for doctering	7	00
to J M Ellsworth for help in sikness	7	00
March the 13/1865 for taxes	52	26
May the 3/1865 to the Surrogate ($7 40)	17	40
May the 15/1865 to the justice for swaring the appisors		40
to Martha + Minnie		15
the expense of witnesses to prove will	5	16
for nales to fix crib		30
to the Surrogate at the time of returne of inventry	1	50
to Lyman Norton for apprisal	6	00
for weying hay		65
to the printer for publishing notice to creitors	5	50
for [...] School tax	1	40
January the 10/1866 for taxes	31	10
to mehim for threshing the grain in 1865	6	42
for weying hay at different times		55
	185	81
to B B Schepel for apprisal	4	00
to J M Norton for coppying the will and other writing for the estate	1	00

Appendix 15b

Expenses and receipts for expenses of the William Ward Estate

$4.00 Rec'd of H. Ward Executer &c
of Mr Ward Deceased four Dollars for serving
as appraiser of said estate
Hainsville N.Y. April 14th 1866
                                    Benj B. Schenck

Baldwinsville Feb 8th 1865
Received of B Vonhosne
thirty two dollars in full
Wm Ward coffin
                    Seth Brown

Appendix 15c

Expenses and receipts for expenses of the William Ward Estate

Rec'd of Hiram Ward one of the Executors of the last will and testament of Wm Ward deceased late of the town of Lysander [...] Dollars for my services as appraiser of the personal property of said Estate and for making copies of Inventory of the same &c

Lysander March 24th 1866   Lyman Morton

Received, Baldwinsville, March 8, 1866, of Hiram Ward Executor of the last Will and Testament of Wm Ward deceased Five 5/100 Dollars in full for publishing Surrogates notice to creditors in the Onondaga Gazette, Baldwinsville N.Y.

James C. Clark

Rec'd of Hiram Ward five Dollars for [...] services attending the funeral of his Father Wm Ward deceased

Plainville Feb 11th 1865   Barnet [...]

Appendix 16a

Internal Revenue receipts for taxes paid on William Ward Estate

UNITED STATES INTERNAL REVENUE.

No., 66   Collector's Office, 23 District, State of *New York*

Baltimousville May 26th 1866.

Received of *Nathan Ward & Hiram Ward*, of *Lysander*, the sum of *Sixty* 100 Dollars, in full for his Excise Tax on—

Legacies .... $ 60.00

Total . . . . $

as per* _____ list of the Assessor of said District sent to me for collection, for the _____ ending _____, 186 .

W. W. Perkins
Deputy   Collector.

$60.00

* Annual, monthly, or quarterly.

Appendix 16b

Internal Revenue receipts for taxes paid on William Ward Estate

Gorham Fulton Co Ohio   June   1866

Received of Nathan Ward and Hiram Ward Executors of the last
will and testament of William Ward deceased — and late of the
town of Lysander Onondaga County and State of New York
one hundred and twenty dollars and twenty-five cents in goods and
cash it being the amount due me as my distribution share of
the personal property of the Estate of said William Ward deceased
and I hereby release said Nathan Ward and said Hiram Ward
from further liability as far as may concern me by
reason of their being Executors of said Estate

Wm. F. Ward

Appendix 17a

Hiram Ward's warranty deed and mortgage
regarding purchase of Ward farm

Appendix 17b

Hiram Ward's warranty deed and mortgage
regarding purchase of Ward farm

MORTGAGE.

WITH BOND.

Hiram & Polly C
Ward

to

James C. Finch

Clerks Office Oxon County, ß.

Recorded on the 29th day
of August 1866, at 12
o'clock M., in Liber 118 of
Mortgages, at page 301 &c and examined.

Carroll E Smith Clerk.

Cancelled
Dec 22 1876
169/ 1306

$290, %. March 28, 1867
a dra, in New York for
Two hundred & Ninety dollars

$150, Received Nov 16, 1867 on
the within Bond
red of fifty dollars

$200 Received by being paid
to N. Ward two hundred Dollars
March 20 1868, on within Bond

$100, Received by being paid to 1868
N Ward one hundred Dollars June 5
on the within Bond

$425.00 Received March 13, 1869 on
the within Bond & Mortgage
four hundred & twenty four dollars
receipt given for the same and Stamp

$100 Received Jany 1, 1870
on the within Bond & M
One hundred Dollars

$100 Received April 9, 1875
on the within Bond & Mortgage
One hundred dollars
receipt Stamped

$285.00 Received on the within
Bond & Mortgage Two hundred and
Eighty-five Dollars
Glens Falls March 25, 1871

$360.00 Glens Falls March 1872
Received on the within Bond and
Mortgage three hundred and twenty
dollars

$150, March 28th 1873
Received on the within
One Hundred and fifty dollars

Appendix 17c
Hiram Ward's warranty deed and mortgage
regarding purchase of Ward farm

(84) *Lysander*

Catharine A. Cook
(formerly Finch)
Admr of James C. Finch

118 f. 881 +c.

TO

Hiram Ward

Satisfaction of Mortgage.

Dated _____ 187

Clerk's Office Onon. County, ss.

Recorded on the _____ 22 _____ day

of _____ Dec. _____ 1876, at 1½

o'clock P. M., in Liber 169

of Mortgages, at page 306 and

examined. _____ W. E. Hubbell Clerk

Cancelled

W. E. Hubbell   Clerk

Appendix 18

Receipt for Hiram Ward's purchase of a cemetery lot in 1876

Appendix 19a

Hiram Ward's Will

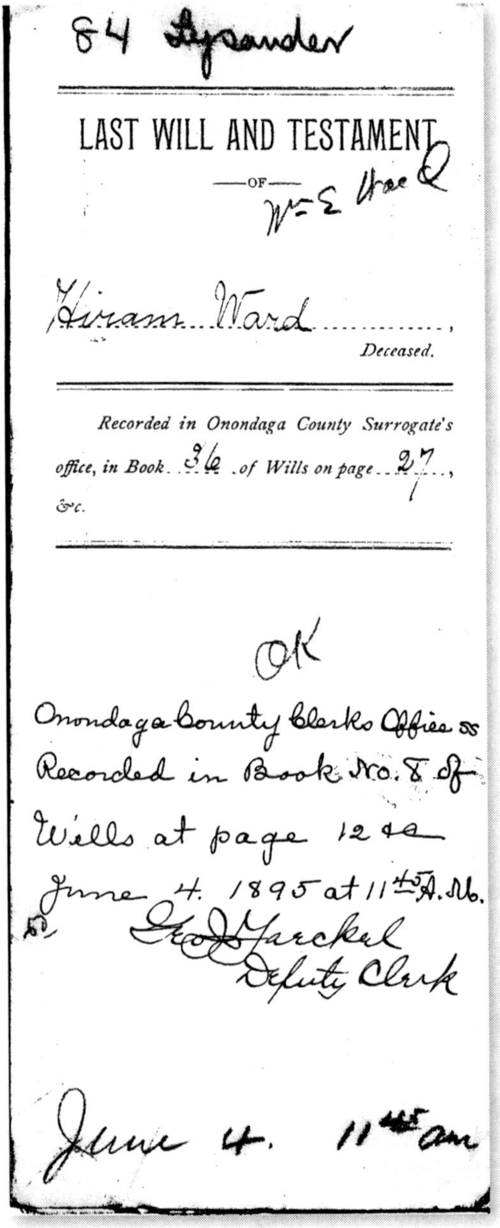

84 Lysander

LAST WILL AND TESTAMENT

—OF—

Wm E Ward

Hiram Ward,

Deceased.

Recorded in Onondaga County Surrogate's office, in Book 36 of Wills on page 27, &c.

OK

Onondaga County Clerks Office ss
Recorded in Book No. 8 of
Wills at page 124
June 4. 1895 at 11 45 A.M.
Geo J Yaeckel
Deputy Clerk

June 4. 11 45 am

Appendix 19b

Hiram Ward's Will

WILL.   173   Williamson Law Book Co., Publishers, Rochester, N. Y. 4-01

The Last Will and Testament

—OF—

Hiram Ward

of the Town of Lysander, County of Onondaga and State of New York.

I, Hiram Ward

do make, ordain, publish and declare this to be my last **Will and Testament**, *in manner and form following, that is to say:*

~~First~~ After the payment of my funeral charges the expence of administering my estate and my lawfull debts I give ~~and~~ devise and bequeath my property as follows

First To my beloved wife Polly C Ward during her life the use of all my property both personal and real and it is my the property to remain as it now is during her life to be kept in good repair

2d After the death of my wife Polly C Ward my estate both personal & real or the proceed than from to be equally divided between my children Ida Ward and Ira E Ward

3d My beloved daughter Ida Ward to have a home and support from my property she to live with my wife Polly Ward untill ~~her death~~ the death of Polly Ward then Ida Ward to share as aard 2d

Appendix 19c
Hiram Ward's Will

Likewise, I make, constitute and appoint
Ida Ward and Wm E. Ward
to be the executrix & executor _____ of this, my last Will
and Testament, and I hereby revoke all former wills by me made.

In Witness Whereof, I have hereunto subscribed my name and affixed
my seal the *30* day of *Jan* in the year of our Lord
One thousand eight hundred and ninety *2* _____

Hiram Ward

The foregoing instrument was at the date thereof subscribed by
Hiram Ward the testator therein named, in the
presence of us and each of us. He at the time of making such subscription
acknowledged that he executed the same, and declared the said instrument so
subscribed by *him* to be *his* last Will and Testament. Whereupon
we, at *his* request and in *his* presence, and in the presence
of each other, do here subscribe as witnesses thereto.

Elias C. Wilson residing at *Plainville* N. Y.
John D Kapl residing at *Plainville* N. Y.

Appendix 20

Receipt for purchase of cemetery lots by William E. Ward

E.M MOORE, President.   J.H.NORTON, Vice Pres!.   F.H.MOORE, Treasurer   J.H.NORTON, Secretary.   C.D.HOWARD, Supt. of Manufacture

HOWARD FURNACE COMPANY,
MANUFACTURERS OF THE CELEBRATED
HOWARD FURNACES,
AND HOT WATER AND WARM AIR COMBINATION HEATERS.

MAIN OFFICE & WORKS,
SYRACUSE, N.Y., U.S.A.
BRANCHES,
NEW YORK, BOSTON, GRAND RAPIDS, TORONTO.

SYRACUSE, N.Y. *June 6. 1895*

Received of William E. Ward, six dollars
in payment for a tin of lots in the grave
yard in Peauville, situated on the north
of a tin of lots set apart to the Wilson
family, and South by the Upson lots.
the lot being directly west of the lot on
which the family of said Ward is buried,
and is twenty one feet by 9 feet in extent
reserving the burying spot on which the
remains of Louisa Babcock are buried
and which occupies a space 9 x 3 feet
on the North end of said Lot

J.H. Norton

CPSIA information can be obtained at www.ICGtesting.com
Printed in the USA
LVOW07s0731151115

462619LV00002B/2/P